DEADLY TEMPTRESS

Sebek surveyed Hathor with hot eyes. His hands darted out with the eagerness of a two-year-old unwrapping a present. His left hand curved round her hip to grasp a buttock and drag her forward. Sebek's breath was hot on her belly as he crushed her to him.

Hathor's hands were soon in motion. Her right hand lashed down at the arm holding her while her left slashed upward against Sebek's face, opening his left cheek from the jawline almost to his eye. Sebek sat frozen on the divan, staring at the blood. Then his face contorted with rage.

One more kick twisted Sebek's head back while tearing the wound on his cheek even wider. Blood gushed down onto Sebek's throat as Hathor's foot descended relentlessly. A strangled croak whispered out of his mouth. "Who are—" That was all he could manage before Hathor bore down ng his trachea.

always known that murder Sebek—just in that she was the going to save and restore Ra's empire. . . .

STARGATE

REBELLION

BILL McCay

A ROC BOOK

ROC
Published by the Penguin Group
Penguin Books USA Inc., 375 Hudson Street,
New York, New York 10014, U.S.A.
Penguin Books Ltd, 27 Wrights Lane,
London W8 5TZ, England
Penguin Books Australia Ltd, Ringwood,
Victoria, Australia
Penguin Books Canada Ltd, 10 Alcorn Avenue,
Toronto, Ontario, Canada M4V 3B2
Penguin Books (N.Z.) Ltd, 182–190 Wairau Road,
Auckland 10, New Zealand

Penguin Books Ltd, Registered Offices:
Harmondsworth, Middlesex, England

First published by Roc, an imprint of Dutton Signet,
a division of Penguin Books USA Inc.

First Printing, October, 1995
10 9 8 7 6 5 4 3 2

 REGISTERED TRADEMARK—MARCA REGISTRADA

Printed in Canada

CHAPTER 1
THREE AWAKENINGS

Dawn was still hours away, but a subtle lightening of the shadows in the suburban bedroom foretold that sunrise, inevitably, would come. Bit by tiny bit, Sarah O'Neil could distinguish more and more details on the dresser and bureaus.

She lay propped on one elbow, silently studying her bedmate in the indistinct gloom. Soon Colonel Jack O'Neil would be up, shaved, starched, and off to the nearby Marine base. Sarah was glad that his classified tasks now involved deskwork instead of killing people in the field—for the time being, at least.

She'd feared his most recent mission was to have been his last. Jack had fallen apart when their son, Jack Junior, died in a gun accident. Their all-American boy had joined the casualty lists in a case of friendly fire—from Jack's own pistol. In the months that followed, Jack had either avoided this bed or lain beside her, his entire body tight as a clenched fist. For hours he'd sat alone in his den, playing with a 1911 Army Colt automatic, an old-line officer's sidearm, .45 caliber—capable of spattering his brains all over the wall if he finally decided to swallow the gun barrel.

When the orders came, sending Jack away on another mission, Sarah believed his superiors were merely aiming him like a piece of ordnance—a combination suicide bomb and detonator.

But Jack had come back. And she had been surprised by joy when, even more inexplicably, Jack returned a healing man. Their son's death wasn't completely behind him, but somewhere on this mission he never spoke about, he'd come to terms with Jack Junior's loss. Jack returned neither as the walking wreckage he'd been right after the funeral, nor the near parody of the spit-and-polish officer he'd transformed into upon getting his orders.

He'd been—himself again. And on his return from wherever, they'd made love for the first time in too, too long. As soon as he'd undressed, Sarah saw he had not had an easy mission. Technicolor bruises marred Jack's ribs and the pit of his stomach—souvenirs of brutal hand-to-hand combat.

She'd tried to be gentle. And the usually gung-ho colonel had been almost shy, as if he wasn't sure the pieces would fit together again. They certainly had, and that had helped the healing.

Silently, Sarah examined the familiar features. From the moment she'd met the cocky young combat corporal, she'd been struck by the contradiction implicit in his go-to-hell eyes and his set, determined jaw. Now the eyes were closed, the jaw softened. In the vulnerability of sleep, the elder Jack looked almost like his lost son.

Sarah slid across the bed, wrapping her arms

around her husband as if trying to shield him with her body. After months of quiet, she knew that today one of those shadowy superiors Jack answered to would be coming to the base.

He's had so little time to be a human being—so little practice, she thought as she clung to her husband. *I hope they won't send him somewhere that will turn him back into a robot again.*

On the planet Abydos, Daniel Jackson looked up at the ceiling and surreptitiously flexed his fingers in an attempt to bring circulation back to his right arm. Not that he minded the reason for the lost blood supply. Sha'uri's head lay across his biceps as she cuddled against him, the fine features of her face burrowing into his chest.

Daniel had followed a strange road to get here. Fellow Egyptologists had dismissed him as a crank for arguing that the sudden flowering of Nile civilization must have its roots in an earlier culture.

But he'd found an artifact of that predecessor civilization on a hush-hush government project. He'd christened it a StarGate from hieroglyphics connected with the find.

Then he'd been put to work deciphering cryptic signs on the StarGate itself, which turned out to represent star constellations. His key had allowed government scientists to unlock the StarGate. And, accompanying a team of recon Marines, Daniel had been hurtled to this strange planet to find Nagada, Sha'uri—and a vengeful semi-human creature who ruled Abydos and other worlds as the sun god Ra.

Daniel helped rouse rebellion among the human slaves while the Marines and a few young rebels battled Ra's guardsmen. Both Daniel and Sha'uri were mortally wounded, only to be resurrected by Ra's extraterrestrial technology—a strange quartz-crystal sarcophagus.

Ra explained that his technology had been the base of later Egyptian civilization, but his earthly slaves had revolted, burying the StarGate. Now, millennia later, he would punish the human homeworld through the reopened gate. He would send an atomic bomb back to Colorado, amplifying its power with his mysterious quartz-crystal.

Revolt and the efforts of the Marines forestalled that plan. In the end, the nuclear blast had destroyed Ra himself.

Daniel decided to stay on Abydos. The local population had not only been used shamelessly, they'd been kept illiterate and ignorant of their past. Daniel could teach them—while at the same time learning the roots of Egyptian culture. Besides, he was living out an adventure of the sort he'd only expected to see on movie screens. He'd even wed the local chief's daughter.

Daniel stared up at the cracked adobe-style ceiling. There was much to be fixed here. He'd started by trying to get the local population literate. In the past months, he had taught hieroglyphics to a basic cadre—Sha'uri, several of the local Elders, and a number of interested townsfolk. This first generation was now teaching basic classes while Daniel gave advanced instruction.

Today, his postgrad workshop had met in the

secret archives of Nagada. Generations of secret scribes had filled the walls of a hidden room with the true history of Ra's infamy, despite the sun-god's proscription on writing. One of Daniel's first actions was to copy these hieroglyphics.

He remembered Sha'uri's halting translation of one section. "When those on Ombos rebelled, Hathor went forth as the Eye of Ra. She covered that world in blood, till, wounded, she entered the vault of Ra to sleep ever since."

Daniel was reminded of an Egyptian myth. To foil a human revolt, Ra sent cat-headed Hathor, goddess of lust and quick vengeance, to slaughter the conspirators. But she developed a taste for blood, planning to kill all of humanity. The gods, concerned at the loss of worshipers, created a lake of beer stained with berry juice. The bloodthirsty goddess drank it up, fell into a drunken sleep, and awoke as her usual light-hearted and sexy self.

Now we have the history behind the myth, Daniel thought. Thanks to hieroglyphics. But a voice nagged from the back of his head. *Maybe you should be teaching these people English instead.*

Nagada depended on agriculture and handicrafts—a subsistence economy, but most of the work force had been miners. The city was near a deposit of that quartz-like crystal used in so much of Ra's technology. It had been a major export, even if the people had gotten nothing back.

It might become a paying export after the scientists on Earth saw some of the items O'Neil brought back through the StarGate. Daniel tried to caution Sha'uri's father Kasuf and other city

Elders about terrestrial business ethics. But it was hard even to explain what a corporation was. For Kasuf and the others, visitors through the Star-Gate were friends, and perhaps heroes.

Daniel could only hope it would stay that way.

Sha'uri shifted and sighed. She opened her eyes, giving him a sleepy smile. "Dan-yer," she whispered, pronouncing his name in her local tongue.

Smiling back, Daniel decided to put his worries on the back burner.

The marble halls on the moonlet of Tuat were not made for raised voices. Especially this hall, with its pyramidal dome of crystal rising to a point far overhead. Not for the first time, Thoth wondered why Ra had topped this particular structure with a dome of viewing. Outside was merely airless rock, unblinking stars, and, hanging in the sable sky, the grayish-blue bulk of the world this moonlet circled. Even after ten millennia, the planet had yet to recover from ecological catastrophe. According to the secret records, this is where Ra had found his first servants, the hands that had built the StarGates, the exoskeletal helmets, and the weapons that marked godhood for Ra's human servants.

The records hinted of a bargain being struck, that Ra would take the inhabitants from their ruined planet to a new one. However, that world had turned out to be Ombos, the world of blood.

Thoth raised his eyes to consider the planet above. Whoever those first servants had been, they'd built well. Even from this distance he could make out the regular lines of their ruined habitations.

"Look at me, Ammit devour you!" Sebek's voice boomed and echoed in the enclosed space.

Sighing, Thoth redirected his regard to the man prowling the pillared central aisle. He didn't know why Sebek kept glancing around. He'd picked this spot for their clandestine meeting. Thoth didn't mention that three other godlets-who-would-be-Ra had chosen the same place.

It was hard to believe that he and Sebek had long ago been part of the same brood of tribute-children sent to serve Ra—pretty boys and girls. They'd grown up very differently. Thoth had risen to head Ra's bureaucracy, becoming the accountant of the gods. Physically, he resembled the headdress-creature that marked his godhood. Thoth was the ibis-headed god—and the ibis was a stork-like bird. Spindly of arms and legs, with an incipient potbelly, Thoth was not an impressive sight in his white linen kilt.

Sebek, on the other hand, was the crocodile god, renowned for cruelty, one of Ra's planetary viceroys, an overseer of overseers. He had the thick, muscular body of a warrior. And if he didn't have the grace of lost Anubis, foremost of Ra's fighters, he certainly had strength to spare.

Right now he looked as if he was just barely restraining himself from using that strength to break Thoth's arms and legs.

Thoth kept his eyes on the prowling warrior. He was reasonably sure that Sebek would not descend to the use of such forceful expedients—at least, not yet. But Thoth had learned to keep an eye on adversaries, even those courting his support.

For that was what all these skulking colloquies were about—on whose side would the machinery of administration fall?

"Several of Khnum's people died in a set-to with some Horus guards serving Apis," Sebek said. "The Ram has been pushing the Bull hard of late."

He turned cold, shrewd eyes to Thoth. "Not that I'm telling *you* anything. Your scribes make excellent spies. I saw it often enough on Wefen. Ra seemed to know my secrets almost as soon as I knew them."

Sebek swerved in his prowling course to confront Thoth. "But," he said, his voice dropping, "such a system can work only if there is strength at the head. I'm sure you know many things. But whom can you tell now?"

Thoth said nothing. In truth, the scribes had provided much useful intelligence for Ra. But now Ra was gone, vanished for months after what was supposed to be a short voyage and visit at the backwater world of Abydos.

From all over Ra's compact empire, warrior-gods came by StarGate to Tuat-the-world and flew up to Tuat-the-moon—for Ra never allowed StarGate access to his personal sanctum.

And on a moonlet where Thoth had once enjoyed a position as second after Ra—as chief administrator—warriors and viceroys now jostled

one another, their servants testing the aggressive-
ness and resolution of other factions. Predators
all, they had been held in check because Ra had
culled the pack. But now it seemed more and
more evident that Ra was no more. The warriors'
minds turned naturally to calculations of succession. And for the more thoughtful minority—such
as Sebek and a few others—those calculations
went beyond quantifying the number of available
bodies and the tally of blast-lances those bodies
could use.

"You could choose worse to back than me,"
Sebek went on. "We ate at the same table as
boys—served Him together."

Throughout this talk, Thoth realized, Sebek had
never mentioned Ra by name. The warrior's voice
dropped to a whisper. "I remember how you
dreaded it whenever you displeased Him—how
you feared the punishment He might mete out."
Sebek speared his old mate with cold eyes. "Think
what punishment I'm capable of. And if you won't
serve me for old affection's sake—then fear me!"

He turned and left Thoth alone in the hall.
Raising his eyes again, Thoth studied the pitiless
stars. Trust Sebek to issue the most direct offer—
and to couch it as a threat. Certainly, there were
worse candidates for the place of power. Sebek
could field a sufficient force to seize the prize.
But even with Thoth behind him, could Sebek—
could any of the would-be successors—*retain*
power in the face of resistance from the other
contenders? Or would the battering of the warriors destroy the prize? Shatter the irreplacable

mechanical and human gears that allowed the empire to function?

Not to mention that backing the wrong aspirant could get Thoth killed. If Anubis was among them, a fighter of such proven ferocity that the pack could be curbed . . .

But Anubis had gone with Ra. No comparable warrior walked the halls of Tuat. Unless Thoth resolved on a far more dangerous gamble.

He had to decide soon, before hand-to-hand brawls became pitched battles with energy weapons. A dubious prospect, with hard vacuum beyond the walls of Ra's pleasure domes. Still worse, there would be no room to maneuver, no chance to temporize with Sebek and the others who wanted Thoth's support.

Thoth activated his headgear, allowing the aspect of the ibis to cover his face. His gangling frame moved smoothly, imbued with sudden purpose. He headed for the lower levels of the pyramid, domain of machinery and the occasional mechanic. But building plans existed, and these had to be recorded, filed, and thus passed into the hands of the scribes.

Thanks to the plans, Thoth had found the airlock, and thanks to other records he had learned of the necessities for workers to wear on their infrequent maintenance jobs outside. The suit accommodated his kilt but tightly gripped his chest and extremities in a sensation unfamiliar on skin that usually went bare. Hookups ran to his helmet so he could breathe.

He cycled through the lock and set off across

the bare rock. Mere yards from the pyramid, the field of artificial gravity died away. That was all to the good. Thoth set off on huge, exaggerated bounding steps for a horizon that seemed unnaturally close. His destination was far enough from the complex of pyramidal construction which housed Ra's palace. It was beyond the view even of the crystal summit of the tallest one—the place where he'd just met with Sebek.

Thoth was gasping by the time he scaled the wall of the small craterlet. Even with the lower gravity this represented unfamiliar exertion. At least this time he had nothing to carry.

The crater floor was of blackish rock, and if the secret records hadn't told Thoth exactly where to look, he'd have dismissed his destination as a shadow or a chance rock formation. Even close by, the contours were irregular enough—and spalled by 8,500 years of micrometeorite impacts—to be dismissed as natural.

One had to look down into the murky hole in the ground to identify the entrance to the *mastaba*, or underground tomb.

Thoth manipulated the entrance controls and slipped inside. A pile of gear, brought by him piece by piece, lay right at the access. He picked up a small hand light, then turned to seal the tomb's portal. Only when he was sure it wouldn't be seen on the surface did he activate his torch. The interior of the mastaba had gotten far less attention than its artfully concealed entrance. The chamber had apparently been chopped into existence with energy beams. Its walls were crude and out of true, the blackish stone melted and slagged in places. In one corner lay the burned and blasted remains of the workers who'd done the excavating.

Their twisted forms made a striking contrast to the sarcophagus resting on the bumpy floor. Exquisitely carved from the quartzose material reserved for the most splendid of Ra's technological wonders, the stone box bulked large in the crude quarters, seeming to glow with a muted golden radiance as Thoth's light flashed on it. A sun disk decorated the head of the funerary bier, which was twice as long as a man was tall. Hieroglyphs ran across the waist-high covering stone—a hymn to eternal life.

Thoth turned to the other materials he'd cached in the tomb. He opened canisters of pressurized air, bringing atmosphere back to the room for the first time in millennia. At last Thoth opened his ibis mask and took a deep breath.

Then he turned to the sarcophagus, tapping several of the hieroglyphics in a certain pattern. The crystal walls of the box shifted as if they were live things. A seemingly solid cover stone split into three sections. The sun disk rose head high, another section of the cover stone moving with it, sliding out in two pieces to give the disk wings.

A pearlescent light flooded the room, coming from inside the box. Thoth stepped forward, his face tight with excitement. The head of the sarcophagus interior was shaped like a pharaonic headdress, forming a sort of halo for the beautiful female face lying in repose there. The woman had an olive complexion, dark but not tanned. Her aquiline features were perfectly formed. With her eyes closed, she looked like a beautifully crafted statue.

Then Thoth noticed the slight rise and fall of the lithe breasts under the pectoral necklace of her chest piece.

The eyes opened.

Hathor lived.

CHAPTER 2
INTELLIGENCE ASSESSMENT

Pain had not merely tinged, but had *been* Hathor's last conscious memory. The battle for Ombos had no longer been in doubt. Step by ruthless step she'd turned the situation on the revolting planet around until the rebels didn't merely face defeat, they faced extermination. Even her own troops feared her as the goddess who had covered a planet in blood.

Hathor had been directing operations against one of the few remaining rebel strongholds, hidden in an inaccessible mountain range. The *udajeets*, single-man gliders, had flown repeated missions, their paired blasters firing incessantly to clear a landing area literally down to scorched earth. But no sooner had she set foot to terra firma than one of those red-haired devils burst out of a pit in the ground. The poor bastard hadn't carried an energy weapon. Apparently, the rebels had learned that the Horus guards could scan for such armament.

But even as Hathor aimed her own blast-lance, the rebel had hurled some sort of metal implement. Spikes of white-hot agony radiated from her stomach. But this was no mere stab wound. Her nerves first seemed dipped in acid, then went terrifyingly numb.

"Poison—" she slurred to one of the Horus guards blasting the now unarmed assassin. Then paralysis set in—and with it, searing pain. Every move on the way back to the StarGate was etched in anguish. She could smell the rot emanating from her stomach even during the brief udajeet ride. Whatever had been smeared on that damnable blade was turning her flesh into a necrotic mess.

If she survived this, Hathor promised herself, she'd track that poison down. A new weapon for her arsenal . . .

Even the flesh on her face was black and splitting by the time she finally reached Tuat. Ra himself was on hand to greet her, and Hathor's heart died a little at his reaction to her appearance.

There was only one hope for her survival. That was internment in Ra's sarcophagus of wonder. Certain others of Ra's servants—the irreplaceable ones—had been placed inside that crystalline box, suffering from a variety of ills. They'd all emerged fit and cured.

So as Hathor came to consciousness, she opened her eyes full of hope. Her strength and looks would be restored. And, of course, Ra would be there to greet her. At the very least, her own servants would be on hand. Instead of Ra's throne room, she found herself in a mean little chamber, more like a cave—or a dungeon. And she had no idea who the single man staring down at her was.

Hathor's muscles screamed in protest as she forced herself upright, reaching for the gawker. What should have been a seamless, easy move-

ment took an extra second—enough time for the
man to take a step backward before she was out
of the stone coffin and grasping him by the throat.

A pair of strides, and she smashed the intruder
against the crude wall. His face turned an interesting mottled color before she released pressure
on his airway. With one hand cocked to deliver
body blows if necessary, Hathor activated his
headdress. She expected to find a renegade Horus
guard engaged in a bit of voyeurism. Instead, she
found . . . Thoth.

"This cannot be," she muttered, pressing again
to unmask the man. "Thoth is an older man, but
not so old that he would die before I—" The room
threatened to revolve around her. "Where am I?"

Thoth sucked air through a bruised throat. "On
Tuat." He managed a soothing tone, at least. "In
a mastaba several miles from Ra's palace."

"A tomb!" She gestured wordlessly, indicating
that her body was whole.

"You slept, O Champion." Thoth struggled to
find the right words. "The records I studied indicated that perhaps you had succeeded in your
mission too well."

"I crushed the rebels as ordered, showing no
mercy," Hathor responded. Her lips twisted. "And
in so doing, I caused even Ra some unease. So
he buried me away, for retrieval in case of some
worse disaster. Is that the case?" Hathor's eyes
narrowed. "Or . . . you mentioned records that *you*
had studied. If you thought to waken me to use
against Ra . . ." Her lips quirked again. "You've
made a serious blunder, conspirator."

Her whole career, pushing her way into the circle of warriors who surrounded the sun god, had
been based on a strategy ancient even in her
time—seduction and dynasty. Even her husband,
engineer of the gods, hadn't dared reprove her for
her "friendship" with Ra. And she knew, *knew*
that the ever young body of her liege responded
to her wiles. But the alien soul inhabiting that
flesh had proven resistant. Yes, Ra's alien *ka* was
doubtless responsible for having her put away.

Even so, it would be unwise of this interloper
to expect that she would nurse a grudge. What
had been done could be done again. She was
awakened now. And the surest way to Ra's favor
would be to bring him the head of a traitor.

Her thoughts must have shown on her face,
because Thoth pressed himself against the wall,
quickly putting up a hand. "I brought you forth
because it seems that Ra is no more."

Now it was Hathor's turn to step back, stag-
gered. For a second she was silent. Then, "How—"
She bit off the question she'd been about to ask:
"How could this be possible?"

Instead, Hathor turned to practicalities. "How
long have I been immured here?"

When Thoth gave her the answer, her eyes went
round with dismay. Eight thousand years was more
than enough time to have wrapped her actions in
the trappings of legend. Her next question was
purely political. "Who now wears the cat's head?"

Thoth looked surprised. "There has never been
another Hathor."

A certain grim satisfaction filled Hathor at this

news. She had been deemed irreplaceable. But it also meant problems. With a successor, she could have challenged for her position—and with a single murder doubtless not only won back her office, but gained a staff of servants and warriors as well. Having no successor closed off that path to getting aid.

She stared at this Thoth, so many generations removed from the First Time. What did he think her capable of? The Thoth of her days had been a scribe and an intriguer—his weapon of choice the pen rather than the sword. She doubted that this soft-bodied Thoth could offer her much in the way of backup—his servants would not be skilled in physical force. Did he count on her to take on the entire warrior caste single-handed?

She turned to him and put her question into words. "What do you expect of me?"

"Ra, it seems, is gone," he said. "Someone must put his house in order."

Ah, Hathor thought, *the dangers of legend. He does expect me to vanquish these would-be successors alone and unaided.*

Still, she felt the promptings of her own ambition. She had thought to create the House of Ra by way of the path of love. Would it be so different to create the House of Hathor by way of the paths of war?

"We have much to speak of." She sniffed and frowned. "And already the air here grows stale."

Thoth gestured to the pile of gear at the entrance to the mastaba. "I have here another suit for traversing the airless plain. And I have arranged apartments—" he made a self-disparaging gesture. "Humble apartments for one of your stature. But they're secure, and in a little-traveled area of the old palace."

Hathor nodded. After more than eight millennia in a stone box, her physical needs were modest enough. And it would certainly be better to retain the element of surprise. "Speak to me of leaders," she said. "What factions contend for Ra's throne? Which of the viceroys has the greatest personal strength? Which the largest following? Is there yet an Anubis? Or did he follow Ra into the void?"

Thoth began the briefing even as he presented the atmosphere suit. Hathor had worn these suits before. She knew their limits. And, of course, in the timeless workings of Ra's empire, technology did not change.

She was ready to leave by the time Thoth had sketched out the short list of candidates most likely to achieve ultimate power. Hathor was most interested in his description of his old crèche mate, Sebek. She had never liked the crocodile god of her days. And this Sebek not only had a reputation as a fierce fighter, he had a strong and well-trained entourage.

In Hathor's eyes that made him a prime target.

"Enough," she finally said. "Let us be out of here." She activated her own headdress, and for the first time in eight thousand years, the face of the Cat was seen once again.

It was well, Hathor thought. The cat, with its supple body and soft purr, was dismissed by many as a creature of mere sensual pleasure. So it had been in her career. Too late, those dismissing her had discovered that this cat had much in common with her cousin the lion.

Perhaps it would be so for this Sebek, and the other godlets who would be Ra.

On the other hand, they might be like this Thoth, believing in legends that gave her an overblown reputation. That could be useful as well. She could make an example of a front-runner—this Sebek perhaps—and terrorize the rest into submission.

Kill one, frighten a thousand. She had learned that equation on Ombos, extirpating the rebels there. Now she would bring this same equation to Tuat. Although, she realized, it had already been instituted there by no less a personage than Ra himself.

From the very beginning of the First Days on Earth, Ra had kept a mastery of the tools of terror. Thus had he bent the slave populations to his will. And, if truth were to be told, terror had also been part of the carrot and the stick which he'd used in leading the gods.

The carrot had been power, of course, and a lifetime extending far beyond that of an average mortal. But if one should fail the sun god, if one should displease Ra, the punishment was death. And Ra could offer death in so many unpleasant guises, like a session with his gem that could turn bones to water.

Like it or not, Ra had shepherded his attendant gods with fear.

Hathor smiled. She could do that.

*   *   *

On Earth, a military transport plane took off from Washington. Its interior was not exactly spartan—after all, there was a senior officer aboard. But General West was smart enough to fly only on regularly scheduled jets—and not the only passenger.

Other officers of similar rank had never bothered to learn that simple lesson, and had managed to blight their careers. A colleague of West's, a head honcho of a European operation, had once flown from Rome to the U.S. in a huge, unscheduled Starlifter with only his female aide on board. After being roasted in newspapers across the country, that unfortunate general had wound up in charge of counting penguins down in Antarctica.

But if he flew by the rules, nonetheless the general had plenty of room to spread out as the plane reached its cruising altitude. Which was just as well—his briefcase was full of reports to be read, and he had to come to a decision on those contents before the plane landed.

West's slightly jowly face took on the stony aspect of the veteran poker player as he reviewed the first of a succession of documents stamped TOP SECRET. This was a technology assessment from the Pentagon big-domes who had attempted to take one of those blast-lances apart and put it back together again. Of course, they were careful to cover their scientific butts, but they were reasonably optimistic. While they did not promise production-line manufacturing of the weapons in two weeks, they did offer the opinion that the technology was accessible.

West frowned. The only bottleneck was that the lances, like all the alien high technology Jack O'Neil and the survivors of the Abydos recon team had reported on, depended on that quartz-like crystal to work. And the only source of that crystal on Earth was the StarGate. West idly speculated on how many blasters they could make if they broke the matter transmitter, or whatever it was, into small pieces. . . .

That would solve two problems—the weapons would permanently tilt the balance of power in favor of the U.S. here on Earth, while dismemberment of the StarGate would close a profoundly disturbing door on a hostile universe.

He went back to reading, this time switching to the survivors' after-action reports. Energy weapons, matter transmission, a working starship. Those were just a few of the technological goodies the recon team had observed on the other side of the StarGate.

On the other hand . . . West shuddered as he went back over Colonel Jack O'Neil's classified report. The StarGate had almost been used as a delivery system for an amplified atomic bomb, with a blast big enough to end civilization on this planet. Were the possible advantages worth the all-too-concrete risks?

Of course, O'Neil had succeeded in using the matter transmitter to plant the bomb on the starship, blowing it up and ending the career of the alien which had styled itself as a god.

But since the three surviving Marines had returned to Earth, no one had gone through the StarGate. West had not only secured the missile silo that housed the artifact, he'd posted the toughest combat Marines he could find for round-the-clock guard duty. Nothing was to go in or out of that alien dingus without his say-so. Managing the threat factors on Earth gave him difficulty enough. He was unwilling to throw an entire new world into his risk calculations.

However . . .

O'Neil's report also stated that among the resources of the planet Abydos was a sizable deposit of Ra's magic quartz-crystal. Much as West would like to decline the proffered invitation to the universe, he had to consider the strategic implications.

With a ready supply of the quartz element, Earth's technical base—specifically, that of the United States—could advance by a quantum jump. Even better, the U.S. would have an absolute lock on this new technology. The Japanese wouldn't be able to horn in and usurp production, because the raw material that was the bedrock for the technological wonders would be available only from America. It would come out of a hole in an American mountain. So what if it had to traverse a million light-years to get there?

According to O'Neil's report, the natives of Abydos conducted their mining operation in an inefficient—in fact, downright primitive—manner. Apparently, that was due to the alien god's strangling grip on the people. All well and good, but the situation would have to change. If this brave new technology were to go into production, the factories would require regular shipments—in bulk. That would be the only economic reason for keeping this portal to the unknown open.

Large-scale mining would require machinery—and, of course, the people to operate it. And those operators would have to be people General West could control. At first he had thought of the Army Corps of Engineers. They certainly had the know-how, and they were *military*, by God.

But he'd quickly identified a drawback to using the military's construction arm. The requirement was secrecy. Could they depend on some short-timer driving a bulldozer not to come home and talk about his building job on another planet?

Once again West wished that O'Neil had blown up the StarGate on the Abydos side and removed this problem before it landed in the general's lap. If nobody knew this stuff existed . . .

But the technology and the crystal did exist, and in the Pentagon's need-to-know culture, it was up to West to make a decision about it. He hadn't reached his rank by passing the buck. He had a reputation for making the right choices in clutch situations.

The decision he was leaning toward was the mining option—with a sizable security comple-ment in case any more unpleasant surprises came down out of the sky. But the miners wouldn't be soldiers. They'd come from the United Mining Consortium. UMC had done lots of government work in the past—including a number of sensitive overseas operations in conjunction with representatives of the intelligence community.

West had done his homework, assuring himself that UMC not only had the resources but the right kind of people to do this job—people who could keep their mouths shut. Even better, the company was used to working in the Third World, which would be a plus in dealing with the primitives on Abydos. And UMC was quite resourceful in keeping up production of whatever ore was being excavated, despite piddling complaints by the natives or annoying shifts in their governments.

The general referred briefly to the newspaper clippings in his UMC file. A native potentate toppled, a separatist movement in the area of richest mining, a recalcitrant president supplanted by a more accommodating military junta . . .

Yes, UMC was certainly a company that could handle itself in the clinch. And for civilians, they would do exactly the sort of job he wanted done. He had the names and numbers he needed to start the ball rolling. No doubt UMC would want to send over some prospectors, advance men, people to do a feasibility study. All under the deepest shrouds of national security, of course.

Well, he had just the man to bird-dog them. Someone who had experience on the far side of the StarGate. A military man who knew how to follow orders and keep his mouth shut.

Colonel Jack O'Neil.

West smiled. Perhaps someday O'Neil would thank the general for putting him in touch with

the right people. Certainly, West expected to be
thanked . . . by UMC. Not immediately, of course.

But a person who puts a company in the way
of making a handsome profit—a monopoly position on a scarce resource with many valuable
uses. Well, such a person deserves a reward. Lu-
crative consulting opportunities, perhaps a seat on
the board of directors.

West leaned back in his seat. After all, the military would expect him to retire one of these days. The
military-industrial complex just wasn't what it used
to be.

Even a general had to think about his future.

CHAPTER 3
INFILTRATION

Shielding his eyes from the brutal desert suns of Abydos, Skaara conducted a quick head count on the *mastadge* herd he and his friends were watching. Sha'uri's brother had to admit that after his brief stint as a freedom fighter, the shepherd's trade was even more boring than before.

He and his friends had become boy commandos almost by accident, rescuing the otherworldly visitors from Ra's wrath. Indeed, Skaara had learned most of his soldiering by observing the man he called Black Hat—after the black beret worn by Colonel Jack O'Neil. *There* was a warrior, despite the dull green clothes he wore. The man had a sharp temper, exacerbated by the language difficulties—the only visitor who spoke the local language was Daniel, his sister's husband.

But Skaara had admired O'Neil, and a certain friendship had grown between them. He'd been vastly disappointed when his idol had disappeared into the StarGate, returning to whatever unguessable world he had come from.

It wasn't merely a wish for action that fueled Skaara's discontent. He'd quickly learned that war did not necessarily mean glory—his mates had suffered casualties, and his friend Nabeh had

nearly been killed. Still worse had been the inno-
cent civilians butchered as the flying udajeet had
blasted the city of Nagada from the air.

Between his days of labor and his work at night
learning hieroglyphics, he had more than enough
activity to take up even the energies of youth. Yet
even his studies spurred restlessness. Translating
the wall paintings of Nagada's hidden archives
gave more tales of Ra's tyranny, and tantalizing
clues about other worlds ruled over by the false
god. What, for instance, had happened on Ombos
after cat-headed Hathor had covered that planet
in blood?

Even the wise Daniel could offer no information.

Slowly as his studies progressed, Skaara also developed a desire to see these worlds on the other
side of the StarGate, to tell their peoples that Ra
was no more—to join with these star-brothers and
fight for freedom as the inhabitants of Abydos
had done.

He hadn't discussed these inchoate aspirations
with his father, the Elder Kasuf, with Sha'uri, or
with Daniel. But when he'd sounded out his shepherd friends, his fellow veterans of the war against
Ra, the response was resoundingly affirmative. So
a new activity had been added to his schedule. In
whatever spare time remained after shepherding
and studying, Skaara and his mates practiced the
arts of war.

They drilled themselves in the arts of conceal-
ment, in quick, darting movement under simulated
fire. They experimented with various weapons,

and zealously worked to maintain the few rifles and pistols the visitors from Earth had left behind. Skaara had organized a careful scavenging operation in the ruins of the visitors' base camp. The search had been rewarded when several boxes of rifle ammunition turned up.

And night and day, as an exercise in war and discipline, Skaara detailed a few members from his shepherds' complement to keep watch on the pyramid that housed the StarGate.

Thus, when the sudden chatter of a rifle on automatic echoed over the dunes, Skaara wasn't exactly surprised. A gunshot was supposed to be the signal that new visitors had arrived. But Skaara wasn't pleased. The signal was supposed to be a single gunshot. He would have some choice words for the watchers about wasting ammunition.

Unless . . . what if the visitors weren't friendly and the watchers were defending themselves?

Skaara had a sickening vision of Horus guards pouring from the carved entrance arch of the pyramid. He'd dreamed of taking freedom out to the other planets of Ra's empire. Suppose one of Ra's lieutenants had come to Abydos with the intention of restoring despotism?

He snapped an order to the others, and in an instant shepherd boys became warriors. They all carried whatever weapons they could. Now, abandoning the mastadges, they formed a rough skirmish line and headed for the watch point, a tall sand dune that commanded a view of the rocky outcrop that supported the pyramid.

Skaara carefully deployed his men, rifles at the

flanks, as they climbed to the crest of the dune. They might be able to get a few shots at the invaders.

But when they reached the watchers, they found a pair of madly capering boys.

"Skaara!" shouted Nabeh, pointing into the distance beyond the dune's face. "They're back! They've come back!"

Skaara threw himself on his belly, slipping another treasure from Earth out of his cloak. O'Neil had given him the pair of black, compact binoculars before leaving Abydos. As Skaara focused on the three figures sliding down the escarpment to the sands below, he saw that Nabeh's eyesight and words were true. The visitors were dressed as people from Earth. And one of them wore a black beret. Fixing his gaze, Skaara saw this was indeed Jack O'Neil.

The black-hatted man wore a different suit: not green this time, but mottled in tans and yellows—the colors of the sands. The camouflage made it more difficult to spot the newcomers. But Skaara had gotten a good look at the colonel's face. That was all he needed to see to tell him that these were friends.

Turning, he reorganized his little command from an ambush party to an honor guard.

But, like any good officer, he still took a moment to lash into Nabeh for wasting their precious ammunition.

Walter Draven, UMC's advance man on Abydos, threw his long, thin body to the sand as the noise of rattling discharges echoed against the face of the pyramid.

"That sounds like gunshots," he said. The hard eyes in his hatchet-like face turned almost angrily to their military liaison.

"At least a clip on an M-16 firing at full auto," Colonel Jack O'Neil agreed.

"You said these people were primitives—that they barely had metal tools when you met them!" Draven's legal background broke out at the oddest moments, like this accusatory speech.

"Well, it sounds as if the locals got themselves some hardware," Martin Preston, the engineering side of the scouting party, pointed out. He was short and stocky, with a round red face and bandy legs. But he was supposed to know everything there was to know about mining in primitive conditions.

"A group of kids helped us," O'Neil explained, a brief smile coming to his lips at the memory of Skaara and his friends. "They used some of our guns. Although," he admitted, "I'm surprised by this date that they'd have any bullets left."

"Maybe they salvaged some from your supplies," Preston's practical voice pointed out. "According to your report, you chose to abandon most of the equipment at your base camp."

O'Neil barely hid his surprise that General West had given classified reports to a mining engineer. He glanced toward the growing mound of sand that entombed most of the cases of supplies left behind. "If so, they showed more initiative than I'd have expected." His face became grim. "More discipline, too."

"How so?" Draven demanded.

"Kids and guns are a dangerous combination. Put a gun in a kid's hand, and it may well go off."

The UMC men glanced at each other, then followed silently as O'Neil led the way down the rocky face of escarpment. No other shots rang out.

"Could it have been target practice?" Preston suggested a trifle breathlessly as he swung down, his foot scrabbling for a foothold.

"I'd say it was more in the nature of a signal," O'Neil opined. He was breathing as easily as if he were on a stroll across the parade ground.

"So these people have someone watching the StarGate." The sharp-faced Draven managed to make it sound like a hostile act.

"Well, they would have a vested interest in knowing if anyone appeared," O'Neil pointed out.

"You think this could be due to that professor who took up with the local girl and went native? What was his name—Jackson?" Draven asked.

O'Neil had to chuckle at the idea. "Daniel? I think he'd be too busy translating hieroglyphics and enjoying married life to organize any sort of civil defense."

"Then who has people out there spying on us?" Draven wanted to know.

"There's an easy enough way to find out," O'Neil responded. "We'll go out there and ask them."

He reached the base of the stony outcrop and

set off for the highest dune in sight. Draven and Preston scrambled down and trailed after the colonel. The sand seemed to suck at their feet, making their steps slow and clumsy. O'Neil, in contrast, seemed to glide along, his Desert Storm surplus uniform blurring his movements as he forged ahead.

Draven cursed under his breath as he slogged along in pursuit. He'd reached a point in his UMC career where he expected to jet in to trouble spots and be met by an armored limo and a few bodyguards. A week ago—even a day ago—he'd have laughed at the notion of traipsing through the boonies with a technical staff of one and depending on a smart-ass Marine for protection.

Yet here he was, preparing for the negotiations of his life. Far better than the military, it seemed, UMC realized the possibilities in opening up an entire world for development. They wanted the best contact man they had for the job.

And that man was Walt Draven.

He mopped sweat off his forehead, glancing up to see how far ahead that damned Marine had gotten.

Surprisingly, they'd reached the foot of the large dune. O'Neil was working his way diagonally up the crusted sand face.

Then Draven noticed movement at the crest. "Colonel!" he yelled, the warning coming almost unbidden from his throat. "Above you!"

O'Neil had already heard the commotion over-

head. He stepped up his pace as he scaled his
way to the top, a grin stretching his face.

Lined up at the crest were Skaara and his rag-
tag band of shepherds. When they spotted O'Neil,
their right arms moved in unison to give him a
snappy salute.

"What the *hell*—" Draven muttered as he
stared up.

The boys' discipline wavered and broke as
O'Neil finally reached them. They gathered
around their hero, and Skaara forgot himself sufficiently to give the thoroughly embarrassed colonel a welcome hug and kiss.

"Seems like a very demonstrative culture," Preston remarked dryly.

The young men were jabbering away, eager to
demonstrate their soldiering skills, but the handsome young fellow with the curly hair and ear-
rings quickly restored order with a few sharp if
incomprehensible commands.

"That's one to keep an eye on," Draven said in
a low voice. "A leader."

The pair of earthlings painfully essayed the
climb, to be met by a dozen helping hands to
make their way over the crest. O'Neil made intro-
ductions. "This is Skaara, and the group of young
men who helped us put an end to Ra."

The boy commandos couldn't understand what
he was saying, but they caught the reference to
Ra. Almost to a man, they spat at the mention of
his name.

Again, it was up to Skaara to restore order.

Draven was not much impressed with the young

men. They had no uniforms, all of them clad in dull, ill-fitting homespun. Their equipment was laughable—the handful of rifles not enough to outfit even half their company. The only other sign of martial equipment was the plastic-compound helmet on Nabeh's head.

But Skaara—there, Draven had to admit, there were possibilities. People followed the young man. He had looks. He had leadership potential.

He could either be dangerous, or, as Draven automatically classified him, Skaara could be used to destabilize the present regime—whatever that turned out to be.

CHAPTER 4
ALARMS AND INTRUSIONS

It was just as well that the Horus guards stationed outside the entrance to Sebek's apartments were masked. If Hathor had seen the expressions on their naked faces, she'd probably have felt obliged to kill them all—and that wasn't part of her plan.

The guards' reaction was only to be expected under the circumstances. Hathor was clad in a shift composed of about ten percent linen and ninety percent air—for all intents and purposes, a transparent wrapping for her abundant charms. Ra's servants were, of course, chosen almost from infancy on the basis of physical beauty. Some, like Thoth, grew up to be ugly ducklings in reverse. Hathor, on the other hand, had matured into a beautiful swan, far outstripping her childhood prettiness. The sinuous perfection of her body offered all the attributes one might expect of a goddess of sex and love.

And Hathor was wise enough not to gild the lily. Glass bangles and a pair of thick-soled sandals made up the rest of her seduction ensemble.

One of the guards moved to block her path—he'd happily have rubbed against her—while ogling her with his eagle eyes. "What brings you here?" he demanded.

She set her eyes demurely on the floor. "My master Thoth sent me hither."

The guard grunted, then turned in communication with someone inside the apartment. "Got a girl out here—a peace offering from Thoth."

A couple of coarse interpretations on that phrase came from within—and then an order.

Outside, the guard gave out with a loud guffaw. "Search her?" he laughed. "She's got no place to hide anything!"

Hathor was then ushered into a large marble chamber filled with warriors of Sebek's faction, obviously at play. The place stunk from a pungent combination of beer and sweat. Men shouted at the tops of their lungs, boasting, arguing, placing bets, all in counterpoint to the incessant rattling of dried knucklebones being tossed on the polished stone floor.

As the crowd slowly became aware of Hathor's presence, the din subsided until finally the room was near dead silence, the men eating Hathor up with their eyes. One of Sebek's lieutenants reached him and whispered in his ear.

The crocodile god's broad body lurched upright, his heavy face flushed from an excess of beer. "So, Thoth sent you, did he?"

Hathor nodded.

"And did he send a message with you?"

Hathor shrugged, knowing it was a good effect. "Only that he sends me as a token of his high regard."

"Well, he certainly knows how to choose a good . . . gift. And he's wise in the choice of recipients as well." He turned to his followers with a coarse laugh. "He certainly wouldn't have enough woman-stuff of this quality to send to *all* contenders, would he, men?"

A loud, boozy chorus of assent rose from the assembled warriors.

"So perhaps you'll excuse me while I enjoy Thoth's offering . . . alone."

Sebek hooked a finger to her and set off across the room. Hathor trailed behind, her eyes still modestly downcast. She was impressed by the discipline evident in the troops. Although they hooted and howled, not a man of them moved to put a hand on the woman destined for their leader.

Hathor left the large common room and followed Sebek to a more secluded chamber. The viceroy dropped onto a heavy divan and surveyed her with hot eyes. "Stay there," he said, gesturing for her to stop. "And turn around. I like to see what I'm getting."

With a slow, sinuous movement she revolved before him, displaying herself beneath the wisp of linen she wore. Sebek's breathing was already heavy as he beckoned her forward. Hathor could feel his body heat as she came to a stop inches from the seated man.

Sebek's hands darted out with the eagerness of a two-year-old unwrapping a present. One fist wrapped itself in the exiguous linen of her shift and yanked downward. As her only covering tore and pooled at her feet, Sebek's left hand curved around her hip to grasp a buttock and drag her forward those last few inches. His breath was hot on her belly as he crushed her to him.

Even as Sebek pulled her forward, Hathor's hands were in motion. Her right hand lashed down at the arm holding her while her left slashed upward against Sebek's face. The razor-sharp glass bangles did their work. The viceroy's gashed arm slacked its grip, allowing Hathor to slip free. Her other attack opened Sebek's left cheek from the jawline almost to his eye.

For a long count he sat frozen on the divan, staring at the blood. Then his face contorted with rage. "Bitch!" he muttered, starting to rise.

Hathor's kick caught Sebek in the midsection, driving the air from his body. Long ago, when she had decided to compete in the ranks of the warriors, she sought out the best trainers available. And she had paid them well, in gold or in the coin of love. Her experts explained that Hathor could never develop the strength of arms and shoulders to match a male warrior. Her legs, however, were stronger than any man's arms—not to mention having longer reach. And the delicate-looking sandals she wore boasted a heavy metal plate in the built-up sole.

Sebek's glare seemed to ask, *who is this devil woman?* as he wheezed, trying to get some air into his lungs. A difficult feat, given his bruised stomach muscles, Hathor knew. She could read his dilemma clearly. One call, and the room would be full of warriors. But what effect would it have on his faction if he needed warriors to protect him from a lone, naked woman?

Hathor feinted a low kick with her left foot. When Sebek committed himself to trying to grab her ankle, she shifted to a roundhouse kick coming from the right. The weighted sole caught Sebek in the temple, toppling him to crash half-conscious on the stone floor.

He lay there for a moment, unmoving. Then he tried to prop himself up on hands and knees. A kick to his left elbow nearly wrecked that joint, collapsing Sebek on his side. Hathor followed up with a kick to his kidneys, then hooked a toe under Sebek's ribs, turning him over to expose his more vulnerable underbelly.

The crocodile god tried to huddle into himself and protect his already bruised stomach, only to have one of Hathor's heavy soles come crushing down on his testicles. In a moan of agony, his breath went whooshing out again.

Sebek tried to turn turtle, but Hathor kicked him out flat on his back again. At this point Sebek *wanted* to scream for help, but didn't have enough air in his lungs to do it.

Hathor didn't help the situation. With a cold smile she moved her right foot toward Sebek's throat. The only response the helpless, gasping man could make was to scrunch his jaw down, trying to protect the soft tissue now at risk.

One more kick from the warrior woman twisted Sebek's head back while tearing the wound on his cheek even wider.

Blood gushed down onto the crocodile god's throat as Hathor's foot descended relentlessly. A strangled croak whispered out of his mouth. "Who—"

That was all he could manage.

Hathor's smile became twisted. The question might have been "Who sent you?" Sebek probably suspected one of his rivals in the succession. Thoth, he was sure, didn't have the resources—human or testicular—to set an assassin on him, much less a trained female killer.

But if Sebek's lieutenant had checked with Thoth, as Hathor had fully expected, he'd have gotten wholehearted confirmation of the "gift."

Because Thoth wasn't a free agent anymore. He was acting in support of—indeed, at the orders of—the champion who was going to save and restore Ra's empire.

So Hathor took Sebek's unfinished question as "Who are you?"

She thought it was only fair to let him know. So Hathor stepped away for a moment, removing a package from under the divan. Apparently, these warrior types had yet to realize that Tuat's housekeeping staff were part of the administrative staff—and owed fealty to Thoth.

Hathor removed one of the pectoral necklaces that converted into god heads. As she resumed her position, one foot on Sebek's throat, she settled the necklace around her neck and activated the smart metal mask. The faintly glowing gold-flecked material formed itself into the semblance of a cat's head—the ancient sign of Hathor.

Sebek's eyes bulged in shocked recognition as he stared up at her.

The mask was the last thing he saw. Hathor bore down with her foot, crushing his trachea.

As Sebek writhed in his death throes, Hathor returned to the package she'd arranged to be pre-set, removing a warrior's kilt and donning it. She waited until the crocodile god was truly and irretrievably dead before she headed to the chamber entrance.

Hathor had never doubted her ability to murder Sebek. That had been the easy part of this incursion. Now she faced the real challenge—stepping back into the room where the men-at-arms were taking their recreation, and uniting all there in fealty to her.

Her breath sounded very loud in her helmet as she pressed the tab to unmask. She wanted the warriors to see her face—to recognize the face of the woman Sebek had taken off for his pleasure returning as the warrior who had killed him.

There remained only one final touch. She reached into the satchel and removed the knife. The blade was of a miracle alloy, sharpened down to the thickness of a molecule. A razor would seem hopelessly clumsy beside it.

Hathor hefted the blade. If she didn't succeed in overawing the crowd out there, she'd need the weapon to slash at attackers, perhaps to use on herself if the beasts tried to use her as Sebek had.

But she had a more practical use for the knife right now. She rested the heel of one hand under the corpse's jaw, forcing his head back. Then she began slicing through the flesh and cartilage of the throat. Ignoring the gore that billowed forth, she worked with the same practical moves as a housewife preparing a chicken. The only problem was the neck bones. Thrusting the tip of the knife between two of the cervical vertebrae, she twisted until they popped apart. Then all she had to do was saw away at the flap of skin that still held Sebek's head to his body.

Hathor wiped her knife on the corpse's kilt, then held up the head at arm's length to assess her handiwork. The slash was a bit ragged, and it was still dripping blood. Luckily, like most warriors Sebek affected the long side-lock of youth. The hair provided a convenient handle.

Knife in one hand, Sebek's head in the other, Hathor kicked open the door and strode down the short hallway to the main chamber. The revels again halted as the warriors realized what she was carrying.

Hathor hurled her bloody burden into their midst. "I and I alone killed this one," she chanted in a loud voice, invoking the ceremony of assassination and offering a tacit challenge to all in the room. "There can be but one Sebek, and I have proven my worth by the severest of means."

Still keeping her knife at the guard position, she moved her free hand up to the tumbler switch on her pectoral necklace. "But I will not take Sebek's place," she went on, diverging from the ancient ceremonial. "For my own worth and position are greater than Sebek's. I am legend. I am Hathor."

She triggered the transformation of the biomorphic metal, the cat's head forming over her features. The gleaming mask panned back and forth over the assemblage of fighting men, its eyes glowing green as Hathor intently studied them for any trace of hostile action.

Sebek's followers sat in stunned silence. Their leader had stepped away to enjoy a ripe handmaid. But the maid had returned as a warrior woman bearing Sebek's head. She laid claim to a name legendary even in their ferocious community. But the grisly proof of that claim had been thrown almost contemptuously to bounce among them.

Hathor could almost follow their thoughts from the looks on the warriors' faces. Sebek had been a deadly master of arms and tactics. That was why this assemblage of fighting men had chosen to follow him. But Sebek's strength and craft had obviously been overcome by this interloper.

A grizzled warrior came to the obvious conclusion. He slowly sank to his knees and made obeisance to Hathor. Others followed, until at last the whole room had abased itself in fealty.

Beneath her cat mask Hathor's lips stretched in a fierce grin as she tossed away her knife. *A legend can be a useful thing,* she thought. *A sharper weapon than the best-forged blade.*

Hathor emerged from her ablutions clad only in a towel draped over her shoulders. As a member of a society based on beauty and used to scant clothing, she had no problem. But she noticed that Thoth turned away from her displayed body.

After what had happened to Sebek, almost all of her new followers had become very careful with their eyes.

She felt very good, her muscles reacting at their accustomed capabilities. And certainly she had worked up a sweat this morning.

Hathor was, of course, not taking over Sebek's position in the godhead. But she had decreed that her followers would not be allowed the traditional round of assassinations to determine who the new Sebek would be. Her faction couldn't afford the waste of good warriors.

Instead, Hathor had invited all those interested in becoming the crocodile god to meet her in single combat. Her practical response to the problem had had several useful results. Considerably fewer candidates had come forward to battle for the Sebek position. And her success in handling them—in a non-lethal way—had greatly increased her standing among her own warriors. Besides, when the stories of the single combats got out— men being the gossips they are—her skill at the martial arts would spread among the other factions as well.

Having consolidated her factional position and arranged a fresh influx of propaganda for her legend, Hathor prepared to reach out to another group that could help her establish supremacy over Ra's empire.

Thoth had brought her the administrative mass of Ra's empire. While the present military men might deride Thoth's people as mere bean counters, they had no experience at large-scale operations. Hathor knew the value of good logistics from her time on Ombos.

But there was another non-military component to Ra's power—the masters of technology led by Ptah, engineer of the gods. These were the ones who tuned the spacecraft engines, built the uda-jeet gliders, who fashioned raw quartz-crystal into Ra's instruments of wonder—including the blast-lances the guards were so fond of using.

To gain control of the empire's technicians, Hathor was going to meet Ptah. The engineer tended to wander the empire, constructing and repairing whatever was needed. The scribe spy system, however, had reported that Ptah had arrived on Tuat-the-world and would visit the palace on Tuat-the-moon.

As Thoth stood with averted eyes, Hathor arrayed herself in the regalia of a warrior. "I am ready," she finally pronounced. "Have your people succeeded in locating him?"

Thoth nodded. "He's in the maintenance section of one of the older pyramids."

"Lead the way."

The two moved off with a small cadre of Horus guards. Thoth led them on a circuitous route, both to avoid strongholds of other factions and to disguise their final destination.

Ra would never have been expected in the maintenance levels of his pyramid palace, as was shown by the spartan decor. Instead of polished marble and wide spaces with columns, Hathor's party marched through dark, narrow corridors of raw stone. The air grew warm and stuffier, with a faint ozone smell, as if the very stuff they breathed had been subtly charged, ionized by great energies at work.

Hathor knew this atmosphere only too well. Long ago the first triumph of her career had been to marry the Ptah of the First Time. The move had elevated her status and brought her under the eye of Ra. She and the head god had consorted together, and there was nothing that Ptah could say. He had suffered his divine cuckolding in cold silence, not even commenting on the brilliant military career Hathor had carved out on the basis of her own competence. When she left for Ombos, Ra had been present . . . but Ptah had not.

Following her guards down the Stygian passageway, Hathor banished her thoughts. Ancient history, she told herself. The Ptah of the First Time must have perished thousands of years ago, as had Thoth, Sebek, and all the others . . . except for Ra. And, of course, herself, suspended somewhere between life and death.

Ahead, Hathor discerned light at the end of the tunnel, not the murky, directionless luminescence that Ra favored but a harsh actinic glare.

"His workshop," Thoth whispered.

They entered to find technicians frantically shifting around some mysterious machinery while a masked man wielded an arc welder. The mask was made of smoked glass, unlike the animal heads surmounting most of the gods. The first Ptah had disdained the practice, and had gone into history depicted as a bearded human.

This Ptah had apparently encountered physical disaster of cataclysmic proportions. The arm holding the welding device was mechanical, composed of golden-glistening quartz. In fact, more than half of Ptah's body seemed artificial, the joints between machinery and meat hidden in mummy-like linen wrappings. The few patches of flesh Hathor saw were dead white, seeming to glow with the decaying luminescence of fungus on a swamp tree.

The welding device clicked off as Ptah became aware of his guests, and the protective eye mask morphed into a decorative torc around his neck.

"Ah," said a dry, whispery voice with its own metallic tang. "So the rumors were correct. My journey here is not for nothing. Welcome back, my dear."

For a second Hathor stood frozen, her face almost as pale as the one that confronted her. Once Ptah's face had been reasonably handsome, but now it was a wreck. Half the features, including one eye, were constructed of Ra's biomorphic quartzose material. The flesh that showed was beyond dead white. It had a waxen greenish tinge.

Even more shocking, however, was the fact that Hathor recognized the ruined countenance. The man standing before her was the first Ptah—her erstwhile husband.

Stark incomprehension stiffened her features. Then she turned in rage on Thoth.

"He couldn't have told you, my dear," Ptah spoke up, forestalling her. "Information is only as good as the system that houses it. And certain facts have been ... removed from the chronicles over the years." A half smile tugged at the human side of Ptah's face. "My own origins, for instance, were known only by Ra. Our relationship was expunged, while your connection with our leader took on nearly mythological dimensions."

"How—" Hathor began, gesturing at his cyborg shell. "What—"

"A mishap in correcting a drive flaw in one of the warships you wheedled out of Ra." Ptah strove for suavity, but Hathor could detect a more metallic note in his whispering voice. "You were already occupying Ra's backup sarcophagus, and he was unwilling to forgo his primary unit for the amount of time it would take to cure me. What if he should unexpectedly need it? So he took a more . . . *mechanical* approach to repairing my ills. Unfortunately, that meant I could never use the sarcophagus again."

Ptah ran a metallic hand down the mechanical side of his face. "But I've managed to survive with these expedients. How ironic that I, who eschewed the use of a mask, now wear one permanently."

What Hathor needed to know, however, was what lurked beneath Ptah's mask. Obviously, he blamed her for his disfigured existence. But she could overlook personal enmity in a political alliance.

"You, more than any other, must know what I intend," Hathor said. "Will you support me?"

Ptah spread his arms, one dull-burnished metal, one wizened flesh. "I've examined your rivals," he said candidly. "Left to themselves, they'll destroy everything unless curbed. Yes, dear Hathor, I support you."

But the unsaid words "for now" hung in the air between them.

CHAPTER 5
BUYING IN

Jack O'Neil was wryly amused—and grudgingly impressed—by Skaara's boy soldiers as they accompanied the visitors to the city of Nagada. Skaara had a point man, rear guard, and flankers out as they marched through the dunes. It was perfect Marine recon patrol doctrine—and a testament to Skaara's powers of observation. His order of march was obviously lifted from the way O'Neil had done things on his last visit to Abydos.

The colonel glanced toward the toiling figure of Walter Draven. Maybe UMC's hotshot negotiator was unwise in equating primitive with stupid.

The moment they came in sight of the city walls, Skaara snapped off an order. Nabeh raised his rifle, this time being careful to fire only one shot. As soon as the strangers were spotted, people in the watchtowers began sounding trumpets that looked like gigantic mutated ram's horns. The low-pitched, penetrating *mooing* sound brought the inhabitants out into the streets.

O'Neil was reminded of his first visit to this city, of the people's almost instinctive courtesy and hospitality. They'd been somewhat frightened of strangers then, thinking they came from Ra. This time the huge, heavy gates opened to reveal a smiling, cheering throng.

It struck O'Neil almost as a physical blow when he realized this hero's welcome was for *him*. The Nagadans were turning out in force to hail the man who had destroyed Ra and won their freedom.

The colonel felt an acid pain in the pit of his stomach as he glanced from the cheering multitudes to his earthly companions. The people will take these snakes to their hearts—just because they're with me, he thought. This is why he was here, not to act as a guide—a bitter fact for O'Neil to swallow.

A familiar face appeared in the crowd. Sha'uri beckoned to Skaara, then whispered in her brother's ear. Skaara led the way to a central square. Kasuf and the city Elders stood gathered outside one of the adobe buildings. As the visitors arrived, Daniel Jackson pushed his way out of the crowd to join them.

"We were expecting visitors by and by. So I'll be acting as translator."

Draven stared. "You mean you haven't been teaching those people English?"

"We've been more busy trying to recapture this people's history, stolen from them by Ra," Daniel replied. "Abydos has been kept illiterate for generations."

Draven's smile indicated that he thought this was an excellent notion.

"But in the past few months, more and more people are learning to write . . . in their own language."

"You had to know that sooner or later, contact

with Earth would be reestablished. We are here to inquire into the export of this world's unique mineral wealth." Draven's gesture took in the dilapidated mud structures around the square. "Let's face it, this world could use a generous infusion of American capital and modern conveniences."

"This isn't Disneyland," Daniel angrily retorted. "These people have a culture thousands of years old. They aren't going to roll over for flush toilets and fast food."

"How about modern building materials and medical supplies?" Draven purred. He nodded to the Elders. "And shouldn't these local leaders make the choice for their people?"

O'Neil shook his head. Watching the unworldly academic go up against the corporate shark was the worst mismatch since Godzilla versus Bambi. As the negotiations began, the Elders drove a better bargain than Daniel. Unless, perhaps, he'd given them some advance warning.

Grudgingly, Daniel offered to start classes in English.

"I don't think it's necessary to divert you from your studies," Draven said smoothly. "My company will take on that job."

And control who can work with UMC and who can't, O'Neil added silently.

"Perhaps our first order of business is to set wages for those who work in the mine," Draven suggested.

"Daniel has mentioned this," Kasuf said, earning the translator a black look.

"We wish you to explain how the system works," the Elder went on.

Draven started. "Don't you pay your miners?"

As Kasuf went into a long, detailed explaination, Daniel looked over at Draven. "Do you want this word for word, or short and sweet? He's going back to the beginning of the mines, about eight thousand years ago."

"You might want to keep to the high points," Draven said, looking a little dazed.

"Okay," Daniel said. "Under Ra's rule the mine was a civic obligation—consider it sort of a sweaty local version of jury duty. The whole community worked whenever they were needed. In return, the Elders here provided food and drink, and shelter from the suns. When you go to the mines, you'll see that the largest construction there—other than the nine million ladders to get up and down—is something the people here call the Tent of Rest. And after you've been down in the heat and the dust of the mine itself, you'll see why it's needed."

"Please tell Kasuf that my company will gladly take over the expense for this rest tent," Draven said. "In fact, I was going to suggest some such arrangement." He gave a sidewise glance toward the Elders. "So you're saying that they have no idea of how to pay for labor?"

"No, they pay wages, but when it came to the mine, people didn't get paid because Ra didn't pay. He just demanded the ore, and if they didn't deliver enough and on time, they died."

"Sounds like an interesting character," Draven said.

Daniel nodded. "I'm sure you'd have loved his labor-management style."

The UMC negotiator's lips twitched. "Anyway, to payment. From the sounds of it, there probably won't be enough local coinage to allow us to pay the workforce we'll need."

Daniel translated, and after some discussion with his colleagues, Kasuf agreed.

"Perhaps we can agree on some sort of interim coinage," Draven suggested.

O'Neil's face tightened. Certainly. UMC could probably provide company coins at a huge profit. They could even manipulate the value of the company currency.

Daniel and the Elders went back and forth several times on this point. "I'm explaining about scrip and company stores," Daniel told Draven with a grim smile.

So much for that proposal. In the end, Draven had to agree on paying American money. But that agreement led to new problems. The Elders—for that matter, no one on Abydos—had ever seen paper money. When Draven provided some samples, they fiddled unhappily with the bills.

"They say they want coins," a frustrated Daniel translated.

"That may not be a problem," Draven said. "Suppose we offer one of these an hour." He pulled a quarter out of his pocket.

Daniel stared. "You've got to be kidding!" he

sputtered. "You want those people to do that
back-breaking labor for two dollars a day?"

"Do you want to flood this city's economy with
American dollars?" Draven shot back. "I've seen
what happens to local industries when people
start buying foreign goods."

He extended a placating hand. "Besides, this is
merely a token payment. I think a fair arrangement would be to offer the government here a
percentage of the ore's value on the world—our
world—market. A royalty, if you will."

A royalty calculated by UMC. O'Neil wondered
how much that would be worth.

From that point the discussion went back and
forth, but the basic payment structure had been
set. Royalty payments would allow the Elders to
buy modern conveniences the city really needed—
a hospital, for instance. Clean water. Plumbing.
The burghers of Nagada fought hard for their people, but they had no idea of the scale of resources
UMC represented.

Daniel's one victory came when he dug a Susan
B. Anthony dollar out of his pocket. "I got stuck
with one of these, and now I carry it for a good
luck charm. Lucky for these people, at least. This
should be the coin you pay the workers."

So Daniel at least had quadrupled the miners's
take-home pay.

The first round of negotiations ended with effu-
sive compliments on both sides. Daniel wanted the
agreement in writing, but Draven avoided that pit-
fall with easy facility. "I'm sure the Elders would
see no need for a written document," he said.

"Certainly a bond of honor is sufficient between men of good will."

Daniel doubted that, and argued the point fiercely with Kasuf and his circle. But Nagada's illiterate civic leaders had done business verbally all their lives. Draven won the point, and Jackson looked too disgusted to enjoy the obligatory feast for the visitors. O'Neil left the UMC men to enjoy the lizardly monster that tasted like chicken. Instead, he sought out Daniel.

"Watch these guys," he warned quietly. "Their company is connected with the CIA—and they're very used to manipulating things in the Third World."

"Well, this is the Fourth World," Daniel responded, but his voice sounded a little hollow. "Why are you acting as great white hunter for these characters?"

O'Neil didn't meet Daniel's eyes. "Orders," he replied briefly.

The next morning, it was Martin Preston's time to take center stage. "I want to examine the mine workings," the UMC engineer said. "It's hard enough translating the expected tonnage of material from the ancient Egyptian system of weights and measures. How do we know these estimates are on the money?"

"They are reduced somewhat from what the locals delivered for Ra," Daniel admitted. "But then, he was liable to kill them if he didn't get enough of the stuff."

The UMC men set off with an escort that included O'Neil, Daniel, Kasuf, some other Elders, and Skaara.

"I understand this is a pit mine," Preston said as they made their way across the desert into an already scorching morning.

"I suppose you'd call it that," Daniel replied. "They bring the ore up from a deep hole in the ground." Ahead of them rose a large, billowing shape—a homespun tent erected on posts as tall as telephone poles.

"That's the Tent of Rest," Daniel said. "The workers need both shade and water under these suns."

Beyond the tent were the works themselves. A thin line of men and women waited to descend one ladder while a matching line rose from the deep, dust-streaming ravine. The members of the climbing line each carried satchels full of quartzose ore. The satchels on those waiting to descend were empty.

Kasuf spoke, and Daniel translated. "They're working with a skeleton crew right now. Most of the miners have been diverted to crop planting and irrigation work." Daniel gave the advance man a lopsided smile. "That's something else they couldn't do in the face of Ra's slave driving."

Preston stood at the lip of the ravine, his mouth wide open as he took in the mining operation. The walls of the ravine extended downward for hundreds of feet, with rough ledges carved out at irregular intervals. The only access between levels was by sturdy but crude ladders, built with two lanes for climbing or descent. The structural members were trunks of whole saplings with the bark removed. The rungs were peeled tree branches.

Bearers moved in an antlike stream up and down the ladders, picking up chunks of ore. On the ledges, but often on ladders themselves, workers swung rough picks or mattocks, physically chopping the ore out of the surrounding rock.

"My God," Preston breathed, staring downward. "They told me it was crude . . . but this is downright primitive."

Sure, O'Neil thought, he's used to seeing Third World mines run on leftover nineteenth-century European technology. This is more like the technical level of sixty centuries B.C.

The mining engineer frowned, still staring downward.

"Something wrong?" O'Neil asked.

"This isn't natural," Preston said.

"Of course not," the colonel responded. "They've been digging here for about eight thousand years."

"That wouldn't account for this ravine." Preston leaned farther out, making O'Neil hope the man had good balance.

"Okay," the colonel said, "so there was a fissure here in the first place, and the locals have just enlarged it."

But Preston gave him a negative head shake. "There's no natural reason there should be a canyon here in the first place—no water, and this couldn't be done by wind erosion." He exchanged glances with Draven and O'Neil. "Look, I know enough about geology—I'm a mining engineer, for heaven's sake."

Preston's eyes returned to the abyss. "It's as though the hand of God gouged a chasm in the rock right where the ore would be. And these folks have been digging and enlarging it ever since."

"Not God, but an alien with the powers of a god," O'Neil said somberly. If Ra had weapons to gouge a planet's crust, maybe they'd been lucky that he hadn't expected much trouble on Abydos. The terrestrial visitors had considered Ra's pyramidal spaceship damned huge and impressive. What if that turned out to be a mere yacht?

In that case, what would a space battleship look like?

"What do you mean, the warships aren't available anymore?" The honeymoon was definitely over in the alliance between Hathor and Ptah. She was crouched over a worktable in his shop, her clenched fists resting on scarred stone.

The creation of a space fleet had been the crowning glory of her influence over Ra. He preferred to exert force through his StarGates, and was reluctant to allow spacecraft even to trusted subordinates. With the StarGates, rebels had nowhere to run. Even in the back of Hathor's mind was the possibility that in case of defeat, she could take off with her flotilla and establish herself as ruler in some other corner of the universe.

Ra did not take kindly to argument, but Hathor had stuck to her point. The Ombos rebels had considerable technology—and they would doubtless have the StarGate targeted. A spaceborne strike proved much less expensive—and it had been successful.

Catching up on history since her internment, Hathor had been baffled that the fleet hadn't been used to put down the revolt on Earth. Now she knew why.

"Where are the ships?" Hathor demanded.

"I'll show you." Ptah turned to a panel and flipped some controls. A holographic image swam into existence. Thoth gave a nervous start when he recognized the scene. It was a supposedly secure crystal-domed gallery where so many clandestine meetings had taken place.

Ptah manipulated more controls, and the viewpoint shifted. They now appeared to be looking through the dome at the surface of the moon outside.

Hathor frowned. "What happened to the spaceport?" she demanded.

She saw only a single docking station, a raw-looking pyramid of medium size. Where the others had stood, there were now two pyramid-domes, obviously representing permanent installations.

"Look more closely at the additions to the palace," Ptah advised.

Hathor examined the image more carefully and realized that despite accretions at their bases, the two new edifices were based on the superstructures of a pair of her old battleships.

"After leaving you to your rest, Ra briefly utilized the ships as escorts for his flying palace," Ptah explained. "The only practical purpose he put them to was on Abydos. Ra used the main batteries to gain access to a deposit of the crystal-element."

Ptah gave his erstwhile wife a sidelong glance. "But your toys, like your ambitions, troubled Ra. While you slept, he finally decommissioned the vessels."

Hathor nodded in silence, well understanding the head god's purpose. Demolishing the ships would deny malcontents any viable chance of escape. "How long would it take to make those vessels spaceworthy again?"

"One of them was completely gutted," Ptah said. "The other at least retains a command deck." He glanced at the technicians in the workshop. "We use it as a training center, preparing backup crews for Ra's yacht."

"How long?" Hathor persisted.

"We could probably refit the drives on one ship. There's also the question of hull integrity. Many access ways were cut in the inner hull, connecting passages within the stone pyramid with companionways in the ship. It would mean a serious patching job. We'd have to remount the offensive batteries, reconnect the fire-control computers, restore life support . . . it wouldn't take as long as building a ship from scratch, but a recommissioning effort would require considerable time."

They stood in silence for a moment, until Ptah finally gave in to the pressure of the dark eyes on him. "The better part of a year," he said at last.

"Three months," Hathor told him flatly. "It should take me that long to establish my position here. I sincerely hope you can manage your work as swiftly. Your immortality depends upon it." She gave Ptah a smile as artificial as most of his body. "How unfortunate, after surviving as long as you have, that I should lose you over so trivial a matter, husband."

CHAPTER 6
PREPARATIONS

The task of turning a pleasure dome back into a battleship was difficult enough, given the lack of dock-construction facilities. Ra had done away with them millennia ago, and Ptah wasn't one to cry over spilled milk. Still worse from the engineer god's point were the delays attributable to political obstacles.

Several of Hathor's rivals maintained suites of apartments in the former battlewagons, or housed their troops in barracks within the construction. These warrior gods were not about to move merely to oblige a strange woman they considered an enemy and an upstart. They'd doubtless become more hostile when they learned the aim of the alterations.

In a couple of cases Hathor managed to achieve her aims by negotiation. She even managed to foment a brief internecine war between two would-be successors by intermingling their troops in the same barracks.

Other faction leaders were more astute—or intransigent. They wouldn't move, forcing Hathor to come to blows with them. She was still husbanding her faction's resources and trying to avoid large-scale combat, so she engineered arguments and duels. The net result was several new openings in the godly hierarchy, an attendant swelling of forces in fealty to Hathor, deeper enmity from the surviving warlords, and a clearance of tenants from the old battlewagon.

Briskly done, Ptah had to admit. His former wife had lost none of her skills during her long sleep. She was, in fact, well on the way to achieving supremacy on Tuat well within the three-month timetable she'd established for herself.

The job of battleship reconstruction was not going as smoothly. Ptah's efforts suffered from shortages of trained personnel. Even by stripping all other projects in the empire, he had little more than a skeleton crew available for refitting.

He hated to admit it, but the lack of technicians was perhaps a sign that Ra's empire was running down. Certainly of late, the sun god had paid more attention to his warriors than to the constructive side of his governmental establishment.

Perhaps it was past time for a successor.

But Ptah might have wished for a leader a bit more flexible than Hathor. She'd have no problem making an example of him, in the expectation of encouraging the next Ptah to meet the deadlines she set.

The fact that she'd be losing an invaluable technical resource, trained by Ra himself, would not matter at all to her. At least not in the short term.

So Ptah was forced for the first time in a few thousand years to devote himself to short-term planning. His technicians worked twelve-hour shifts. He himself got his hands dirty, performing manual labor while simultaneously managing everyone else's work. When he bothered to check into it, he realized he was getting by on only a couple of hours' sleep each day—one of the advantages of a mechanically assisted body.

Even so, the project fell inexorably behind schedule.

Ptah stood in the ruins of an arcaded hall, welding a steel plate across what had been a delicately fashioned archway. Rough welds stood out like scar tissue against the inlaid metalwork of the arch. The craftsman in Ptah cried out against the quick and dirty job.

But the plate, ugly as it was, did serve to seal off yet another passageway entrance. While the ship's structural integrity hadn't been compromised by all this peacetime construction, the multifarious openings to adits in the former docking station had turned the vessel's inner hull into a sieve. All such orifices had to be closed.

Ptah put down his arc welder. Well, at least that joint should hold against hard vacuum. Although they wouldn't be able to test for leaks until the engines were up and calibrated. Then there'd be the navigation tests and, finally, physical disengagement from this rock.

The godly engineer shrugged that prospect aside as being far distant in the future. He was consulting a holographic plan to see which leak next needed caulking when one of his foremen came down the companionway.

"What are my people to do when they're scheduled for two jobs at the same time?" the man com-

plained, pressed beyond tact by exhaustion and
the exigency of work. "We can either install those
new secondary weapons mounts, or test the fire
control for the main batteries," he said bluntly.
"We simply can't do both."

"Install the new weapons," Ptah replied after a
moment's thought.

The foreman stared. "Half those fire-control circuits are original with the ship," he reminded
Ptah. "We just patched them into new consoles.
And there aren't any backups." This was unlike
his usually perfectionist master. Ptah insisted on
redundant systems and extensive cross-testing.

But the engineer of the gods only shrugged. "I
tried to get a year, expecting to finish the job in
half that time," Ptah said. "But I have only a quarter of a year, which I estimate to be half the time
I really need."

His ghastly face gave the foreman an even
ghastlier smile. "Under those constraints I am expected to present Hathor with a ship that can fly
and shoot. I will do so. *We* must do so."

He sent his dubious craftsman off to execute a
mass-production job.

Given Ptah's already papery voice, the foreman
wouldn't be expected to catch his master's muttered comment: "I simply won't warrant *how long*
it will do both."

Eugene Lockwood had made himself a reputation in UMC as a site manager who got things done.
He prided himself on being equally at home in an
office or on the bottom of a mine shaft. But

though he tried to keep it off his almost handsome, boy-next-door face, Lockwood found it
vaguely off-putting to be working in an office at
the bottom of a mine shaft. Or, to be more spe-
cific, in the bottom of the missile silo that housed
the StarGate to Abydos.

He was eager to establish himself on this new
planet, to get hands-on. But there were a few million administrative details to be settled on Earth
before he could get to work on his new assign-
ment. A major annoyance was dealing with
UMC's technical advance man, Martin Preston.
Because of his expertise in primitive mining tech-
niques, Preston had been moved to Lockwood's
management team as a consultant.

Lockwood just hoped the old boy didn't expect
his advice to be taken seriously.

"You've got to see these people at work to believe it," Preston was saying for about the doz-
enth time.

"I've looked at photos," the manager said dis-
missively, depriving the engineer of eye contact by
looking through some reports.

Preston didn't get the hint. "Pictures don't give
any real hint of the *scale* of the operation," he
went on. "And they're doing it all by brute-labor
methods. No steam hoists. Not even tracks and
ore cars."

"Right, right, you've pointed this out." Forget-
ting himself, Lockwood directed an impatient
glare at the engineer. "The people at corporate
level tasked me with three directives. One, I'm
supposed to get this mine up and modernized.

Two, I'm to handle any disruptions from outside sources—that means marginalizing this Daniel Jackson character."

He shrugged. "I don't see any problem there. He's offered to teach the locals English. But we'll offer English classes that will knock the natives' socks off. Audio-visual. Multimedia. We've already hired an educational TV company to make it as slick as possible. I'm figuring how many portable generators we'll need to run the video screens."

Lockwood brought himself back to the task at hand. "And finally, I'm supposed to do all this while managing a profitable production of ore from the mine operation as it exists now."

"But you're holding to production figures that I told you are too high." Preston's pudgy face was tight with disapproval. "I thought the figures cited by the Elders at Nagada were excessive, and you've inflated them."

"It's a level of production that this mine has achieved in the past, according to our military sources."

"Yes. I was there with one of those military sources. He told me the only way those figures were achieved was by using the whole city's population as slave labor. This great god Ra or whatever was working them with guns to their heads. How do you expect to match that?"

Annoyed, Lockwood went back to riffling through reports. "My mandate is to achieve the highest production possible from the get-go. You copy? This quartz stuff is apparently very valuable, judging from its price per ton. It's also very versatile, because research centers all over the country are screaming for it. And we've got to provide the stuff—in bulk."

He tried to sweeten this annoying subordinate. "So I'll have to ask you and the local labor force to sweat a little until we get modern methods in to pick up some of the slack—"

" 'Pick up the slack?' " Preston echoed. "There's no way we can modernize part of that operation without disrupting the rest of it. These people have been working that deposit in the same manner for thousands of years. There's no way you're going to come in with hoists and ore conveyors and not joggle their elbows. You're not even considering a training curve for using your new technology. Production at that mine is going to go down—perhaps steeply—before it heads up."

"Thank you for your consultation," Lockwood said. "I think you're wrong. Why don't you let me worry about modernizing the place while you do the job I need you to do. You just keep these Abydos people as productive as possible during our teething pains." Lockwood gave Preston a wintry smile. "Until we have the machines in and can afford to get rid of most of them."

"Meals, Ready to Eat." The bald supply officer looked dubiously at the amount O'Neil was requisitioning. "For the number of men you're taking, this will be a six-month supply."

"We don't know if reinforcements will be needed," O'Neil replied.

"I thought you were expecting to get supplies from the local people."

"We expect to," O'Neil said. "But I want to make sure we don't strain their resources—and I want a reserve."

"It's just a case of trucking the stuff here and getting it through that StarGate thingie," the supply man said.

O'Neil hid a smile. There spoke a man who'd never been through the StarGate. He wondered how the man would feel about the "StarGate thingie" after it tore him down to atoms and squirted them a million light-years through a tunnel that didn't obey three-dimensional geometry.

The bald officer moved on, his hand scratching in puzzlement through the fringe of hair around his vast expanse of scalp. "Now, about all this ammunition." He squinted at the quantity requested. "You intend to run a whole lot of live-fire exercises?"

"I don't know who or what we may end up shooting at," O'Neil said. "But I don't want the balloon to go up and have us stuck without enough ordnance to handle whatever happens. Besides, we may get reinforcements, and I want bullets for them as well as food."

"Um-hmmm," the bald man said. "A chicken in every pot, and a Stinger missile for every man." He tapped another figure on the requisition list. "You want more Stingers than we sent to Afghanistan for their entire holy war. And the towel heads on this—um, Abydos—are so backward they'd probably think a bow and arrow was hopelessly high-tech. Why do you think you'll need so many hand-held missiles?"

O'Neil restrained himself with difficulty. "I need the Stingers because General West turned me down on building some hardened SAM sites."

The officer stared at O'Neil in disbelief. "You wanted to set up fortified surface-to-air missile sites on this planet? What for? You think the Russkis are going to sell the towelheads—"

This time he caught O'Neil's disapproving look.

"Ah, the *natives* have a couple of Air Force-surplus MiGs that we'll have to defend ourselves against?"

Then understanding dawned on the officer's face. "Oh, maybe you're concerned about flybys from the people who built the StarGate."

He tried a joke. "Are you sure Stingers are effective against flying saucers?"

O'Neil didn't laugh at the man's heavy humor. "I could give a rat's ass about flying saucers." His face grew more somber as he remembered the combat gliders his second in command, Lieutenant Kawalski, had had to dodge. Not to mention Ra's own spacegoing palace.

"It's the big flying pyramids that worry the crap out of me."

CHAPTER 7
LEARNING THE MOVES

On the Abydos side of the StarGate, a sudden wash of energy spurted outward from the toroidal quartzose ring, then formed itself in a vortex pointing in the opposite direction. Then the energy flux stabilized into a shimmering lens shape, like a glowing liquid jewel in a golden quartz bezel. An instant later, that jewel-like illusion was destroyed as a ripple disturbed the shimmering surface, and a human figure formed and was spat out.

Eugene Lockwood's first step on an alien planet was more like a humiliating belly flop. From his briefing, he knew he was inside a giant pyramid, in a good-sized hall. What he didn't expect was the godawful racket of a gasoline-powered generator powering a temporary light system. The explosions of the machine's internal combustion engine echoed off the dressed-stone walls.

Lockwood moved from the StarGate chamber down a hallway to a wider room set with what appeared to be beaten-copper disks vertically arranged on the floor and ceiling. His briefing described this room as the site of some sort of short-range matter transmitter. Beyond was a rising ramp, a huge stone gallery, which then widened into a pillared entrance hall.

Here he caught up with the people he'd come to see—the UMC blasting team assembling demolition charges around the narrow exit to the outside world. In contrast to the generous proportions of the inside passages, the entrance itself was a virtual bottleneck, barely as wide as the height of a tall man. Lockwood cast an anxious glance at the planted explosives as the team wired up the detonators.

"You're sure this will work?" he asked the head blaster, a short, red-faced man who worked with a slightly soggy, unlit cigar clamped between his teeth.

The look the explosives expert gave his boss was almost hot enough to set off the blasting charges. "We've checked the load-bearing limits of the stones, and we know how to site a blast. All our shaped charges will do is widen that doorway— unless you want to bring all the equipment you send to this joint in small pieces."

"But it won't harm the StarGate?" the nervous Lockwood pressed.

"That doodad is about as far from the discharge as you can get," the demolitions expert replied. "But we're gonna set up some blast shields just in case."

He ran an experienced eye over his subordinates' work. "Perfect," he declared, his cigar at a jaunty angle. "When this blows out, we'll use the rubble to help widen the ramp leading up to the door."

They unspooled detonator wires backward to the StarGate chamber. More men and materials were arriving from Earth. Heavy steel shields and braces moved forward to block the entrances to the StarGate and transporter rooms.

"We're ready to go," the blaster announced. So Lockwood did, heading back to Earth.

It seemed that no sooner had he arrived and pulled himself together than the blaster came hurtling out of the StarGate.

"Crank 'em up, boys!" he cried to the other workers in the converted missile silo.

If the noise in the StarGate chamber had been loud, the roar that filled the converted missile silo was deafening. The heavy engines of the earthmovers stationed in front of the StarGate throbbed with power, a low counterpart to the cycling of the gate itself. Lockwood felt a moment's sympathy for the Army sentries permanently posted at the transition point. The tumult was like a physical blow. Those poor grunts must be practically numb.

Three bulldozers stood ready to move to Abydos. The first ground its way up the expanded and strengthened ramp to the rippling energy lens, moved through, and disappeared. Remembering his own disorientation, Lockwood fervently hoped that the driver remembered to cut the engine as he hit the threshold.

The StarGate cycled down, giving the first machine time to move out. A few minutes later, power was fed again to the alien construction, and the second earthmover passed through.

Lockwood waited until the third construction digger had arrived on Abydos before risking the

StarGate again. He arrived to find that the bulldozers had already cleared the blast-shields from
the passageway. Following gingerly after the
throbbing mechanisms, Lockwood and the blasting chief retraced their steps through the chambers and up the ramp.

As they reached the entrance hall, the executive
could see that there was much more light coming
in. The slit-like gap in the wall was no more. Instead, a much wider opening allowed the glare of
Abydos's three suns to pour in through a cloud of
rock dust.

The new, improved portal would require some
work—broken stone at the ragged ends of the
blast needed to be shorn straight, perhaps a con-
crete arch would have go in place. But the new
adit was more than wide enough to accommodate
an earthmover, as one of the bulldozer operators
demonstrated as he jockeyed his machine forward
to push away the first load of rubble.

"It's a start," Lockwood conceded.

And we didn't bring the roof down on ourselves,
he silently added.

The outward-directed force of the blast, combined with the long, tube-like set of chambers behind it, had the same effect as the *crack!* of a rifle
shot—except on a much more massive scale. And
this "rifle" was aimed directly at the city of
Nagada.

The blast wave didn't hurt anything—the explosion was too far away and the city too sturdily
built. But the sound struck the inhabitants like a

sonic boom, a more impressive experience, since
only one of them—Daniel Jackson—had any experience of jet planes.

Daniel abruptly declared an end to his advanced
hieroglyphics class when the dull booming sound
pulsated through the air.

"What the hell could that be?" he muttered
as he set off through the streets in search
of Kasuf.

Daniel found the town leader in consultation with several of the other Elders. They
adjourned to one of the spidery watchtowers,
hoping to get a long-range glimpse of whatever
was going on.

Kasuf's face was stiff with dread, and Daniel
could understand his concern. The last things to
come from the great pyramid had been udajeet
gliders lancing down out of the sky on a terror
mission, lancing bolts of destruction into the helpless city.

A couple of Skaara's home-guard members
came into view, running madly up the dunes. One
fired off a rifle shot into the sky while the other
gesticulated in the direction of the pyramid.

Kasuf drew himself up. Whatever was going on
out there, it would have to be met and dealt with.
He called an order, and several howdah-equipped
mastadges came galumphing down the crooked
streets. Well, Daniel thought, they'd ride out in
comfort and the best possible local speed to investigate events.

The massive gates of the city opened, and the
cavalcade—or was that mastadge-cade? a be-

mused Daniel wondered—set off. Skaara had turned up from somewhere to join them as they careened their way over the brownish dunes.

Soon enough they reached the young watchers, who accorded Skaara snappy military-style salutes. Their report, however, was less precise. Apparently, there had been a tremendous explosion at the pyramid where Ra's spacecraft had docked. Afterward, a roaring yellow machine appeared. Seeing this, the boy commandos had fled to spread the word.

Daniel frowned. Could something have gone wrong with the StarGate? For a second an unworthy part of him hoped so. Better that he lose his connection with Earth than see the culture of Abydos torn apart by corporate wolves.

They topped a dune and came into sight of the pyramid. Daniel saw bulldozers and wreckage, and a red haze descended over his vision.

The front face of the pyramid was no longer a perfect sweep of limestone. The base had been blasted, and a huge rent had been torn in the stone. Instead of the severe, tight arch of the old entrance, rubble was now being shoved to either side of the old entrance ramp. Among the wreckage were the pair of stone obelisks which had once flanked the ramp.

Kasuf and his compatriots sucked air between their teeth in shock. More workers marched out of the violently expanded gateway. Some went to work shoring up the breach they'd created. Others began laying gravel over the stony rubble and mixing cement. Apparently, they intended to expand the rampway to three times its original width. That would allow heavy machinery like the bulldozers to roll down without problems—not to mention big trucks.

Daniel was so angry, he flung himself out of the howdah before the mastadge stopped moving—and nearly got himself stomped on.

After managing the avoid the mastadon-like beast's huge, klutzy feet, Daniel began running for the ramp. "What the hell are you guys do—"

He skidded to a stop after confronting something he hadn't noticed in his anger. There was a military presence around the pyramid. Marine troopers in desert camouflage were aiming rifles at him.

Slowly, Daniel spread his arms to show that his hands were empty. "Hey, guys. No gun, see? I speak the same language you do, right? You can't shoot me. I'm the translator."

An all-American civilian type with the word *executive* written all over him came storming down the ramp. "What are you people playing at—*Lawrence of Arabia* on mutated camels? You could have gotten hurt, wandering into a construction zone."

"Yeah, well, we didn't see any warning signs up about getting crushed or shot," Daniel retorted. "Our only clue was the explosion when you blasted our pyramid."

"*Your* pyramid? I believe our Mr. Draven made it clear that we required unlimited access to the StarGate."

"But we didn't know 'unlimited access' meant blowing holes in an eight thousand-year-old monument so your bulldozers could roll. The least you might have done is given us some warning."

The executive looked at Daniel as if the Egyptologist were something extremely unpleasant he'd scraped off his shoe. "You must be Jackson."

"Daniel Jackson, Ph.D. And you?"

"Eugene Lockwood. I'm the UMC site manager. And right now we're preparing the site."

"Way to go, Lockwood. You've got a start on your truck route, and all it cost you was any goodwill Draven built up among the people who live here. Take a look at them."

Daniel gestured to Kasuf and the other Elders, who stared at the wreckage Lockwood's plans had created. Their expressions were critical, to say the least.

"On the other hand, the sooner we get into production on the mine, the sooner UMC can offer things this world needs." Lockwood nodded toward Kasuf and the Elders. "You might tell them *that*."

"I'll tell them that—it's about time *you* turned up!" Daniel was looking over Lockwood's shoulder at a newcomer to the confrontation.

Jack O'Neil was not in a good mood. "I got here as soon as I heard that UMC requested a security team for their . . . alterations."

"Your guys nearly shot us when we came to investigate the blast," Daniel accused.

"A calm, laid-back investigator like you?" O'Neil raised an eyebrow. "How could that be?"

One week later, Skaara took his seat for Daniel's third English class. Actually, it was a joint teaching effort, with Daniel and Sha'uri at the front of the room.

What concerned Skaara was the growing number of empty seats. He counted only half as many students as had appeared at the first class.

Daniel noticed it, too. "Is it something I said?" he asked, trying to make a joke of his misgivings. "I may not have the world's greatest accent in your language. That's why I asked Sha'uri to join me."

"It's not your teaching—or your accent," one of the students apologized. "It's the classes those others are giving at their camp."

"The camp" had quickly crept into the vocabulary of everyone in Nagada. In mere days, Lockwood had created a tent city on the rocky plateau that supported the StarGate pyramid. A constant stream of material seemed to be transiting over from Earth. In addition, the security force of Marines commanded by Jack O'Neil had taken up defensive positions.

Although the Marines offered far more protection than his home guard unit, Skaara had maintained the watch on the pyramid. It was more of an exercise for the young men, but Skaara had gotten reports of a continuing trickle of Nagadans visiting the encampment.

"So what have they got that we don't?" Daniel

asked. "Prettier teachers? Or are they grading on the curve?" He waved his hand. "I'm sorry. I'm making bad jokes—and nobody here even understands what I'm joking about."

Daniel glanced at Sha'uri. "So let's start working on some things we *can* understand." He started to work on the lesson.

When the class ended, Skaara set off from Nagada's gates and across the dunes. He stopped briefly at his watch point, then went on to the UMC camp. He looked for a Marine uniform and put his fledgling English into use. "Ko-ro-nel O'Near—O'Neil," he corrected himself.

Surprised, the Marine pointed the way to the command tent.

Jack O'Neil was surprised to see Skaara. But he was even more surprised when the young man spoke to him. "Hello, Colonel."

"Hello, Skaara."

"My sister teaches me. Daniel, too."

O'Neil smiled. "They're doing a very good job."

"They teach here, too." Skaara frowned, trying to get his point across with a limited vocabulary. "People Daniel teaches. They come here . . ."

"You want to know why?" O'Neil had to smile at Skaara's eager nod. "Good idea, General."

The young man looked confused. "General," O'Neil repeated, snapping a salute. "You General, I salute."

Skaara touched his chest. "General."

"You're scouting." O'Neil shaded his eyes with

his hand, miming the action of scoping things out. "We call that intelligence."

Poor Skaara looked totally lost. O'Neil toned down his conversation. "I'll show you the classes. You look around."

UMC's English classes were being conducted in a large, airy tent. Skaara's eyes were big as he took in the banks of computer and video monitors. Some showed incredible machines, like the earth-movers he'd seen at the pyramid. There were other pictures of great, boxy wagons that moved on many wheels, but had no mastadges to pull them.

There were also brightly animated figures on other screens moving to cheerful music. The young man had wondered how people who didn't speak his language could teach theirs. The flashing figures explained how. The UMC teachers were using hieroglyphics—and besides deserters from his English class, Skaara also saw faces he recognized from Daniel's literacy courses.

The strangers were using Daniel's own work to lure away his students!

It certainly wasn't perfect. Skaara saw several signs he didn't understand, and some that were just plain wrong.

One of the teaching staff approached him. "You want to learn my tongue?" he asked in a broken, fumbling sort of dialect. "You must help teach me yours."

"The teacher in the city speaks my tongue better," Skaara replied. "Why shouldn't I learn from him?"

"That one is not . . ." The teacher tapped the side of his head. "In my place, he is a failure."

Skaara kept his face noncommittal. But when he returned home, he'd have much to discuss with Daniel and Sha'uri.

CHAPTER 8
HARSH EDUCATION

Daniel couldn't believe what Skaara had to tell him. "Televisions. Computers. All the bells and whistles." He saw the incomprehension on Skaara's and Sha'uri's faces and apologized. "Sorry. An expression from back home."

Listening to the content of what Skaara had seen, he scowled. "So. Part of this show is to impress people with the wonderful machines Lockwood intends to bring here. He may even be looking for people with an aptitude to run them. They'd be a lot cheaper to pay than bringing people from Earth. Most of that can be done with pictures. But how can they talk to people? I can't believe the Marines picked up enough words . . ."

When Skaara explained about the dancing hieroglyphics, Daniel's eyes went big behind his glasses. "They're trying to learn ancient Egyptian from the people *I* taught how to write? Using hieroglyphics?"

"Some didn't make any sense," Skaara said. Using chalk on a piece of slate, he drew one of the odd figures he'd seen on the glowing screens. "I can't get the colors, of course," Skaara apologized.

Daniel, however, was staring at the glyph

Skaara had drawn. He began to laugh. "No wonder you couldn't understand what this means. Those idiots are using Budge's work—and it's full of mistakes."

His good humor restored, he turned to Sha'uri. "Looks like we'll have to reopen enrollment for our English classes," he said. "This time we choose people we didn't teach how to write. You'll handle the spoken word, and I'll teach them the English alphabet." He frowned and muttered in English, "Wonder if I could send away for that phonics course I always used to hear advertised."

The strangers made great progress in a very short time. A road now stretched from the pyramid housing the StarGate to the mining site. Trucks roared back and forth. Work began on the first mechanical hoist system to carry the ore from the depths to the surface. But in the meantime the quartz material still had to be dug and transported by hand.

Lockwood made several visits to Nagada, bargaining with the Elders for more workers and harder effort. He wasn't meeting his production estimates. He brought staff members along, and as his teachers became more proficient in the local idiom, some of them accompanied the manager as well. At least they verified that Daniel Jackson was translating Lockwood's requests fairly and accurately.

The UMC man was not happy to hear this. He had a sizable gap developing between what he'd promised his superiors and the amount of ore being loaded. And Lockwood wanted someone to blame. He tried incentives, raising the rates of workers who produced more than usual. It didn't represent *that* much of a monetary drain. The elders had agreed on daily wages that would produce coronaries in most mineworkers' unions. The only problem was that the locals demanded payment in coin. They didn't mind if it was U.S. coin. But a lot of American banks were wondering why the demand for Susan B. Anthony dollar coins was rising.

Production rose slightly, but not enough to reach Lockwood's goals. Having failed with the carrot, he next decided to try the stick. He began by arranging private meetings with his field foremen—a much more corporate title than *overseer*.

"They're lazy," foreman Tony DiBlasi complained. "No discipline. I don't know how they managed to produce as much as you say they did. Just a few trips up and down those ladders, and half of them are off to that refreshment tent of theirs. Especially the women and old men."

DiBlasi didn't mention that just one trip up the ladders was enough to put him out of commission for a good half hour.

Lockwood smiled. "So what we need to do is set standards. These people can't declare breaks on their own. Let's try for a minimum of five round trips before they can take a rest. Does that sound reasonable?"

Sitting in the boss's air-conditioned trailer, out of the broiling heat of Abydos's three suns, anything sounded reasonable to DiBlasi. "But how do we enforce it?" he asked.

Lockwood's face looked as if he'd suddenly bitten into a sour persimmon. "I'll apply to headquarters for some security people. Knowing what a soft heart this O'Neil guy has, we'll never get the Marines to back us up on this."

"And what about the Abydos people? What if they complain?" DiBlasi wanted to know.

"The Abbadabbas?" Lockwood smiled derisively, speaking aloud for the first the name he'd privately been using for the natives. "What are they going to do? File a grievance with the union?"

DiBlasi chuckled. "Abbadabbas," he repeated. "I like that."

"I want you and the other management people to monitor the workers," Lockwood said. "Identify the weak links—the ones who don't produce. As we mechanize the operation, those will be the first we'll get rid of."

His clean-cut features twisted into a smirking wink. "Just don't work them to death, all right? For the time being, we need these people."

Perhaps Lockwood considered himself clever dubbing people "Abbadabbas" and calling them dirty and lazy. But he underestimated one of his listeners. While Lockwood and DiBlasi had been talking, one of the locals had been cleaning Lockwood's trailer. She was a older woman, who reminded one of the foremen of his own mother, so he'd secured this light duty for her. What neither the foreman nor Lockwood knew was that the woman was also a student in Daniel Jackson's English classes.

The voices coming through the paper-thin partitions of the trailer had been clear enough. And although her English wasn't up to translating the whole interview, the woman had an illiterate's facility for remembering sounds.

When she recited the conversation at class that evening, Daniel felt as though he were listening to a human tape recorder. Some of those more fluent in English, like Sha'uri and Skaara, were angered and offended. The ill-will grew as the less fluent got translations from more advanced students.

Daniel merely felt sick. *Abbadabbas*, he thought. *The bastard has come up with a perfect demeaning name for us.*

But he had other concerns at the moment, heading off a ground swell of anti-UMC feeling in his classroom.

"Who does this Lockwood think he is?" an angry student demanded. "Ra himself? He at least had the excuse of being a god—not human. But Lockwood is as mortal as the rest of us."

Daniel picked his words carefully. "On my world," he said, "when big jobs must be done, large groups are organized, called corporations."

"Large jobs—like mining?" another student asked.

"The bigger the job, the bigger the corporation. Some of them begin to take on lives of their own. Those who work for the corporation—especially those near the top—begin to think only of the good of the company. For them the corporation becomes a god to be worshiped—like Ra."

"And with their power, they begin to act like Ra," Skaara said shrewdly.

"But how do the people on your world protect themselves against arrogant corporations?" a young man in the back row wanted to know.

"There are different ways," Daniel said slowly. "In some cases the people ask our leaders to make laws protecting them. Other times the workers organize to bargain with the corporation."

"Little good that would have done us with Ra," an older woman scoffed. "If we had protested mistreatment, the Horus guards would have beaten us more severely."

There was a moment of silence as the class considered her words. Ra's followers had treated the people badly—until the people had finally risen up. When they were finished, Ra and his people were dead.

Daniel didn't like the obvious train of thought he could read on his students' faces. "We've gotten very far from the point," he said abruptly, turning back to his slateboard. "We were talking about why some words are spelled one way but sound another . . ."

The next day, Daniel, Sha'uri, and Skaara were called to meet with Kasuf and the Elders. The older men were frankly baffled.

"We hear of strange things in the camp of this man Lockwood," a white-bearded leader said almost peevishly. "Those who go to learn the strangers' language are shown pictures of great machines that can do the work of a hundred men. Some are offered the chance to learn more than the language—how to ride these great devices themselves. They are told this will make them valuable workers. And there are hints that others may lose their jobs."

"Not hints," another Elder put in angrily. "I have heard a report that Lockwood was saying as much to his overseers."

"I, too, have heard this," Kasuf said, turning to Daniel. "And I have heard that it was said in your class. Is this true?"

"A woman who cleans for Lockwood heard it," Sha'uri spoke up. "He laughs at us, calls us silly names. But he wants his overseers to keep track of who brings up more ore and who brings up less."

"Well, of course some can carry more than others," an Elder said. "In my day—in the days of Ra—" he amended, "everyone dug for ore when it was demanded. The children, the elderly, women—they could not carry as much up the ladders as a strong man. But they could bring *something*."

"They carried their loads for fear of Ra and his warriors," Skaara pointed out. "The people now working in the mines do so freely, for the coins the strangers offer."

"And Lockwood complains they do not work hard enough." Kasuf looked baffled. "If they do not work hard enough, why does he want less workers?"

"He will get rid of them as he brings the machines in," Skaara declared. "Until then he needs many laborers—and he intends to work them hard. None will be allowed into the tent of rest until they have made five circuits of the ladders."

The Elders muttered among themselves.

"Five circuits—that is difficult enough for a strong man under the suns at this time of year."

"What does Lockwood know of the suns?" Whitebeard demanded angrily. "I am told he spends most of his days in a box where it is always cold."

As good a description of an air-conditioned trailer as I ever heard, Daniel thought.

"Let him and his overseers stagger under the suns before they set such conditions," another oldster angrily declared. "Even under Ra, the tent of rest was open to all who needed it—*whenever* they needed it."

Daniel frowned. The Elders were obviously talking about a tradition that had survived for thousands of years. But Lockwood apparently felt the tradition was insufficiently businesslike, and intended to change it.

His attempt might blow up in his face even worse than the blasting at the pyramid. There he had merely destroyed an artifact of the people's past. Here he was attacking an institution that affected the health and welfare of every Abydan who worked in the mines. The Elders, all of whom had spent time in the pit, were getting worked up. And understandably so. As older men working under the broiling suns, they had probably needed the amenities of the tent of rest.

"Tell them how it is on your world, Daniel,"

Skaara suddenly urged. "About the corporations, and the laws, and the workers protecting themselves."

Daniel Jackson suddenly found every eye in the room on him. It was an uncomfortable feeling. He'd experienced it other times—standing in front of a horde of skeptical Egyptologists when he'd presented the theories that got him branded as a crackpot. He'd experienced the near adulation of the people of Nagada on the first day he'd come to Abydos. Back then these people had thought he was some sort of messenger from Ra.

But now, after he had finally convinced them that he was just a man, the leaders of Abydos were turning to him for advice. After ignoring so many of his warnings, Kasuf and the Elders were beginning to suspect they were out of their depth in dealing with Eugene Lockwood.

What could Daniel tell them? He wasn't a lawyer, or a labor consultant. He was a scholar, an ivory-tower type who'd made some right guesses about history but couldn't get a job. By dumb luck his theories and knowledge of hieroglyphics had gotten him into the StarGate project, and he'd managed to parlay that knowledge into a chance at the greatest adventure in his life.

Daniel gulped, looking around at the expectant faces.

I'm only an expert on the dead past, not current events, he thought. *This is a hell of a situation for an Egyptologist to get himself into.*

CHAPTER 9
TROUBLE IN MIND

"Colonel O'Neil? Vernon Ballard. I've been brought in as head of security for the mining operation."

Jack O'Neil smelled problems the moment this latest newcomer from Earth entered his command tent.

The stranger was a big, beefy man, holding himself ramrod straight but with the beginnings of a beer belly ruining the line of his uniform. It was the gray-brown of the camouflage suit that caught O'Neil's eye. One glance told that it was definitely government issue—but the uniform didn't come from the U.S. government.

Ballard removed his matching combat cap, revealing balding brown hair cut so close, it was hard to tell where haircut ended and five o'clock shadow began. The line of Ballard's chin was also slightly softened by excess flesh, as if he'd spent more time recently at a desk than out in the field.

The security man caught O'Neil's speculative gaze on his uniform. "I thought it would be best to differentiate between our forces. UMC was able to pick up a shipment of old Rhodesian uniforms—most suitable, I think, for dry bush operations."

O'Neil responded with a noncommittal grunt. Lockwood had been whining for some time about the need for company police. Trust UMC to outfit them with relics from a twenty-year-old black-white African war.

"Well, I trust you do better than the soldiers who last wore that uniform," O'Neil said dryly. "Rhodesia, after all, is now Zimbabwe."

He gestured for Ballard to sit, but the man remained standing at parade rest. O'Neil's distaste deepened. Civilians who played soldier made his teeth itch. If, on the other hand, this guy was a pro taking UMC's pay, that made him a mercenary. And the Universal Mining Consortium's record with mercenary troops in the Third World was scarcely what one would call exemplary.

"So, how many people are you bringing in, Ballard?" O'Neil inquired. "Does this mean I can send some of my Marines home?"

"I'll be transshipping approximately a hundred security consultants." A fine euphemism for hired guns, O'Neil thought. Ballard's face stiffened when he caught the soldier's expression. "I expected you'd be bringing in reinforcements as well, Colonel. I mean, considering the uncertain temper of the mine workers."

"The people who delve into that mine have been working at it since time out of mind," O'Neil said, trying to keep his voice even. "UMC is stirring up its own problems, trying to change things overnight. Besides, I'm tasked with external security."

"But surely your troops must be prepared to safeguard American interests."

O'Neil gave Ballard the look of a man finding something stinking and sticky on the sole of his shoe. "I've yet to be convinced that the national interest and UMC's are exactly concurrent." He nodded at the security man. "That's why you and your bully boys are being imported. Your pay probably costs Lockwood as much again as the wages he's offering the people doing the real work down in the pit."

Ballard pulled himself to full attention again, his pale face going red. "Perhaps you doubt our professionalism, Colonel. But I assure you my people know their jobs—as do I. You may be Marine recon, Colonel, but I trained as a Navy SEAL."

O'Neil's expression was flat, unimpressed as he gazed up at Ballard. "A SEAL, huh? What happened? You get skinned?"

The flush in Ballard's face deepened. "Excuse me, Colonel?"

O'Neil jerked a thumb toward the entrance of his tent. "Take a good look outside, Navy boy. I'll bet you were trained in underwater demolitions and wetlands operations. But this is a goddamned desert planet, bucko. Your areas of expertise mean nothing out here—except one. So you can talk about security, but you've been brought in here as UMC's leg breaker. And I wish you joy of it."

Ballard was already storming his way out of the tent as O'Neil finished: "When they got sick of being mistreated, the people here went up against gods and killed them. I don't think they're going to be scared of an ex-SEAL and a hundred guns for hire."

The atmosphere was equally hot in Eugene Lockwood's air-conditioned trailer, where Martin Preston had barged in on the site manager's privacy.

"You're going to put *guards* around the rest tent?" Preston exploded. The UMC engineer had just heard of Lockwood's latest edict from one of the supervisors. Although Preston was supposed to be consulting on the project, the new system had been implemented without any input from him.

"We'll be able to tighten things up with our own security people on-site." Lockwood sat behind his desk, completely unmoved by the headquarters man's ire. "We're going to impose our standard of five round trips before the ore carriers are allowed to take a break. After the fifth trip, our supervisors will issue a chit to the worker. The guards will be on hand to ensure no chit, no entrance to that tent."

"From the lowest part of that mine, the trip to the surface is the equivalent of an eleven-story climb on those ladders." Preston had tried to make it on an uninterrupted climb—once. Since then he had carefully paced himself and took frequent rests on various levels.

Lockwood, who monitored progress only from his office on the surface, merely shrugged. "The local workers must surely be used to the climb."

He turned to more serious matters. "These people have ignored our supervisors when we tried to establish the standard on a voluntary basis. Even when they're docked in pay, they still take unauthorized rest breaks."

The site manager thumped the desk with his fist. "I will not allow a bunch of rag heads to flout management's authority. We're still operating below our production projections—"

"Below *your* projections," Preston challenged. "You severely underestimated the logistical impact of having a single-lane road for a supply line. It's not easy scheduling the movements of ore and supplies. I hear you've had to start buying food in the city."

"That damned O'Neil puts his supplies at a higher priority than ours," Lockwood growled. "He ties up the StarGate when he's got huge stockpiles already on the ground here."

"You can't blame O'Neil for your delays in upgrading the technology in the mine. It's taken weeks—*plural*—to get the first elevator installed in the pit, because of the difficulty in getting the pieces to the bottom of a missile silo and then over here."

"All the more reason to get better work out of the locals," Lockwood snarled back.

"Define 'better' when your work rules will result in people dropping from heat prostration." Preston unearthed a copy of his latest report, which lay unconsidered under a pile of dead-item papers. "You're ignoring the most elementary safety concerns which I outlined—"

"I can't be bothered with your baseless complaints," Lockwood cut him off. "I've got a mine to run."

"I think you mean an ass to cover," Preston accused. "You were going to be a corporate hero, offering the board of directors profit estimates grossly in excess of the projections I made."

The mining expert favored his superior with a mirthless smile. "But now the mine's actual production falls laughably short of your inflated guarantees. You're falling behind on construction. You tell me you can't afford to implement anything in the way of safety, but you bring in a small army of thugs and call it 'security.' "

Preston jabbed an angry finger at Lockwood. "You're not an engineer anymore—-just a lousy bean counter!"

"A bean counter who happens to be *your boss*," Lockwood emphasized. "And there's a good reason for that. You engineering types are supposed to find practical answers to problems. But do you? No. You have no conception of the bottom line."

"We're talking about human lives here," Preston said desperately, "not beans. Don't you worry—"

"There's nothing to *make* me worry," Lockwood cut him off. "No unions, no OSHA—no feds. We're on another *planet*, for chrissake. So who's going to worry about a few Abbadabbas more or less?"

Azar was one of those whom Lockwood had mockingly christened Abbadabbas, a humble member of the *fellahin*, the thousands of simple laborers who toiled in the deep, stony gash that was Abydos's quartzite mine.

Leaning on one of the myriad ladders that climbed the ravine walls, Azar wiped stinging sweat from his eyes with the tail of his head rag.

The triple suns of his world had seemed to align themselves with diabolical accuracy to beat down mercilessly into this deep crack in the planet's crust. Shade was nonexistent, coolness a forgotten memory.

Sucking on a pebble to generate some sort of moisture within his parched mouth, Azar leaned far between the rungs of the ladder he occupied, hacking into a surface vein of quartzite with a crude copper mattock.

One, two, three times his digging tool chopped into the bright ore with dull *chunk*. At last a fragment of ore about half the size of a man's head broke loose to fall to the floor of the terrace below.

Azar paused for a moment while a collector stepped beneath the ladder to grab the piece of gleaming rock and pack it into the bag he carried.

"Come on, Gaden," the miner jested to his workmate. "Gather that up and get out of there before I drop another piece on your head."

"Ah, no, I've enough to carry to the top now," Gaden replied. "Perhaps I'll even stop by the tent of rest—while it's still allowed."

Azar glanced over at the lines of *fellahin* toiling their way up the multiple ladders that led to the surface. "Why not take your load to the box-that-flies? It stops right over there—" he gestured two ladder lines over. "A lot closer than the top of the gorge."

"I hope you haven't been doing that while *you're* collecting," Gaden said. "I hear the overseers— the *soo-pah-vai-sas*—have been noting the names of the workers who deliver to the box. They're marked as weak—and they'll be the first to be discharged as more of the boxes are built."

"That will take a long time," Azar scoffed. "Have you seen the strangers building the frames to hold the boxes? I don't even know their language, but I know they're cursing. They keep starting and stopping their work."

"But someday they will finish their work. The parts will come. The boxes will fly up and down. And many, many of us will no longer have work." Gaden cast a sharp look toward his friend. "No more of those odd, shiny coins. They'll only be for the ones who run the machines—and perhaps for a few others."

"But none who'd be listed as weak," Azar said in a meditative voice. The flying box *whoosh*ed past on its way to the surface, shaking slightly in the cage that held it. The ladders shook more.

Azar climbed down the smooth-worn rungs and headed over to the ladder rising right beside the framework that enclosed the box that flew. When the hoisting machine had gone into operation, Azar had examined it with interest. A great rope made of metal wires wrapped around each other was attached to the top of the box, pulling it up or letting it down. The open-sided car also ran on tracks.

Gaden stood, watching, as Azar waited for the box to come back down, pretending to hew at rock where there was no ore. They heard the *whoosh* of the approaching box and glanced upward. Azar's eyes narrowed, gauging distances. The bottom of the square receptacle reached their level. Abruptly, Azar suddenly heaved his mattock to intersect with the joint of track and box.

The elevator was empty except for the bulk of a heavyset young man leaning against one corner of the cage.

Charlie Morris had been known in his Texas high school for two things: being a formidable linebacker and having the largest collar size in town. Unfortunately, college had not brought another growth spurt, so his dream of playing in the pros had faded. He'd taken a number of jobs that generally depended more on brawn than brains. Like this one, keeping an eye on a bunch of rag heads to make sure they didn't screw up too much on the job.

How could they screw up digging in the ground?

Charlie's head naturally thrust forward in a simian manner off his thick neck. In school it had earned him the nickname "Vanilla Gorilla." On Abydos his posture left him suffering from what felt like terminal sunburn on the back of his neck. No way was he climbing down with those suns blazing like the hinges of hell.

Not when he could ride.

Charlie leaned forward into the air flow coming

around the dropping elevator car. It would be the last breeze he'd enjoy for the next four hours, down on the floor of this crack deep between the cheeks of Mother Abydos.

Instead, it nearly turned into the last breeze he *ever* enjoyed.

From the corner of his eye Charlie caught the gleam of copper. He glanced around to see one of the miners' primitive digging tools fly outward to jam the elevator's tracks.

Beyond he caught a glimpse of a miner—a burnt-dark face like a thousand others, registering shock as he realized that what they called "the flying box" was occupied.

A clang, a screech, and the open-sided elevator jolted to a stop, flinging Charlie into the air. His frantic hands managed to catch hold of the framework he'd been leaning against a moment before.

For one horrible moment it looked as through he'd be flying down the last five floors worth of shaftway without benefit of the elevator. But with a wrenching twist he managed to throw himself back into the cage of the now stalled car.

Charlie landed on the floor with a brutal thump. He pushed himself up dazedly on hands and knees, then glared over toward the ladder that had been occupied by the towel head who'd just tried to kill him.

Of course, the rungs were vacant now.

"Sabotage," Lockwood muttered as he raged around the UMC encampment, trying to track down Colonel Jack O'Neil. He'd repeatedly asked the local military commander to post Marine guards to protect UMC's improvements to the mine. But O'Neil had laughed him off.

Now, just as the site manager was about to move in his own security people, the damned Abbadabbas had wrecked the elevator—the one bit of modern technology he'd gotten up and running in their primitive cess pit.

Still worse, his construction people told him it would take days before the blasted machine would be running again. They'd have to replace part of the track, importing it from Earth, and then getting it down those Stone Age ladders to the spot where the sabotage had taken place.

His supervisors had no clue as to what had happened. The cause of the elevator wreck had been one of those local digging tools, something that by all rights should be in a museum of ancient Egyptian artifacts.

The wooden handle of the mattock had been ground to splinters. But the soft metal head of the implement had smeared itself between the elevator car and its tracks. The havoc wreaked by some illiterate digger with dirt under his fingernails was as bad as the most sophisticated high-tech saboteur.

There was no way to trace the mattock, of course. Thousands of them were scattered across the mine workings. And asking any of the workers in the area was equally futile. Lockwood moved in the best of his language teachers, the ones who had picked up the most of the local lingo. He might as well have sent in his dullest grease monkeys fresh from Earth. The Abbadabbas not only suffered memory loss, but apparently they'd lost all their language skills as well.

Lockwood himself had engaged in a long, sweaty climb down the crudely built ladders to the sabotage site. He'd always considered himself to be in excellent shape, but after climbing five stories down and three stories up, Lockwood had been left panting on one of the mine terraces. Vernon Ballard, the new security chief who'd accompanied Lockwood, had been forced to climb to the rest tent and bring back water and salt tablets for the weak and sweating site manager.

After Lockwood recovered, he'd climbed back to the surface, rested a bit in his air-conditioned office, then set off to complain to O'Neil. To his fury, the Marine commandant seemed nowhere to be found.

Lockwood had covered the Marine encampment and his own establishment. No O'Neil. The UMC man was on the verge of setting off for the city of Nagada when one of his people reported that the colonel had been spotted driving a Humvee into the desert.

The mine executive requisitioned one of the all-terrain vehicles and set off in the same direction.

Moving through the deep desert was like riding a small boat across the heavy swells of a large ocean. The Humvee topped the crest of one sandy rise to reveal a vista of seemingly identical dunes stretching to the horizon.

"Where the hell could he have gone?" a frustrated Lockwood demanded of his Marine driver.

"Uh, sir," the rattled grunt replied, "maybe they've gone to Hogan's Alley."

Lockwood rounded on the man. "Take me there. *Now!*"

Hogan's Alley turned out to be a valley inconspicuously tucked between two dunes. Part of it was a firing range, using one of the sand mountains as a backstop. The rest of the valley had been transformed into an obstacle course.

Lockwood stared down from the summit of a sand hill. "What is this place? Some sort of training ground for your people?"

"Well—" the gyrene began, but he didn't need to answer.

The ATV was suddenly surrounded by a squad of homespun-clad young warriors who seemed to erupt from the sand itself, aiming an assortment of weapons. Lockwood had a moment of terror before he realized that the guns had no ammunition clips, the crossbows no bolts.

"Abba—" Lockwood quickly revised his terminology. "Abydos natives?"

The squad leader, an intense-looking young man with the dark skin of someone continually outdoors, growled a brief, disgusted word in the native language. "You not in *ex-uh-size!*" He pronounced the English words carefully.

"Exercise?" Lockwood repeated in bafflement. "What's going on here?"

His answer came as another squad of young native men appeared to engage the first group in mock combat. Suddenly, the dunes seemed to be covered with struggling figures. A platoon-sized war game was underway, the two teams of Abydos natives battling not merely with zeal but obviously with well-trained skill.

The first ambush team was taken down with a speed and adroitness that took Lockwood's breath away. Still more astonishing, however, was the referee who appeared to listen to the first squad leader's complaints.

Lockwood had studied his files carefully before taking over the Abydos operation. He immediately recognized Lieutenant Adam Kawalsky, O'Neil's second-in-command on the initial Abydos reconnaissance, from photos in those files.

The lieutenant was serving as a junior officer in the present expeditionary force. He patiently listened as the intense young man who'd led the first group of Abbadabbas complained in broken English about the accidental triggering of his ambush. "Not in *ex-uh-size!*" he complained.

"Sorry, Skaara," Kawalsky said. "You should have seen that before committing your forces— um, before you moved in."

This young Skaara character showed not only spirit but discipline. He accepted Kawalsky's ruling with a smart salute.

Lockwood turned to view the rest of the battle and spotted another referee—Feretti, the other survivor of the reconnaissance team.

And standing on another dune, binoculars in hand, stood Colonel Jack O'Neil, observing the whole training exercise.

CHAPTER 10
DEPARTMENT OF COMPLAINTS

General West maintained a small office in the Pentagon, a working space whose size grossly undervalued his true influence in the military establishment. For the general, however, this seemed to be S.O.P.—standard operating procedure. Eugene Lockwood could appreciate the appearance of being only a small cog in the large Pentagon machine as useful camouflage for West's true, if somewhat shadowy, power.

The pokey little room didn't even boast a window. But West kept a formidably dragonish WAC posted at a desk outside his door to discourage unwanted visitors.

Lockwood had traversed a million light-years by StarGate from Earth to Abydos. He'd moved forward in terms of civilization eight thousand years, from ancient Egypt to an ultramodern missile silo in Colorado. He'd survived a jet trip to Washington. But as he drove through the Virginia countryside to the Pentagon, he glanced at his gold watch, hoping he'd budgeted enough time to make his official appointment.

Lockwood negotiated his way through the Pentagon labyrinth with the ease of a true bureaucrat, arriving at West's office precisely on time. The female Cerebus led him in with a growl. But Lockwood faced far worse attack after the WAC had closed West's door.

"Problems on Abydos?" the general asked, riffling through some papers on his desk.

Lockwood noticed the UMC logo atop the sheets. The military man had been going over his supposedly secret progress reports!

"We've had some setbacks," Lockwood chose to admit. "Our language-acquisition program has not progressed as quickly as we'd hoped, in part due to native antagonism generated by Daniel Jackson, your former expert who remained behind on Abydos."

West nodded, his slightly fleshy face carefully blank. A bureaucratic in-fighter from way back, he wasn't about to accept responsibility for someone else's snafu.

"I was more concerned about your failure to install more modern mechanisms in the mine workings." West riffled through more reports, penetrating Lockwood's careful wording. "On this side of the StarGate we're gearing up for serious use of that quartzose material. But your actual production is far below the estimates that UMC presented us at the beginning of the project."

He's trying to hang me with my own projections, Lockwood thought, trying to keep his own poker face. But he hadn't come to Washington to defend himself from this general's annoying questions. He was launching an attack of his own—not to mention setting up a scapegoat for the mine's production problems.

"We have more serious problems than supply bottlenecks and delivery delays. The locals have started a campaign of sabotage." Lockwood paused for a second. "And I personally have seen them engaged in paramilitary training—apparently with the approval and aid of Colonel O'Neil."

West shuffled a new set of papers. "Yes, I've received a report from the colonel."

Covering his ass, Lockwood thought. *But it won't help him.*

"O'Neil has just become aware that two, ah, alumni of the Abydos reconnaissance have offered some help to the young locals who helped them escape the alien forces. The young men had organized a sort of militia, as the colonel had earlier reported—along with Messrs. Draven and Preston of your company."

West shrugged. "Lieutenant Kawalsky and Corporal Feretti believed that organized activities would help release some of the young men's high spirits. It would also allow them to keep an eye on what this group got up to."

"According to my briefing, there were barely a dozen of those shepherd boys," Lockwood objected. "I saw considerably more than that number engaged in war games."

He leaned over the general's desk, pressing his advantage. "The colonel has consistently refused to guard the new mining machinery from the locals. Now he allows them to train and become more dangerous to my people."

The mining man glanced sidewise at West. "I know you initially appointed O'Neil to the expeditionary force because of his experience on Abydos. Perhaps, though, he's had *too* much experience there—too many contacts. O'Neil is blind to any danger that doesn't come from outside the planet. With this Ra person dead, the possibility of an outside attack seems remote to me. The real problems on Abydos come from disaffected elements in Nagada, not from some bogeymen beyond the StarGate."

Again General West nodded, his face still revealing nothing of the thought processes going on behind his bureaucratic mask. "It is true that O'Neil was sent to Abydos because of his familiarity with local conditions." The general's voice held a considering note. "But you raise a reasonable concern. Perhaps he's grown too familiar with the autochthones."

"So what are you going to do about him?" Lockwood wanted to know.

"I still need someone on site who knows the terrain and the people," West finally said. "But it behooves me to recognize your own requests for an additional military presence on Abydos. If we add counterinsurgency forces to our troop strength on Abydos, we'll need an officer of sufficient rank to take command."

Lockwood nodded as if he were hearing the judgment of Solomon. Behind this respectful facade, however, he nearly quaked with fiendish glee. *Do it, West,* he silently urged the general, *kick the bastard downstairs!*

On Abydos, Daniel Jackson finished another

lecture for his English class. As the students left the room, he beckoned Skaara over.

"What's this I hear about some kind of fighting out in the desert?" he asked. Rumors were flying around Nagada about the perfidy of UMC, about destruction of mining equipment. If he hoped to be useful in his new position of adviser to the Elders, Daniel had to listen to them all and boil out the truth. After a week of fantastic stories the young academic was prepared to take anything he heard with a grain of salt.

When Skaara began telling of the training ground in the desert, of the war games, Daniel's eyes went wide. This story went far beyond any of the apocalyptic tales he'd heard in the city.

"You had maybe five friends who survived the fighting against Ra," Daniel said. "How could you—"

"A lot of other young men joined us," Skaara interrupted. "More and more keep joining every day. By now we have more than a hundred training regularly. Some of your friends have helped us—the tall one who yells—"

"Not O'Neil," Daniel protested.

"No, the other one—Kawalsky." Even with his English lessons, Skaara had tough going with the lieutenant's name. "And the quick one—Feretti. They set problems out for us and judge how we fight one another."

Daniel shook his head in disbelief. "You've got a pair of combat Marines training you?"

"Even the one in the black hat came to watch us fight—O'Neil himself," Skaara said proudly.

"But that snake Lockwood turned up. I think he hopes to make trouble for the colonel."

When he saw Daniel's surprise at his use of the title, Skaara explained. "That's what the other two call him."

Daniel tried to get the conversation back on track. He'd just discovered that his brother-in-law had organized an army—however small, this was a first for the natives of Abydos. They might not have much in the way of modern equipment, but knowing Skaara, they certainly had spirit. They'd also benefited from the training of two Marines who'd fought shoulder to shoulder with them against Ra.

"Okay," Daniel finally said. "You've answered two of my questions—what and how. But that leaves one that may be the most important. Why are you getting ready for a war?"

He was almost afraid he'd get a speech of the "kill the foreign devils" variety. Although, he privately admitted, some of it might be justified. In mere months UMC had generated more hatred than Ra had managed to stir up across the millennia.

But Skaara surprised him again. "In the days of Ra, we had only rumors—vague traditions of other worlds beyond the StarGate. When you arrived, you made those traditions real—and you helped us destroy the god who sucked our blood for so long. We were free."

"So what is it? Are you afraid some of Ra's stooges will come back through the StarGate?

That's what O'Neil and all the soldiers are guarding against."

Skaara nodded, a little shamefaced. "At first we were like boys playing at warriors. I did establish a watch on the great pyramid. But we had a dream—a larger hope. When you taught us to read the hidden writings, we learned more about those other worlds."

He spread his hands, trying to communicate his feelings instead of just the words. "We have brothers out there, Daniel. They're still slaves to Ra, or the vultures who served him. Our brothers don't even know that the monster is dead. But we hope to change that."

Daniel stared, wondering when Skaara's almost delicate features had hardened and matured with such purpose. "Change?" he echoed. "How?"

"I didn't want to approach you until we were ready," Skaara said. "You're the one who knows the StarGate best. We know you could find the keys to other worlds—Ombos, Wefen—perhaps even Tuat, the home of the gods. Then we could take the struggle to those living enslaved—and bring them freedom!"

Daniel stood almost slack-jawed in dismay. *This is what happens when you get the reputation as the local wise man,* he thought. Often enough before the advent of UMC, he'd stolen off to the pyramid and the hall of the StarGate. In daydreams he'd manipulated the enigmatic twenty-foot-tall torus.

The face of the Abydos gate was carved with completely alien figures, representing constellations as seen in the local sky. Some Sha-'uri had taught him. Others had been lost in the tides of local history. Nonetheless, Daniel had fantasized about shifting the chiseled figures into new configurations, opening the doorway to unknown worlds.

But it had been mere fancy. Daniel hadn't even experimented. And with the coming of the Earthlings he had avoided the portal. O'Neil would have had a stroke at the idea of opening the window of Earth's vulnerability any wider. And, of course, UMC would want no interruption on its Earth–Abydos lifeline.

Even if he had experimented, there was the problem of finding the right constellation configurations out of the quadrillions of possible combinations. Daniel's probability math was a bit rusty, but he quickly figured that he'd have better luck guessing the numbers for a multimillion-dollar lottery.

"Skaara." Daniel took a moment, trying to let the young man down as gently as possible. "You were there when we found the pillar engraved with the cartouche holding the coordinates for Earth. From our troubles then you must know how hard it is to find the routes between StarGates."

Skaara's face fell. "But, Daniel," he said, "your wisdom—"

"I'm merely a scholar," Daniel quickly interrupted. "I'm not Ra. And I'll tell you honestly, I could spend all the rest of my life trying to find

StarGate coordinates for somewhere—*anywhere*—
and not find the key to another world."

Bitter disappointment showed on Skaara's
downcast face. Daniel uncomfortably cleared his
throat. The people here should know better than
to bestow him with infallibility. Surely they'd seen
enough of his klutziness in dealing with the real
world. Children still did imitations of his chicken
impersonation from his first meal with Kasuf. The
people of Abydos had had no knowledge of barn-
yard fowl. Their feast food of choice was a pig-
sized lizard, broiled whole in its skin. To Daniel
the delicacy had tasted like chicken. In trying to
convey that message to Kasuf, he'd resorted to
pantomime. Even today kids flapped their arms
and called "Bwark! Bwark!" when he walked by.

So why, with such knowledge of his shortcomings, did Kasuf, the Elders . . . and now Skaara—
expect him to be unerring in his answers?

The answer left a cold hollow in the pit of Daniel's stomach. They're facing greater unknowns
than their culture has ever dealt with before. They
need to believe.

"Besides," Daniel finally said, "you may not
need to take your struggle to other worlds. We
may have more than enough struggle around here
before too long."

Beneath the base of the renovated battleship,
Ptah watched his vacuum-suited technicians moving like a flock of ungainly storks. He had cut
local gravity control to facilitate the installation of
the ship's drive units. The minuscule pull of Tuat-

the-moon had allowed his skeleton crew to hoist and maneuver the huge instrumentalities for lift and stardrive. But they weren't used to movement in near zero G, and gladly fled when he announced that he was personally taking on the job of tuning the drives.

Ptah turned in annoyance to find his head technician still standing beside him. "I realize my idiom is sometimes antique," the godly engineer said. "What part of my instructions did you fail to comprehend?"

"Lord," the technician replied, "I know that it was in a test such as this that your corporeal form was almost destroyed. I thought"—he swallowed his words—"I *wish* to serve you by attending to this task myself."

"Ah." Ptah's voice was almost gentle as he inquired, "And how many times have you calibrated stardrive units of this size, worthy servant?"

"I—" Again, the technician's voice failed him. "Never have I done the operation, sire. But I have studied the relevant instructions—"

"There will be numerous guards aboard this conveyance when it sets off for Abydos, not to mention their leader, the great goddess Hathor. I do not think we should risk their lives on inexperience, even inexperience that has studied the relevant instructions. Go. Enter the docking station, proceed to the next dome, and continue with the fabrication of the external controls. I wish all to be in readiness when I return."

With a bow and a worried frown, Ptah's lieutenant made his exit.

The calibration of the drives was a grueling chore, best undertaken in minimal gravity and near-vacuum. Perversely, Ptah found his cyborg body was far better suited to the labor. His mechanical arm could control tool movements to millionths of an arc. His flesh body had failed in a minute adjustment, triggering a flawed circuit that should have been inert. The drive unit had blasted for a nanosecond—with Ptah and his crew deep within the killing radius.

Ptah made his final connections in each of the four corners of the empty pyramid. Then he entered the docking station, making his way to the external control center. His servant had done well. The center was already in operation, a holographic image of the docked battleship hovering over the heads of the operations crew.

"Disengage from the docking station," Ptah ordered. On the image above, close-ups appeared of the clamps that had anchored the battleship to the stone structure for millennia. The refurbished mechanisms retracted smoothly.

"Energize drive." Ptah's voice sounded almost dry as he gave the order.

Hands danced across control panels. An eerie glow lit the golden quartzose sides of the pyramid ship. It seemed to leak from within.

"Lift!" Ptah commanded.

The glow from the ship intensified as the vast bulk of the vessel rose gracefully into the air. Lethal radiation reflected off the polished stone of the docking station. Thanks to the lack of atmosphere, there was no thunder to accompany the drive's operation. But dust and debris from the renovation project blew away at the dreamlike speeds of low gravity. And even from the distance of the next pyramid dome over, Ptah and his technicians could feel the shaking transmitted through the moonlet's stony crust.

Its glow almost too intense for human eyes, the resurrected battleship climbed smoothly into space until even the holographic imaging system recorded it as one more star in the black satin sky—albeit a balefully glaring star.

"At this point stardrive translation would be effected," Ptah announced. "But that test will await the arrival of the ship's full crew. Bring the barque back to station and dock."

He cast a glare around at his jubilant navigation trainees. "And try to be careful not to scratch anything."

Ra's empire had never been a participatory democracy. But in the absence of a head god, the warrior godlings had taken to the expedient of council. Hathor arrived at the meeting chamber with a small retinue—and last, as befitted the leader of the most powerful faction on Tuat.

In the intervening months, she had expanded her power by co-opting rivals or killing them in single combat, and elevating members of her clique to fill the vacancies. Some dangerous adversaries abandoned the cockpit of Tuat's politics, retreating to the safety of their home fiefs. They had not been eliminated, but they had been neutralized as long as Hathor kept tight control of the StarGate on the surface of Tuat-the-world.

Success had left Hathor with a host of restless allies ready to turn on her at the slightest misstep, as well as one major enemy. Ram-headed Khnum had fought a rear-guard action against Hathor's march to power. With Hathor's every victory, Khnum's ranks swelled as frightened lesser gods joined his confederates. And when Hathor killed a great god, there were always some members of the conquered god's factions—favorities of the deceased leader, or very loyal followers—who turned to Hathor's main rival to gain their revenge.

Hathor didn't mind having all her enemies in one camp. Her last duel had delivered her a majority on the council. That fact, and the report of the successful drive test, impelled her to make public her plans.

Hathor didn't kid herself. She knew that a couple of godlings had established effective intelligence operations. At least two of Khnum's followers—and three of her own—were merely waiting for her to leave for Abydos. Then they would make their own snatches for Tuat.

Such opponents didn't worry Hathor. The best of the would-be overlords' troops would accompany her to Abydos. No, the real problem was Khnum, and how he would react. . . .

"My lords," she addressed the assemblage, "I have important news. Today at the third hour my people successfully demonstrated the refurbished drives on Dome Five, formerly the battleship *Ra's Eye.*"

A hologram filled the room, showing details of the liftoff.

"Ah," commented ape-headed Hapi, one of the minor gods who knew of the work in progress on the old vessel. "And here we all thought it was a Tuat-quake, or a meteor impact."

Khnum, however, surged through the three-dimensional representation, eyes wild with fury. He was a slender, handsome man, with whipcord muscles. They bunched across his chest and arms as he confronted Hathor.

"I thought perhaps you were establishing your own fortress in that dome when you dispossessed the others who lived there," he began.

Hathor smiled at the notion of pinning herself down on an airless moon under a dome vulnerable even to blast-lances. What could Khnum be thinking of?

"But to reactivate devices forbidden by Ra—"

Here was the true problem among the would-be successors. Even as they fought to assume Ra's throne, they could not escape the playing field where the former head god had penned them.

Oh, she understood Khnum's agitation. With a working spaceship at her command, the godlings' fief defenses—a watch or even a mine at the Star-Gate—had been sidestepped. Khnum might have the cream of his forces at his side, but the planet that formed his power base was now vulnerable to attack.

Hathor ground on over Khnum's objections. "The battleship has been recommissioned to *search* for Ra and discover his fate. Although I will command the expedition to Abydos, I call upon all here to provide detachments of your best warriors for the effort. In that way we can field the largest possible force—and, of course, each of the gods here present will have observers on the scene."

"Enough!" Khnum burst out. "Not only does the demon goddess threaten us all with her forbidden warship, she expects us, her rivals, to provide forces for our own undoing!"

The ram god's hand went to his pectoral necklace, plucking loose one of the hanging decorations. The seeming doodad pulled free to reveal itself as the gold and jewel-encrusted handle of a throwing knife. The thin blade, however, was plain utilitarian steel.

"Die, you usurping bitch!" Khnum howled, hurling the blade.

Hathor moved with economical violence. She seized Hapi, the too wise godling who'd commented on her ship tests, and spun him into the path of the knife. It sank into his heart.

Even as Hathor's human shield sagged, Khnum plucked a new jeweled dagger.

Hathor raised her right hand palm out, almost in a warding gesture. But the move revealed that she, too, wore dangerous jewelry. A tracery of gold wires ran around the back of her hand. They came together in her palm, creating the setting for a marble-sized mottled black jewel that glowed with a baleful light.

Before Khnum could hurl his second blade, Hathor unleashed a rush of energy that hit the ram-god like a blast of cyclonic wind. He hurtled backward until he struck a wall, then oozed downward to a seated position.

Hathor was on him before Khnum could even exert some semblance of control over his stunned muscles. He could only look helplessly upward as the hand with that damnable jewel came down in contact with his shaven head.

Every one of Ra's servants knew of his punishment jewels, bizarre offshots of the technology from the StarGates themselves. But rather than reassembling one's component molecules across space, the black gem *rearranged* body molecules. Ra had used the glowing stone to turn failed servants' bones to water. Of course, the process killed the recipient.

Khnum was a strong man, but his whole body began to shudder and spasm as the gemstone exerted its awful effect. His eyes bulged as his very brain began to boil off. His arms, no longer under his own control, made little spastic motions. Air rushed from his lungs through a constricted throat in a bubbling, coughing rattle.

As Hathor pressed the deadly stone ever harder into Khnum, the ram god's head became spongy under her hand. He drooped to the floor. Hathor dropped to one knee, maintaining the contact until at last the once great Khnum lay still and literally boneless at her feet.

"I will name a successor at my earliest convenience," the goddess announced to the silenced assemblage. Her hand rose to give them one last glimpse of the deadly stone. Then she curved her fingers over what had been Ra's personal weapon.

"See to the preparations for your guard detachments."

There was not even a whisper of dissent as she left the chamber.

CHAPTER 11
NEWCOMERS

Jack O'Neil's first warning that a new commander had even been contemplated for the Abydos expeditionary force was the appearance of an Army one-star general in his command tent. "At ease, Colonel." The officer drew a thick envelope from the breast pocket of his olive drab battle dress. "Francis Keogh, brigadier general, U.S. Army."

Keogh slapped the papers with more than necessary force on O'Neil's desk. The movement brought prominence to the West Point ring on the general's hand, its heavy gold sounding a muted timpani against the wood.

"These orders second your troops to my command," Keogh went on briskly. "You will remain as second-in-command, under my orders." He glanced around the tent. "I believe we can leave the paperwork—signing for stores and all that—for later."

Keogh finally looked O'Neil in the eye—his own eyes were a surprisingly bright blue, set deep under massive orbital ridges on either side of a sharp, beak-like nose. In the intensity of their gaze Keogh's eyes were like a pair of lasers mounted in twin caves—with the jut of his nose acting as range finder. The general's face was craggy more than handsome, and his expression was not a pretty one. "I want two of your men—Kawalsky and Feretti—here. *Now!*"

With a sick feeling in his gut O'Neil passed the call to the guard outside the tent. In moments, the lieutenant and the corporal arrived. Spotting the strange general, they immediately saluted and stepped into the brace position.

"Kawalsky and Feretti, sir," O'Neil said with a crisp salute of his own. "Present as requested."

"Gentlemen," Keogh said, though his tone of voice made the honorific doubtful. "You see in me the new commander of this force. Sizable reinforcements are arriving even as I speak. The new troops will present a major logistical drain on our stockpiles. Because of this, Lieutenant, I am appointing you supply officer. And you, Corporal, will assist him."

Supply duty was a slap in the face to a pair of combat Marines. But Keogh wasn't finished.

"To insure your full and undivided attention to these great and serious duties, I am confining you to this base. Departure—even going into the desert—will be construed as desertion. In addition, your sensitive employment will preclude all fraternization with the natives of this planet. Is this understood?"

Faces blank, Kawalsky and Feretti both snapped salutes like a pair of automatons, their eyes not focusing on the general. "Yes, sir!" they chorused.

"Excellent. Dismissed, the pair of you."

As Kawalsky left, his hard-bitten features lost

their rigid cast as he glanced at O'Neil. *Damn!* his eyes seemed to say, *we dropped you right in it!*

O'Neil carefully schooled his own face into mask-like blankness. He shouldn't have let Kawalsky talk him into seeing what progress Skaara and his boy warriors had achieved. The colonel had been expecting some fallout from Lockwood's discovery. But he'd hoped for more support from General West.

Keogh waited until the tent was empty before he addressed O'Neil again. "In studying the supply situation for this base, Colonel, I noticed an excessive stock of hand-held surface-to-air missiles. These seem unnecessary given local conditions. Perhaps you can put Kawalsky in charge of shipping them back."

"Sir, when we were fighting Ra's guards, our greatest problem was their air mobility. Their udajeets—flying gliders—and blasters pinned Lieutenant Kawalsky and a group of native auxiliaries—"

Keogh interrupted with an aphorism: " 'The military mind,' " he quoted, " 'is always prepared to fight the last war.' What you're talking about is ancient history, Colonel. Our concern should not be with incursions from the air, but with counterinsurgency preparations." He glared at his subordinate. "You not only ignored such a danger, you actually allowed the training of an insurgent cadre."

Keogh's body was long and lanky, and he made himself taller by drawing himself up stiffly. "I'll continue to use you, O'Neil, as local liaison. But you are to limit yourself to formal contacts with the local government. I am not happy about this home-grown militia you fostered. Neither is General West."

The general turned to more mundane matters, demanding a map of the plateau that served as home for the base camp and UMC's local presence. "We'll need to expand the camp significantly to accommodate the new troops. In addition, we'll require a maintenance area for the armor I'm bringing in—"

"Tanks, sir?" O'Neil said.

"Best weapons available for projecting strength in a desert environment," Keogh replied. "North Africa in World War II. The Arab–Israeli wars. Desert Storm. By my calculations the StarGate's size should accommodate both Abrams heavy tanks and the lighter Sheridan units. We will, however, need assembly areas for the helicopter gunships. They'll have to come through in pieces."

Although O'Neil struggled to retain his military mask, Keogh trained keen eyes on his second-in-command's face. "You don't believe all this is necessary, do you? Well, I think it's *required* to undo the damage you've caused. Heavy ground strength—so we'll have lots of rifles in case the worst happens. But I'm still betting we can overawe these Abbadabbas when they see our technological edge. The tanks and helicopters are key to that strategy."

"Yes, sir," O'Neil said tonelessly.

These people fought anti-gravity gliders and energy weapons, he thought, *and this clown thinks he's going to cow them with a few helicopters and a demeaning name.*

Keogh was again examining O'Neil's force dis-
positions on the map. "I'm not impressed with your
defensive arrangements, Colonel. These strong
points and guard posts wouldn't stand up to a
human wave assault—which is, I think, the only
tactic the locals could conceivably use. Almost all
of their weapons are hand-to-hand, are they not?"

"Yes, sir," O'Neil replied again.

"Starting immediately, I want a defensive wall
around this entire plateau. An earthen berm
should do—reinforced with strong points—perhaps some defense towers. We'll leave that to the
engineers. Requisition materials and earth-moving
equipment from the UMC people as necessary."

Lockwood will love this, O'Neil thought.

"You can also tell Mr. Lockwood that effective
immediately, I am dispatching troops to support
the UMC security personnel in the mine."

O'Neil's mask slipped as he saluted again.
Keogh caught the shift in expression. "Look,
O'Neil, I don't need you to like me to get this
job done." Scorn poured from the general's voice.
"That's the problem with you short-timers. You
don't really understand the military mystique."

"Sir," O'Neil replied, "I've been in the service
for more than twenty years."

"My family have been officers in this man's
army for *generations*," Keogh snarled. "Since the
Civil War!"

"Of course, sir." O'Neil gave him another salute
as he left the tent. "There was a Keogh with Custer, wasn't there?"

*   *   *

Lockwood waited until O'Neil left his office before he indulged himself in a full-scale gloat. In almost frosty-cold air-conditioned comfort, the mine manager rubbed his palms together as a show of satisfaction. *How the mighty are fallen,* he thought. *The hot-shot Marine Colonel reduced to the level of messenger boy!*

Turning from the clutter on his desk, Lockwood picked up the radio communicator he used to keep in contact with his subordinates. "Get me Ballard," he said into the receiver.

A moment later, Vernon Ballard's static-fuzz came out of the box. "Mr. Lockwood?"

"Get over to the military camp and introduce yourself to the new commander there. He's detaching men for pit security, so it's up to you to figure how they'll work with your people. One thing—I want a complete cordon around the rest tent. Got it?"

"Yes, *sir!*" Ballard happily signed off.

Lockwood's lips stretched off his teeth in a hard grin. *Now* they could get down to business, he promised himself.

"Here's another one that needs explaining." The company security guard, clad in gray camo fatigues, turned to Charlie Morris.

The image of an ice-cold beer vanished like a pricked thought balloon as the mine supervisor moved to deal with the latest recalcitrant. "Hey! Underwood!" Morris yelled to the language expert hiding from the noonday suns under the shade of the rest tent.

Today they had finally implemented the rule of five round trips before a rest, no exceptions. A cordon of gray-clad UMC security guards and newly arrived Army men in olive drab cut all access to the rest tent.

The baffled worker whose way was being barred was pure *fellahin*. His skin had been broiled to the color and consistency of dark leather by at least forty years of exposure to the three suns of Abydos. But there was an ugly grayish tinge to his complexion, his white beard was matted with sweat, and he wobbled slightly on his feet. The worker seemed unable even to summon the strength to protest as Morris raised a hand before his face.

"Five times," the supervisor said loudly, as if volume could push his meaning into the man's mind. He spread his fingers wide. "Five times around before you can come in here."

The worker spouted a brief string of gibberish. Morris turned to Underwood, one of the UMC language specialists. "You tell him."

In halting ancient Egyptian, Underwood tried to explain the situation.

The workman protested again, seizing Underwood's hand and trying to draw it to his head.

With brisk economy of movement the UMC guard swung his rifle butt and knocked the hand away. "Don't know what diseases they got," he said laconically.

Underwood shot Morris a nervous look. "This fellow says the suns are getting to him. He needs water and salt."

"Bastard's probably faking." A grim expression

settled over Morris's simian features. On closer examination, this Abbadabba looked remarkably like the one who'd screwed around with the elevator. "If we let him in, we'll have a whole parade of 'em, all claiming to be sick. Underwood, you tell him to get back to work and not come back here till he's got a chit."

"I dunno," said an Army pfc who'd been standing off to the side. "This guy looks pretty much out of it. Are you sure—?"

"How long you been on this planet, soldier?" Morris loved using that comeback. He'd been waiting for someone with even less experience than he had.

Since the soldier had only been on Abydos for hours, and the alternative to guard duty was shoveling sand to make a defensive wall for his camp, he subsided.

Underwood again set off on a limping speech. The elderly worker gave a vehement negative, pointing toward the rest tent.

"He's not listening, Sullivan," Morris said to the guard.

In a single jerking move the security man rammed the butt of his gun into the pit of the workman's stomach.

Argument ceased as the older man folded in half, clutching himself and gasping.

"Now go. *Imshi!*" Sullivan yelled, using some Arabic he'd picked up in the Middle East. He had a hard time distinguishing the natives from the Muslims he'd guarded UMC executives from.

The man was down on his knees. Sullivan

yanked him upright and sent him tottering back to the ladders that led down to the pit.

They watched the man's slow progress as he joined the line of carriers, half leaning on the man in front of him. He reached the ladders and disappeared below the lip of the gorge.

"See?" Morris said harshly. "You gotta show 'em who's boss or they'll—"

A cry came from the mine pit, a wordless yell of terror that was obliterated yet amplified by the shouts of many voices. The line of carriers abruptly stopped.

Leaving his place in the cordon by the rest tent, the Army pfc walked to the edge of the slash in the earth. He shuddered, then headed back.

"What?" Morris asked, his mouth suddenly very dry.

"That guy you turned away—he fell off the ladder." The soldier's face was pale under his incipient sunburn. "He fell all the way down—ten, eleven stories? And it looks like he bounced off a couple of those terraces."

He glared at Morris. "I guess you showed 'em good—huh?"

Azar and Gaden were both on the carriers' line when their fellow worker died. They heard the scream. Then something flashed past their places on the ladder and struck a glancing blow to the terrace below them.

They heard a sound like a ripe melon smashing open after a fall. When they looked down, they saw a smear of blood and a limp, twisted human figure growing steadily smaller as it fell into the depths of the pit.

First came shock and horror as the men slowly learned the identity of the accident victim. Old Zaid lived in the same neighborhood as Gaden. He was a widower with a sickly daughter. Every coin he got for his mine work went to doctors and medicines for his girl.

Then the mood turned to anger as various versions of the events before Zaid fell began to filter down the pit.

"The gray-clothes beat him with sticks because he fell on the line and couldn't get up!"

"Whelps of *mastadges*!" one man swore. "I heard the gray ones threw him into the pit."

"They're worse than the Horus guards!" Another worker contributed the story he'd heard. "But bad as they are, the ones in green are worse. I hear that they *shot* Zaid as he begged for mercy."

"The green ones can't be that bad," Gaden objected. "Black Hat and the ones who followed him wore green. So did Daniel. Most of them died helping us defeat Ra."

"Well, the new ones in green must not be the same," the first worker said. "They stand around the tent of rest drinking water and not letting anyone in."

"Yes," said his friend, who'd propounded the green men as murderers story. "Besides, the ones friendly to us now wear the colors of the sands," he added, as if that were a clinching argument.

"One thing is certain," Azar finally said, turning

to the ladders. "Someone must carry word to Kasuf and the Elders."

Daniel was not at his best after a wildly bounding journey by mastadge across the dunes. Kasuf had acted as quickly as possible when reports of trouble at the mine had reached town. He'd gotten the Elders mounted and riding, along with Daniel and Sha'uri to act as translators. Skaara had disappeared at the news. Daniel sincerely hoped he wasn't out activating his militia.

The jouncing ride ended just as motion sickness was about to set in. Daniel's legs were rubbery as he made his way down from the mastadge howdah.

How I know I am not a hero? Proof #999, he thought. *Heroes do not have an urge to vomit right at their big entrances. I do.*

The light of the suns was striking him like a physical blow, not merely blinding him but accentuating the churning in his gut. Daniel blinked, gulped, and tried to concentrate.

A dead body lay on the sands in front of the rest tent. The late Zaid, Daniel figured.

Behind the dead man stretched a vast crescent of angry miners. It looked as if all work had ceased by the time the Elders arrived. The workers looked like a sea of humanity at a low boil. Angry muttering from thousands of throats struck Daniel's ears, nothing that he could make intelligible—except as proof that the workmen were in a fury.

He could tell that by the way some of the men

handled their picks and mattocks. From the expressions on their faces, they wanted to hew more than stone.

The Abydans had come a long way from the time when a blow from one Horus guard could make the whole workforce lower its head and scurry. That had been before one of Ra's guardsmen had made the mistake of striking Jack O'Neil—and gotten his guts blasted in return. Before Daniel Jackson had removed the Horus mask to reveal that Ra's slave masters were human, after all.

This was history that UMC and its overseers had apparently never heard. The cordon around the rest tent had now extended itself into a rough skirmish line. Lockwood's gray-clad company police readied their assault rifles. Beside them, fingering their weapons much more nervously, stood regular Army troops in green fatigues. Skaara's watchers had sent word of the arrival of reinforcements. The fresh troops must have come with a new commander if they were being deployed beside UMC's bully boys. Jack O'Neil would never had allowed his people to get dirty by such associations.

Daniel looked from one group of men to the other. The miners were nerving themselves for an assault, First Dynasty digging tools versus top-of-the-line assault weapons. The guards, both corporate and government, prepared to drive the Abbadabbas back into the pit with a storm of lead.

Cool heads would have to prevail, or else there'd be a slaughter.

"Daniel. Come." Kasuf beckoned him over to kneel by the dead man's body. The old man gently probed. "He is broken from the fall and his flesh is torn, but I see no effects of the strangers' weapons on him."

Daniel breathed a sigh of relief. The messenger who'd arrived, a miner named Azar, had reported several conflicting stories on how Zaid had fallen. At least now one of the most damning versions had been disproved.

As Kasuf announced his findings to the crowd, Daniel noticed a small knot of men rubbing themselves with sand to remove the blood clinging to their arms and torsos.

"We helped bring Zaid up from the pit," one of them, a brawny young fellow, told Daniel in decent English. Noting the teacher's surprise, the young man explained, "I was learning the strangers's tongue from . . . *those*." He gestured to the UMC battle line. "Now, no more."

They had to get this settled, and quickly. Daniel spotted plumes of dust coming their way from the base camp. With reinforcements, who knows what the UMC people might do?

He raised his voice. "We need to speak with those who saw what happened to Zaid before he went into the pit." Daniel was surprised at the authority in his voice. "Not those who heard things, or *think* they saw. We need men who were on the line to go down, or who were in the tent of rest."

It took precious moments to separate the wheat

from the chaff, but at last Kasuf and his associate Elders had eyewitnesses to Zaid's last minutes.

Armed at last with an accurate story, Daniel headed for what appeared to be the UMC man in charge, a supervisor in white shirt and khaki pants. The guy looked like a gorilla who had undergone a body shave and a blond hair-dye job. Daniel hoped that looks were deceiving.

"You," the supervisor said, "you're that Jackson guy. You speak the local lingo. Certainly better than Underwood here." He gestured to an obvious academic type cringing behind the battle line.

"I came to see what the problem was," Daniel said.

The Vanilla Gorilla scowled. "The problem is that these Abbadabbas are taking one guy's accident and making it an excuse to screw around. So if you'd just tell them to get back to work—"

"We'll have to wait on that," Daniel interrupted. "The Elders—that's the local government around here—are questioning eyewitnesses. And from what I'm hearing, they're saying that one of your guards roughed Zaid up."

The supervisor glanced for a moment at one of the gray-clad men, then said pugnaciously, "Well, who the hell are you going to listen to? Us or a bunch of savages?"

"Those savages, as you call them, welcomed me to this world and saved my life." Daniel couldn't keep the anger out of his voice. "What have you and UMC done for me lately?"

He returned to Kasuf, who was worriedly conferring with his fellow Elders. "We can keep the men from attacking these warriors," Kasuf began.

"Which is just as well. Their weapons would slaughter the miners," Daniel told him.

"But we must have justice," Kasuf insisted. "The warrior who beat Zaid and the overseer who allowed the beating must be punished."

"They're not even admitting that their people touched Zaid," Daniel reported. "But I think I know who did it, and if we can keep things from getting out of hand here—" His voice faded as he saw truckloads of Army soldiers and marines rolling up. Inspiration struck.

"Right now we have to get our people out of here without getting them shot. We have to do it nonviolently."

"Nonviolently?" Kasuf echoed.

"Just follow my lead," Daniel said, turning to the crowd. "In my world, we have ways of showing those who run things the errors of their ways. If you would make this mine safe, if you would have it run better, you must withdraw your work!"

"Right!" Azar shouted, catching on quickly. "How much ore could the strangers dig out without us?"

"So throw down your tools! Leave the pit right now!" Daniel cried, carried on by his own oratory. The earth seemed to rattle with the sound of tools being abandoned to drop to the earth.

"What the hell is he telling them?" Daniel heard the Vanilla Gorilla mutter behind him.

"I don't know, but at least he's disarmed the bastards," one of the guards answered.

The people of Nagada needed something quicker to squeeze UMC than a strike. Daniel was suddenly struck by a memory from his college days. A protest . . .

"Friends!" he cried. "The strangers come to the city to buy their food, don't they?"

"Yes, they do!" shouted the crowd.

"Well from now on, no one in the city must sell them food," Daniel shouted. "If anyone does, no one must buy or sell with them. This is a very powerful weapon from my world. It's called the boycott!"

"BOIK-ODD," the enthusiastic miners took up the cry, mangling the pronunciation. "BOIK-ODD! BOIK-ODD!"

"Take the word to the city! We'll march now!" Daniel led the miners past the line of gunmen stretched before the rest tent, away from the arriving troops.

"BOIK-ODD!" his enthusiastic new followers chanted.

At least I stopped them all from getting shot, Daniel thought.

Then he remembered what the great college protest had been over. The students had boycotted the cafeteria, trying to get better food.

Daniel also remembered that the protest had been a complete failure.

Except for the fact that Froot Loops had been added to the cafeteria breakfast.

CHAPTER 12
A QUESTION OF BLAME

Walter Draven was not in a forgiving frame of mind. He had been enjoying a lobbyist's luncheon in one of the finest Washington restaurants when his office called him with the new emergency. He refused to eat airline food, and landed in Colorado hungry. Stepping through the StarGate, he found UMC's Abydos operation under a local boycott and with no food at all.

"Dam-*nation!*" he exploded at Eugene Lockwood. "How could things have gone so badly in so short a space of time?"

The site man looked on the verge of peeing his pants. "We've had growing problems from a variety of different sources," he began. "But—"

"Oh, I know the next line," Draven sourly assured him. "But it's not your fault. Where are the geniuses responsible for the incident?"

Lockwood got on his radio. A moment later, Morris and Sullivan, the supervisor and the guard, marched into the office. Draven noticed that both had shaved and apparently spiffed up as much as possible, given the frontier conditions on Abydos.

"I want to hear what happened," Draven told them, "from the horse's mouth, so to speak."

At least from one end of the horse, Draven thought, taking in Morris's almost simian features.

The pair exchanged a glance. So. They'd decided to collaborate on telling their story. But the report they gave seemed reasonably straightforward—as did the defense Morris offered.

"I was only carrying out company policy," the supervisor said. "As of that date, no workers were to be allowed into the rest tent unless they had proof of making five round trips carrying ore. This Zaid guy didn't have a chit. So we made him go back to the line."

"Nice try, Morris," Draven told him. "The Eichmann defense—'I was only following orders.' But the witnesses say that Zaid had been complaining he felt unwell. Shouldn't that have changed your mind?"

"Sir . . ." Morris faltered to a stop, looking now at Lockwood, who of course was perfectly willing to let his subordinate hang in the wind. "We thought he was faking—malingering. If we let him in, we'd have to let anyone in who complained about the heat. And, well"—he rubbed his arms in the almost arctic comfort of the office trailer— "it's *brutal* out there. Our translator couldn't stand the suns—he'd gotten under the shade of the tent. Both the Army guys and our own people were out in the sun, but they were drinking from canteens."

"So you were upholding a company policy you yourself could not have lived with," Dravan finished. "And you," he demanded, turning to Sullivan, "I'm told you struck the dead man—twice."

"I broke the guy's hold on Mr. Underwood— the translator," Sullivan specified. "This Zaid guy grabbed his hand. I made him let go. If he really was sick, I didn't want him spreading germs. Besides, the guy looked as if he already had fleas."

"You've described one alleged blow," Draven said, shifting well into prosecutorial mode. "What about the other?"

"That was more a move-along kind of thing," Sullivan explained. "Mr. Morris told him to go. So did Underwood, the translator. Me, too. When the wog didn't move, I gave him, well . . . a poke, like."

"With the butt of your rifle, apparently in the solar plexus," Draven amplified. "So, we have a man who seemed to be suffering from heat stroke having the wind knocked out of him. Then he was ordered to climb down eleven floors' worth of ladder." The engineer shook his head in disgust. "What a surprise that he wound up on the express route down."

He raked the pair with glaring eyes. "It's too bad neither of you came up through the mining business," Draven finally said. "If you had, I'd have you, Morris, drilling blast holes in the lousiest mine in Zambia. And you, Sullivan, would be right beside him, setting charges with the most chancy, deteriorated, *volatile* blasting compounds I could find."

The troubleshooter jammed his hands in his pockets. "But then, you're used to playing around with volatile mixtures, aren't you? These people were virtually slaves less than a year ago. They were working for somebody whom they considered a god." He glared again at Morris and Sullivan. "Maybe that makes them sound primitive to you.

But if you'd been working for a *god* and told him where to get off, how much crap would you take from a mere man? Even a man with an assault rifle?"

The pair was silent.

Draven's lips twisted. "But you pushed this new policy like good corporate minions. Didn't you see that was like juggling nitroglycerine? You're very lucky, damn you—lucky your stupidity didn't result in things blowing up in your face. Instead, you've apparently caused the first strike in the eight-thousand-year history of Abydos. Congratulations."

Lockwood spoke up. "It was that damned Jackson's fault. He's been a thorn in our side ever since I arrived here."

"I was wondering when we'd get around to the 'outside agitators' plea," Draven said. "Frankly, Dr. Jackson was a pain in my ass when I arrived here. That's why I wanted him marginalized—which apparently didn't happen."

For a long moment Draven surveyed the three men. "Besides, Jackson did you a favor, though you don't realize it. He managed to get the miners away without bloodshed. If they'd tried to storm your line, there'd be a hundred dead tonight instead of one."

His comment took another moment to sink in, so Draven pressed a little harder. "And you, Lockwood, would be inside the Army compound walls, watching this lovely office burn."

He flung himself into a chair. "I guess my next stop is the city, to see if I can sweet-talk those

Elders. I'd prefer not to do that on an empty stomach. So, Lockwood, you might make yourself useful and order something—"

"Ah," Lockwood said quietly.

"What?" Draven demanded.

"When Jackson led the miners off, he was already organizing a boycott against us. For supplies as well as labor. We, ah, haven't been able to get any food from the natives. And with all the traffic through the StarGate to bring the military reinforcements in—"

Draven had seen the military build-up, the men and machinery still waiting to get to Abydos. He himself had transited the StarGate at the end of a marching infantry platoon.

"Perfect," the troubleshooter muttered, rising from his chair. "Just bloody perfect."

"Mister Draven?" Lockwood asked as the troubleshooter left the office. "Where are you going?"

"Change in plans. I'm going to see the local military commander before I see your friends in the city. I've got to see how far he'll back us.

"And maybe," Draven added, "I'll get something to eat."

General Francis Keogh was a disappointment. Oh, he looked every inch the model of a military man, even in the bustle of making the command tent his instead of Jack O'Neil's. A cot had been moved in so the general could catnap if necessary while conducting operations. O'Neil had seemingly never needed that. The Marine colonel had impressed Draven as more of a machine than a man—a machine that would keep going until it broke down or blew up.

Keogh was all too human, Draven decided. It showed in the touches he was adding to the tent—a regimental flag, a photo of a younger Keogh shaking hands with the president—two incumbents had held the Oval Office since. It especially showed in the ring that gleamed on the general's right hand. Certain men went to West Point and emerged superlative officers. Others attended the academy and came out convinced they were God's gift to the military—whether they were or not. An officer who took along his battle flags and West Point class ring for a million light-years probably fell into category number two.

That didn't mean the general was stupid, however. Stupid officers didn't get chosen by General West for sensitive postings. O'Neil, for instance, had been nobody's fool.

But O'Neil had been the commando type, flexible in his approach to tactics and life. Draven sensed a rigidity in Keogh. Lockwood had complained about O'Neil, and West had obliged by sending Keogh—a by-the-book type who would be more likely to view the natives as potential threat than O'Neil, who had fought beside the Abydans. Frankly, Keogh was an administrator, a bean counter of battle, the military equivalent of Eugene Lockwood.

They'd have deserved each other, but for the crisis caused by the cessation of ore flowing from the mine. Back on Earth, research facilities were already screaming for their rations of this magic quartz stuff. If politics began entering the equation, unraveling the curtain of secrecy West had placed over the StarGate, the result would be a scandal worse than Iran-Contra.

A political general like Keogh had to sense the powder keg he was sitting on. But even as Draven introduced himself, he could see there'd be no help forthcoming.

"My orders are clear," Keogh said. "I'm supposed to protect the StarGate and defend American interests here on Abydos."

"Well, this strike is imperiling those American interests you're supposed to defend," Draven snapped. "And I don't merely mean UMC, although I work for the company. This mineral we're mining has strategic purposes. Important research is going on—but now it's hampered by a lack of supply."

He decided on the patriotic pitch. "Are you going to let a bunch of towel-head primitives hold up the military research of the United States of America?"

"My orders say nothing about compelling the natives to go out and work for you," Keogh demurred. "As I understand it, forced labor is what caused the last rebellion here. With paramilitary groups arising in the population, surely the last thing you want is to foment trouble."

"I hope to negotiate a settlement," Draven said smoothly. "But my negotiating position will be much stronger if I know I can depend on your support. This entire project is of special interest to General West. Failure will look bad on *all* our records."

"I have my orders," Keogh repeated.

"But you do stand ready to protect American rights and citizens?" Draven worded his question carefully. The natives would no doubt be demanding Morris and Sullivan for scalping or some such punishment. If he could get an undertaking from Keogh to protect them . . .

"I don't know about individuals," Keogh said, stepping around the verbal land mine. "I'm to protect American interests. UMC personnel will of course be welcome inside this fortified camp in case of attack. But I do not intend to undertake offensive or inflammatory action."

Draven suddenly switched battlefields. "Then how about some humanitarian aid? Professor Jackson has apparently taught the locals the principles of the boycott. Native merchants are no longer selling food to my people. The StarGate is being tied up with your reinforcements and their logistical tail. Perhaps you could share your rations—"

"My own people are living on what Colonel O'Neil stockpiled," Keogh said. "Until our own supply situation is stabilized, I think sharing our food would be . . . unwise."

Draven's empty stomach rumbled in unhappiness. Still, he attempted to put the best face on the situation.

"Thanks very much for your input, General. I guess I'll go and talk to the city Elders. Perhaps you could lend me an all-terrain vehicle and escort?"

Keogh gave him the smile of a man who has just discovered vinegar in his wineglass. "I'm sure UMC has transport available—and security people to provide an escort."

Draven shrugged. It had been worth a try. Arriving at Nagada in an Army truck with a military guard could have given him the *appearance* of enjoying Keogh's support. But the general had seen through his strategem.

No, Francis Keogh was definitely not a stupid man.

Rigid, yes. Draven tried to push away hunger pangs. But stupid, no.

UMC's Abydos operation used jeeps instead of the government Humvees. When Draven announced his intention of going to Nagada, Lockwood immediately offered him a jeep and driver, plus a three-man security detail.

"Fine," Draven had replied, "just get those boys out of their camouflage suits and into civvies." If the locals had developed a hatred for gray suits, it did not behoove UMC's negotiator to turn up surrounded by those uniforms.

From the looks of his escort, some of the mercs hadn't bothered to bring civilian clothes with them. One had a gaudily patterned Hawaiian shirt that hung around him like a tent. Another wore a white shirt that strained over his shoulders and had to be left unbuttoned because it wouldn't stretch across his beefy chest.

Between their guns and the expressions on their faces, they looked more like a lynch mob than a guard of honor.

Well, a lynch mob might well be what Draven would encounter inside Nagada.

They fired up the jeep and headed out of the camp. Draven enjoyed the smooth ride as far as the mining pit. Whatever Lockwood's shortcomings, he'd planned and executed a well-graded road.

"Does the native militia still maintain a watch post?" Draven asked his driver.

The mercenary shrugged. "Sure do. We usually find a couple of slopes peeping at us up top of the next sand dune."

"Then pull up the jeep," Draven ordered.

"Hello!" he called, feeling like a perfect fool. "We're going to Nagada. Will one of you come with us?"

A voice came out of the shadows, replying in passable English. "You're going to Nagada? I'll come."

A young man seemed to flick into existence about halfway down the face of the dune, riding the hard-packed sand as if it were a slide. He was slim but sturdy-looking, and he seemed to notice neither the hostile looks nor the weapons of Draven's bodyguards.

The young militiaman enjoyed riding on the jeep, much more so after they'd passed the mine and the road for all practical purposes seemed to disappear. Draven's jeep shifted and swooped over what seemed to be the best path for a mastadge to take through the shifting dunes.

Draven noticed that their local guide didn't bother to fire a warning shot for the keepers of the gate. Then he realized that the sound of the jeep's engine obviated the necessity. Trumpets mooed, but when they arrived before the great gates, they remained closed.

"My name is Draven. I've come through the StarGate—all the way from Earth—to speak with Kasuf and the Elders."

"Thought so," the youthful militiaman said. He called up to one of the adobe towers flanking the gates. After an exchange of shouts the portals grudgingly swung open.

"You know where are the Elders?" the self-sufficient young man asked.

"Ah, no," Draven admitted.

"I'll take you," the boy soldier offered.

Following their youthful guide's directions, the driver jockeyed the jeep through the hodgepodge city's twisting streets. Draven had paranoid visions of ambush, of the young militia seizing the jeep and his guard detail's weapons.

Certainly, Draven didn't remember this part of town from his first visit. But then he'd been on foot, surrounded by cheering crowds. Now the streets were empty. The evening meal was either just on the stove or just ended, because smells of cooking filled the air.

Yet again Draven's stomach rumbled, more deeply and despairingly.

Draven noticed something else. Most of the

mud-brick structures in this area showed signs of recent repair. The patch jobs didn't stand out ostentatiously. The new walls were already bleached by the desert suns and scoured by sandy winds.

"This was all built over?" Draven asked their guide.

The young man nodded. "Blasted by Ra. The houses we fixed, but many died."

He abruptly shoved back part of the homespun cloak he wore, revealing the scars of a huge burn that had seared his arm. "Also blasted by Ra. I fought where your camp is. At the pyramid."

Draven nodded, catching the unspoken message. These people had suffered destruction and death for their freedom. They wouldn't be pushed around.

A few more twists and turns, and Draven found himself in familiar territory—the large square fronting the building where he'd met with the Elders.

The jeep coasted to a stop, and the young man vaulted out.

"Thank you," Draven said.

"Glad to help," the boy soldier said. "Maybe you can help us."

"Maybe," Draven said almost to himself.

The Elders had obviously been alerted. Kasuf and his *confrères* sat in a large room. At their side was Daniel Jackson to act as interpreter.

Draven took a shot at grabbing the initiative. "You've been busy making a lot of trouble, Jackson," he accused.

The academic gone native gave him a look of pure disgust. "I wondered how you were going to start," he said, "but that has to be the biggest load of crap I've ever heard from you. This afternoon there were a few thousand miners who were just aching for a piece of your so-called company police. Compared to the trouble you could have had, this strike is a walk in the park."

"So, you admit it's a strike." Draven made his voice as portentous as possible.

"Yes, the people here won't work for that clown Lockwood and his idiot flunkies. But you don't have to take my word for it." He turned to the Elders and spoke in the local dialect. All Draven got was the name Lockwood and the expressions of anger and dislike that appeared on the leaders' faces.

"We made an agreement," Draven threatened.

"Yeah," Jackson retorted, "and it's worth the nonexistent paper it was written on. Remember your wonderful words back then? These people do—that's the wonderful thing about folks who grow up in illiteracy: they've got a real memory for the spoken word. That's how Homer's poetry survived for thousands of years—and how the lies of Draven come back to haunt you. You didn't want a contract because, and let me quote: 'Certainly a bond of honor is sufficient between men of goodwill.' "

Draven stood with his mouth open as Jackson pressed on.

"The only problem is that UMC has shown neither honor *nor* goodwill. Remember your last visit here? The Elders greeted you with a feast. Well, you don't see any food for you here now. When it comes to boycotts, these people catch on quickly."

Draven pressed a hand to his empty stomach. "Some might consider this action precipitate."

"Your boy Lockwood has taken all sorts of precipitate actions—unilaterally, too. He blew up part of a pyramid that's been here for thousands of years. He set up work rules that don't seem to have any connection to conditions in the mine. And he hired guns to enforce them. Not once has he come to the Elders, even to discuss situations with them. They might have explained why that rest tent was set up—and how difficult it is to lug stuff up and down those ladders."

He glared at the UMC man. "*I* tried that climb when the Marines and I took on Ra's overseers. And I can say it was no picnic. Have you tried it? I know Lockwood hasn't."

"Oh, I'm sure you'd like to put all the blame on Lockwood," Draven shot back. "But the locals haven't exactly been angels. Some of them are responsible for sabotaging the new equipment my company is installing in the mines."

"I've heard rumors," Jackson replied. "But that's all anyone here has heard—because Lockwood never came to the Elders. If he'd given Kasuf and the others something to go on, they might have been able to get to the bottom of things. But Lockwood has treated his plans for the workforce as top secret. He's excluded the Elders, and when he had a real reason to turn to them for help, he went to Earth to get hired guns—like your body-guards over there—and a new commander for the military forces on Abydos. Lockwood obviously doesn't trust the Elders, so why should the Elders trust him?"

"Couldn't you have done something?" Draven burst out.

"Since when did I start working for UMC?" Jackson shouted back. "You guys didn't even want me in the business of teaching English!"

The renegade Earther calmed a little. "I've tried to explain to the Elders about corporations. It doesn't make much sense to them. But they understood about the strike and the boycott. Your people got a man killed today—a man named Zaid who worked his guts out in a back-breaking job because he had a sick daughter. And what did he get? A handful of Susan B. Anthony dollars. Or perhaps you'd like me to translate while you explain UMC's death-benefits policy?"

"Perhaps we can come up with something," Draven carefully allowed.

"Like the medicine you promised for the local clinics here?" Jackson asked. "That was a big incentive to allow your company in—and we haven't seen squat."

"Well, we were actually thinking of a company clinic when the operation expanded a bit more," Draven retired to lawyerspeak. "After all, dispensing drugs would require appropriately trained personnel."

"It's nice to hear that UMC is so finicky about the law when it comes to health-care issues,"

Jackson said sarcastically. "Because you've been downright illegal when it comes to pay and safety."

Draven's complexion went ruddy. "You've had a lot to say, Jackson, but I'm not hearing much from the Elders. Kasuf," he said, turning to the town's leader, "are you sure it's a good thing for your people to turn away from the mine?"

Jackson carefully translated the speech. But Kasuf turned to the young man as he began answering. Jackson nodded. "Draven, you've never understood about the mine here. It's valuable to you, and it was valuable to Ra. But for the people who lived here, it's been a centuries-long drain on the economy. They've broken their backs and gotten *nothing* in return. If the people sweating in the mine were out digging irrigation ditches instead, agriculture would boom. The mine stayed open because of the goodwill of the Abydan people. Their friends from Earth wanted the quartz mineral, and they were happy to provide."

Kasuf's bearded face grew angry. Jackson continued to translate. "But now our friends feel belittled. Strangers tell us how much we should work, people die. And what do we get?"

The leader of the city tossed down a handful of American coins.

Draven sat in a moment of silence.

Then Jackson spoke again. "You don't have the economic clout you imagined. UMC needs the people to work that mine. But Nagada can survive without it."

The renegade stared hard at the troubleshooter. "If you want the miners back at work, you've got to give them justice—and give the government here a voice in planning for the future."

CHAPTER 13
BACKDOOR POLITICS

Draven returned to the UMC camp in thoughtful silence.

His guards, however, were more vocal.

"You going to left that blond poofter and a gaggle of wogs tell you off like that?" an obviously British merc complained.

"I only went into the city to see how much give there was to the local government," Draven said.

"Not bloody much," the mercenary observed. "They are a tough bunch of old men."

"So we'll have to change that," Draven replied. "But first I think I'll rip a patch or two of skin off the three who got me into this."

The gang of three was still in Lockwood's office, waiting like little children for Daddy to come in and tell them all was well.

Needless to say, Daddy was not in a good mood. "You fool!" he raged at Lockwood. "I walked in to try pushing that council of Elders, and what do I find? We have absolutely no leverage. Zero. Zilch. *Nada.*"

"But sir, I assure you—" Lockwood began.

"Don't you assure me of *anything!*" Draven shouted. "Thanks to your mishandling of affairs, we've got a mine that's far behind on production, a strike and a boycott, *and* a military commander who won't stick his neck out to help us."

He rammed a finger hard into Lockwood's chest. "The end result? These 'Abbadabbas' you've been so busily laughing at have you right where it hurts. They have UMC right where it hurts. We're not a penny-ante outfit, Lockwood. Are we?"

"Of course not, sir," the sweating manager replied.

"Are we, Morris?"

"No, sir."

"Are we, Sullivan?"

"You've always paid me a good buck," the mercenary responded.

Draven's empty gut began to hurt. Three people he'd have to save, and the only one with a hint of spirit was the hired gunman.

"We're a major multinational corporation, gentlemen. We have resources. And this is the biggest undertaking we've ever been offered. I came to this planet, to this city, to make the arrangements with the locals. I'll admit something here. In my first contact I underestimated the natives. I thought they were primitives, that the problem would be the leftover American, Jackson."

The thin man's eyes began to glare. "But as I spoke with the Elders tonight, Kasuf was throwing my own words at me. How could this be? I left this world with considerable goodwill from the people here. What went wrong? The answer is— *you three.* The locals want justice—that means you, Morris and Sullivan."

Lockwood's voice was wobbly as he spoke. "Maybe—"

"Shut up," Draven said briefly. "Don't even *think* of turning them over to the natives."

The two subordinates glanced at each other in alarm.

"If it would restore the workforce—" Lockwood was almost whining.

Draven glared at the manager in complete disgust. It was only luck that Sullivan didn't have a sidearm. Or perhaps it was *bad* luck. Lockwood's removal—even with a bullet in the head—could only be a benefit.

"We don't turn over our personnel to local justice," Draven said flatly. "That's company policy. And I think it's a good policy when you consider some of the rather primitive notions of justice that obtain in some of the places where we operate."

His voice was flat and dispassionate. "I've seen cultures where hands get cut off for minor infractions. For all we know, the Abbadabbas might feel that the proper recompense for this Zaid person's death is to throw those responsible into the pit."

Charlie Morris's gorilla-like countenance began to show the realization that he was in real trouble. Sullivan's face looked a bit pinched.

"We have practical reasons for not backing down and giving our people away," Draven added. "The Elders are demanding more of a voice in running the mine, thanks to what they call your precipitate actions, Lockwood."

"Mr. Draven, I can't belive you're paying any

attention to these people." Lockwood sounded really desperate.

"Oh, attention *must* be paid," Draven replied. "The company has a policy for dealing with recalcitrant governments." He smiled thinly. "We replace them. And since such operations involve military action, you may want to call for that SEAL you hired as security chief—Ballard, I believe his name is?" Draven glared at the other two men in the office. "I'm hoping you could recuit *one* capable subordinate."

Daniel Jackson found himself still full of energy after the meeting of the Elders. Kasuf took the wired academic back to his house, where they were joined by Sha'uri.

"Your husband did well," Kasuf told his daughter.

"I expected no less," she said with a smile.

"I'll judge my performance by its results," Daniel replied, still so full of nervous energy that his body quivered. "I think I hit Mr. Draven with my best shot. But did I convince him? That's the big question."

Pushing his blond hair out of his face, Daniel began walking jerkily back and forth. "What I had hoped—what *we* hoped—is that our strike would force UMC to send someone to negotiate."

"And it did," Kasuf said. "This Draven arrived."

"Yes, but I was hoping he'd offer us a deal. Instead, all he did was attack us."

"In our markets, the merchants never make an offer until they have listened to the customers and judged what they'll pay. You gave the stranger much to think about, Daniel. Do not be surprised if he takes time for that thinking."

Daniel raised his hand and bit the cuticle of his left thumb—a nervous habit he thought he'd conquered years ago. He winced as blood flowed. "I just wish we knew *what* Draven is thinking."

Sha'uri shook her head in gentle incomprehension. "Why all this worry about one man's opinion?"

"Draven represents much more than a single man. He's a troubleshooter—" Daniel went on quickly to explain the unfamiliar English idiom. "Draven acts as an agent for his company. His word can bind UMC—as it did when he arranged for the use of the mine. But his words to his superiors can also make things happen." He glanced at Kasuf. "I've told you often enough I paid little attention to the doings of corporations on my world. But even I had heard of UMC. They wield great power—more than some governments on my world." Daniel frowned unhappily. "And here they're not even hampered by considerations of public opinion. Only a handful of people on Earth know that Abydos even exists. And they're all bound to secrecy."

One look, and Daniel could see that he'd lost his audience. "Let me put it this way. Draven's relation to Lockwood is the same as Ra's to a Horus guard."

Comprehension dawned for the Abydans. Powerful as a Horus guard might appear to a run-of-the-mill human, Ra represented infinitely more might—and danger.

Kasuf gave Daniel a thoughtful frown. "This Draven is king of the company?"

"No," Daniel explained, "but he has the ear of the kings of the company. That's why it was so important for us to talk to him—to go over Lockwood's head."

He sighed, realizing he had used another Englishism. "Imagine that the Elders had to make a decision on a matter of arbitration. But one side of the argument had arranged that only their case would be heard. That's the situation Lockwood had us in."

"But now Draven has heard our side," Sha'uri said.

Daniel nodded. "The only other way would have been for me to go back to Earth."

He glanced away from his wife's shocked face. "To plead our case we'd need someone who knew both English and the ways of my planet. The others who might be willing to help—O'Neil, Kawalsky, or Feretti—while they're our friends, they're also in the military. Their superiors have bound them by orders to stay here on Abydos."

Daniel gave Sha'uri a lopsided grin. "I, on the other hand—well, their superiors know that I'm not one to take orders."

Sha'uri had to smile. "Only too true, husband. Why, you wouldn't even take orders from Ra."

"I can't take much credit for that," he replied. "Ra ordered me to kill my friends. It's lucky that you and Skaara were on hand to get me out of that situation—by helping us all to escape."

He glanced around. "By the way, where *is* Skaara? I thought he'd be there for the fireworks at the council meeting."

Kasuf shook his head. "My son is off practicing to be a warrior again. Something called 'night operations,' whatever they may be."

"I hear that he's done great things with those boys," Daniel said. "They may not have uniforms like Lockwood's or Keogh's men, but he seems to have turned them into an effective force." Daniel hesitated for a moment. "Maybe we should ask to see them in action. It might be time for the Elders to take formal notice of Skaara's militia."

"You think we'll need warriors?" Kasuf asked in concern.

"It's just that I've been talking with Skaara— about his ambitions. They're bigger than this planet."

"How so?" Kasuf asked.

Dubiously, Daniel described his conversation with Skaara about the StarGates. Surprisingly, he found Kasuf in agreement with his son's proposed crusade.

"I have often of late found myself thinking about our brothers in the stars," Kasuf admitted, "and what a great thing it would be to let them know that Ra was no more. How strange that my son has taken those thoughts and tried to put them to action."

"Well, there won't be any action unless we find more StarGate coordinates, as I told him," Daniel said. "I don't see that happening unless we stumble across another treasure trove of ancient records."

He still strode back and forth, as if he were lecturing a class. "Maybe it's just as well we *don't* have coordinates. Because then Skaara would face the same problem I would if I wanted to go to Earth and plead our cause. The StarGate isn't ours anymore. It's in the hands of the military—who are no longer led by our friend O'Neil."

Daniel's hands bunched in his pockets. "Maybe I should have seen that coming. But with Keogh taking charge, it means for all practical purposes that the StarGate is now controlled by UMC."

"They have a need for it," Kasuf said. "To what use would we put the StarGate?"

"Suppose Draven hadn't come," Daniel pointed out. "If I wanted to go to UMC and tell them of Lockwood's misdeeds, do you think he'd give me free passage? Most likely, he'd refuse." He frowned. "Or, being the rat he is, Lockwood would allow me into the pyramid, where I would disappear. An 'accident' in transit." Daniel's face twisted. "Even if I got to Earth, whom could I tell? I've explained how my colleagues thought I was too eccentric, to say the least. If I went public with a story about going to another world, I'd be put away as insane."

He smiled gently as his wife began to protest. "Remember, to my people Ra is nothing but an ancient myth."

Then Daniel's smile faded. "I don't know anyone at UMC. If I wanted to complain about Lockwood, I'd have to go to General West. You haven't met him. But my impression of this guy is that he's so twisty, he'd make Draven and Lockwood look straightforward. On this side of the StarGate, I learned that he uses people like tools. I was his translating tool. O'Neil was chosen to lead our expedition because he'd be West's wrecking tool, if necessary. Should the StarGate seem dangerous, O'Neil was willing to blow it up."

Daniel glanced at Sha'uri again. "To tell you the truth, I wouldn't like to put us—or myself—in West's hands. What if he's finished with this tool? If I went to talk to him, he might not let me back."

"Don't worry yourself so much about possibilities," Kasuf said.

"I feel that I've got to weigh them," Daniel protested. "It seems that, step by step, I've been leading you down a path to—I don't know what. I'm not a leader by nature, Kasuf. It worries me."

"We can do no more until we hear a counteroffer from Draven. Perhaps he will see the rightness of our concerns. We will get more of a voice in the running of the mine—and those who caused Zaid's death will be turned over for judgment."

"I meant to ask about that," Daniel admitted. "What sort of punishment would those two guys face?"

"It's not a question of punishment," Kasuf said. "Rather, it's a question of recompense. Zaid had a sick daughter. That girl no longer has a father to support her. Were I to judge the case—which

I can't, because I fear my dislike of Lockwood would cloud my faculties—I would have the men whose negligence caused Zaid's death take responsibility for his daughter. If they could have her cured, they should do so. If not, they should arrange that she be cared for."

Daniel's eyebrows rose. "Your system of law sounds quite pragmatic. I was afraid that the penalty would be boiling in oil—something like that."

Kasuf gave him a bitter smile. "The law of Ra—well, he did not rule by law but by whim. We could not live so."

Sha'uri saw her father smother a yawn. "It grows late," she said. "Come, husband."

As they walked the silent streets of Nagada, Daniel's nervous energy sent him striding ahead of his wife. Sha'uri took his arm, then looked at him in surprise. "Clashing with this Draven fellow has left you on edge. You're quivering like a mastadge sensing a sand storm."

"I'm not afraid of the guy—just concerned," Daniel said.

She gave him a teasing smile. "I didn't say you were trembling. Just that you're a-quiver—like the difference between the night we were wed and—"

"That's not fair," Daniel complained. "With the language barrier, I didn't realize that was a wedding. When I did—"

Sha'uri's smile grew broader. "Exactly."

The two of them extended their strides to reach their quarters all the more quickly.

*   *   *

The next day, Draven took over Lockwood's office, banishing him from his precious air conditioning. Seated behind the manager's desk, the troubleshooter met with Vernon Ballard.

"I'm extending feelers toward our counter force through the language teachers," Draven told the security man. "If all goes well, we'll contact them tomorrow evening." Night was always best for plotting, especially when one was plotting the downfall of a government. Darkness brought out the best qualities in coup leaders.

"You're sure these guys will overthrow the old men?" Ballard asked.

"They're young. I'm sure we can depend on them to be . . . impetuous."

The mercenary chief shook his head. "Just a matter of business for you, isn't it? If you can't get in from the front, you'll take the back door."

"But we'll still need a key," Draven said. "And I expect you to provide it."

"My great-grandad, he used to trade with the Indians," Ballard said. "There were two prime trade goods—whiskey and rifles." He smiled. "I don't see as how these folk are much in the way of drinkers. But those boys sure do love guns."

Draven nodded. "But we don't want them getting their hands on guns that are too good."

"Like Great-grandad and the Indians. These guys'll need something that will give them an edge over the local competition—but my boys will still have an edge over them."

He squinted, thinking. "I might be able to get my hands on a couple of cases of Garand rifles.

1942 vintage—adapted for the Marines during Double-ya Double-ya Two. Bolt-action guns, five rounds in the clip."

"And fifty years behind today's technology," Draven said. "I like it."

"Garand's a workhorse gun. They were using them back in 1903," Ballard said.

"All the better," Draven smiled.

"I didn't mention the best thing of all," Ballard said. "The Garand takes a .30-caliber bullet. Ammo for later guns is a lot smaller—more on the order of a .22, to fit more in the clip."

"So they can't use our stocks—or the military's—for supply."

"So, sir," Vernon Ballard drawled. "These boys want bullets, they'll have to go through us."

"Head back through the StarGate and do your deal," Draven ordered. "I don't imagine it will cost us much. And I want a sample on hand for our meeting with our new friends-to-be."

His smile was absolutely without mirth. "These primitives do love a big bang."

The three visitors from the mining camp entered Nagada disguised in homespun robes. Skaara was amused by the cloak-and-dagger aspect. What did the strangers think they were plotting at?

Several of his followers had approached him the day before. Students from UMC's English classes had sought them out. The important man who'd arrived to speak with the Elders also wanted to speak with Skaara. But he wanted to do so in private.

Skaara was unwilling to meet until one of his lieutenants—another former shepherd who'd proven himself fighting the Horus guards—spoke to him about Draven.

"He was smart enough to ask at our watch post for a guide to the city," the young man said. "Whatever he has to say, it might be interesting to hear."

So, a rendezvous was set for tonight, starting with the entrance of the three disguised strangers—badly disguised, at least in Skaara's eyes. One of them simply towered over the average height of the city folk. When O'Neil and Kawalsky had pretended to be from Nagada, the tall lieutenant at least had had the sense to hunch a little. This tall man stood erect and almost strutting as he came through the gate. And what was in the long package he handled so carefully?

The strangers had specified that the meeting place be secluded and noise-proof. Skaara had chosen a warehouse built against the walls. It had thick walls, but had been blasted by Ra's udajeets and not yet repaired.

A couple of oil lamps provided wavering illumination as the strangers were ushered into an inner room. They threw back their cloaks to reveal the faces of Draven, Lockwood, and the head of Lockwood's guards—Ballard.

"You lead the boy soldiers?" Lockwood spoke a mangled version of the local idiom.

"'What is it you want?" Skaara asked them in English.

"I thought you'd speak our tongue," Draven said. "Your man who guided me last night was quite understandable."

To Skaara, he sounded like one of the merchants in the marketplace, flattering the customer before setting up a sale.

"You wanted to see me," he said.

"I came to see what it is you want." Draven smiled. "The company I represent is large and powerful. We could give you wealth, women—and power here on Abydos." The negotiator leaned forward. "So I ask again. What do you want?"

Skaara gave him a whimsical smile. "I want the stars. Can you give them to me?"

Draven was shocked out of his smooth manner. "What do you mean?"

"You and the new soldiers—the greencoats—control the StarGate," Skaara said. "I want our scholar, Daniel, to have access to the gate. There are other worlds besides yours and mine out there. Our people have brothers still under the yoke of Ra. Shouldn't we at least *try* to search them out?"

Draven was so taken aback, he sought time by pretending to consult with his companions.

"The kid thinks big," Ballard whispered. "Who'd have thought he'd want to stake a claim on other worlds?"

"We have a profitable setup now." Lockwood's voice was almost a whine of complaint. "Do we really want to waste time allowing Jackson to tinker with our lifeline? Every moment the StarGate is off-line means lost shipments of ore—or missed deliveries of supplies needed on this side."

"We're getting neither ore nor supplies unless we get a more complaisant government," Draven whispered. He sized Skaara up. Despite his idealistic pose, this young man might go for the bread-and-butter pitch.

"I don't know if I can give you the stars," he said frankly. "Our wise men say it would be very difficult to find other worlds."

Skaara nodded. "That's what Daniel says. There are many combinations. But surely we might make some attempts."

"Perhaps," Draven said smoothly. "What I can offer you is a better position here on Abydos. Supplies for your militia—uniforms . . . weapons." He turned to Ballard. "Show him."

The hired warrior unwrapped the bundle he'd carried. Inside was a rifle, longer than the sort Skaara was used to. Ballard took a clip of long bullets, slapping it into a hole in the belly of the weapon.

With a *klick-chak*! he operated some sort of bolt atop the gun. Then he fired into one of the adobe walls, creating a huge pockmark. The blast was deafening, even in the large-sized room. Militia members came boiling in, fearing their leader was in danger.

Ballard, carefully keeping the muzzle away from Skaara, operated the mechanism again and fired.

"A fine weapon, isn't it?" Draven said.

"It seems slower than the weapons we saved from Colonel O'Neil's camp," Skaara observed.

"More to do before it can be fired . . . and the bullets are larger than the ones we use in our guns now."

Draven's smiled curdled. Apparently, the UMC man hadn't expected him to notice these things. "The guns are of simple design because, well, things are simpler on this world. But they're also easier to repair. And if they don't fire so quickly, they also won't jam so easily in the sand."

"All right. As you say, they seem to be fine weapons. How are we to earn them? Do you expect us to work in the mines for you?"

"We'll give you the guns to help you take your rightful place here in Nagada. Use them to overthrow the old men who hold you—and your city—down. The mine can bring you riches. Just send the people back to work for us."

"So, we can have guns, and I can have riches, if only we will overthrow the old fools who rule us."

Draven nodded eagerly.

"I have advice for you, Mr. Draven." Skaara pointed at Lockwood. "Fire that man. He's been here for months, now, and he never discovered that I am the son of Kasuf, the head old fool."

Draven aimed a lambent glare at the manager. Ballard began desperately manipulating the bolt on his rifle again. Skaara snatched up a long pole with what looked like a stylized lotus flower at its top. Draven had dismissed it as some sort of torch or decoration. Swinging the pole like a quarterstaff, the young man knocked the rifle from Ballard's hands.

Then he worked some hidden control, and

flanges sprang out at the head of the staff. Skaara aimed, and a bolt of energy leapt from the staff. The rifle's stock burned, the metal bolt vanished. The barrel melted.

"I don't think we need your . . . simple weapons, either." The young man was every inch the leader as he aimed the blast-lance at them.

"Now go—be out of here before I show you how this works on flesh!"

CHAPTER 14
EVEN THE GODS ARE MORTAL

To an exterior observer, the battleship *Ra's Eye* made the transition from stardrive to normal space in a soundless blaze of glory. Vacuum, of course, does not transmit sound. But it does convey light, and at the moment of its appearance, incandescent sheets of luminescence emanated from each face of the starship's pyramidal structure.

On the bridge, Hathor felt the familiar queasy sensation of shifting from the unreal hyper-realm back to reality. Starship jumps were different from transiting the StarGates—they seemed curiously unfocused. One had a sense of rushing through the void with no destination.

One of Ptah's technicians ran her hands over the lit panels that made up the navigation controls. A holographic screen flashed in front of her face. "We have arrived in the star system Amentet," she announced, "precisely as calculated."

Ptah himself roved the bridge, checking readouts at all stations. At Engineering, he activated the communications system. "Engines! I'm reading a power fluctuation from the drive. Modulate!"

Hathor beckoned the engineer god over. "If you keep doing their jobs, they're never going to learn," she said in a whisper.

His own voice was rough. "They're only trainees, with a surface indoctrination in shipboard systems. A skeleton crew able to move Ra's flying palace in small jumps—that's very different from handling this behemoth."

Hathor knew all too well. Ra's ship, for all its apparent size and majesty, was a mere yacht, a toy, next to the grim bulk of the warship. In addition, most of the royal starcraft ran on automatic systems. That wasn't possible on a ship going into combat.

Ra's ship had power in abundance. But even with the quartz wonder stone, power was precious, being juggled between the stardrive and the weapons systems. It didn't help that in spite of months of refurbishing, most of the power connections were millennia old.

Hathor felt a sense of edginess as she paced. Feeling the bridge under her feet awoke uncomfortable memories—mere months old for her, but dating to the age of legend for almost everyone else aboard.

She turned to Ptah. "How do you deal with it?" she asked.

"With what?" her erstwhile husband returned.

"How do you manage your status as legend? The reactions of today's ones to the fact that you lived in the First Time?"

"Simple," he replied with a shrug. "I don't let them know."

Ptah's solution wouldn't work for her, she thought. And it certainly wouldn't help her fit into what she considered a degenerate age. The engi-

neering crew was not the only skeleton complement aboard *Ra's Eye*. Resources and manpower
were being hoarded on godlings' distant fiefs.
Even some of Ptah's technicians were being kept
against their god commander's orders.

Worst of all, however, was the shortage of warriors. The ground force attached to *Ra's Eye* was
seriously under-strength. Far more than on
Ombos, Hathor would have to depend on slashing
attacks by the udajeets to project firepower. There
simply weren't enough dependable warriors to use
as foot soldiers, except as a tiny reserve. She even
lacked warriors for the battleship's fire-control
posts. Whole batteries had been slaved together
and would be fired by conscripts from the ranks
of Thoth's administrators.

Still, the ship's shake-down cruise had taken
them as far as the star system nearest to Tuat.
Hathor remembered doing the same with her new
fleet before moving to quell the Ombos rebellion.
The Amentet system was barren of planets that
could sustain life. But there was a sizable band of
space debris where the third planet should have
been.

Hathor proposed to use the rocky asteroids for
target practice.

"Activate the system drive," she ordered her female navigation officer. "Set course for one of the
thicker meteor swarms."

The eerie glow of normal-space drive illumi-
nated the base of the pyramid ship. It accelerated
toward a collection of space junk.

"Closing, Lady Captain," the nav officer reported.

"Sensor nets at maximum gain!" Ptah called. The ceiling of the bridge disappeared as a holographic representation of nearby space appeared. A stylized pyramid in the center of the projection showed the location of the ship. Glowing multifaceted shapes depicted the asteroids.

"Gunnery!" Hathor called, opening a new communications line. "Secondary batteries, engage and fire!"

In seconds, the holo-projection began showing the breakup, and in some cases disappearance, of the orbiting rocks. The margins of the representation began to crawl with hieroglyphic information scoring accuracy and fire-to-hit ratios.

"Satisfactory," Hathor said to Ptah. "It seems that time on the simulators imparted a fair degree of skill, even to Thoth's accountants."

She turned to the Nav station. "Sensors, find me a good-sized chunk out there. Something about the order of Tuat-the-moon."

A scan of nearby space turned up a piece of cosmic debris that an Earth astronomer would have classed as similar to Ceres. The pyramid shape on the holographic projection shrank to represent the larger scale. Minor space junk appeared in dimmer shades. The worldlet became a glaring orange.

"Gunnery! Main batteries target—and fire!"

The designated target blazed brighter in the holographic view, expanding as if it were a cloud of gas, then vanishing.

Which is pretty much what happened. Blast-bolts of enormous energy had vaporized the plane-toid. During the Ombos campaign these batteries had obliterated entire cities from orbit.

In the present, however, the single barrage led to disaster. Instants after showing the devastation of the moonlet, the holographic projection winked out. So did most of the light on the bridge. Essential stations were represented by the fox-fire glows of emergency illumination. Warning sirens howled.

"Engines! What did I tell you about that fluctuation?" Ptah shouted in fury.

"Lord, the energy drain for the main batteries caused a power cascade!" A panicked voice replied. "We are now trying—"

Screams echoed over the communications link.

"Report! Report, Ammit eat you!" Ptah swore.

Hathor aimed a glare that would have made the ship's main battery look like a birthday candle. "If your people strand us here, I swear I'll feed you to Ammit myself!"

"I'm sorry, lord." The voice from the engine room sounded harassed but no longer panicked. "Some of the ancient circuitry could not handle the load. We'll have to bridge and reroute, but I assure you the drive will be on-line shortly. Life support is operational, and passive sensors show us to be in no danger."

"I thought there was supposed to be redundant circuitry for all drive and navigation equipment," Hathor hissed at her husband.

"In the normal course of events," Ptah said

smoothly. "But in a rush job . . ." He shrugged. "I suppose we should be glad we discovered the defect. My people will have to learn to be more careful."

Hathor preferred not to know how long they drifted almost helplessly. At last, however, power returned.

"Take us back to Tuat," she briefly ordered.

She stood looking calm and unflappable as *Ra's Eye* transited into stardrive. But the muscles in Hathor's stomach were clenched.

They arrived at the edge of the system, and proceeded on systemic drive to Tuat-the-world.

"I want a runthrough on a planetary landing," Hathor said to Ptah quietly. "Unless you think it's too . . . *dangerous*."

"No more hazardous than any of the other maneuvers we've undertaken," Ptah replied.

The glow from the drive flared as the battleship swung majestically into the atmosphere of the derelict planet. With peculiar delicacy for all its bulk, *Ra's Eye* settled onto the ruinous docking station in the midst of a huge, decayed cityscape.

"Launch the udajeets," Hathor commanded. "Our warriors come from six different factions. They have to learn how to fly—and fight—as a team."

With a brusque gesture she then beckoned Ptah aside. "And while our fighters get themselves together, you will get every technician in or on Tuat and make absolutely *positive* that there will be no more embarrassing systems failures." Hathor glared. "If that had happened during a combat situation—" She throttled back her voice. "You would be the first casualty."

"Are you so sure you'll be taking *Ra's Eye* into combat?" Ptah asked. "Ra's ship could have failed somehow between here and Tuat. He had no technicians aboard—just the children and a few warriors."

"What has happened to the empire?" Hathor burst out. "You can't gather together enough technicians to refurbish one ship. Lack of warriors—they're little more than a ceremonial guard."

"This isn't the First Days anymore," Ptah said. "The empire isn't expanding—we're no longer dealing with the active threat of revolt from the *fellahin*."

"And the result is that our expedition to Abydos has been pared down to something more like a scouting mission," Hathor said bitterly.

"And what if your scouting expedition discovers Ra?" Ptah asked.

Hathor's face stiffened. "We will serve him, of course."

The pallid flesh on Ptah's cyborg face twitched into a smile. "And if he turns out to be helpless?"

Hathor remembered those uncannily glowing eyes that always seemed to know her thoughts. Whatever secrets she kept here, *he* would know.

"You haven't answered my question," Ptah mocked.

"And I don't intend to." Hathor strode off. "I'll be taking the shuttle up to Tuat-the-moon."

*   *   *

Hathor elected to pilot the shuttle up to the royal palace by herself. She could operate the small spacecraft, and frankly, she wanted some time to herself. Her performance on the bridge of *Ra's Eye* had been more draining than she expected. Besides, she had flown shuttles and uda-jeets in the days of the First Time. And the controls hadn't changed.

The shuttle itself had the same pyramidal construction that marked all spacegoing vehicles in Ra's empire. But it only accommodated ten people and a pilot. Its small, gleaming, golden-quartz contours added an incongruous note as it perched atop the cracked and weather-worn pyramid that housed the StarGate to Tuat-the-world.

Attempts had been made to patch the irregular stone bulk, but they were almost hidden under a coating of hardy lichen that had climbed almost to the apex of the pyramid. To a passing Earthling the docking station would have looked like a squat Christmas tree with but one ornament—the star at the top.

For Hathor, the sad state of the spaceport seemed a metaphor for the slapdash attitude afflicting all of Ra's empire. In her day the pyramids had been flawlessly maintained, although the city they once served had already fallen into ruin.

Two stations over, the bulk of *Ra's Eye* had settled, looking like a mountain of glassy gold. Even as Hathor glanced that way, heavy face plates retracted to reveal the launching decks and the firing slits for the blaster batteries. The battleship seemed the grimly purposeful artifact it had been in the days of the First Time—at least from the outside.

As Hathor prepared for liftoff, a pair of udajeets launched. The graceful, rakishly designed anti-gravity gliders had the sharply curved wings of a striking falcon. The white wings even had stylized pinions picked out in gold.

The atmospheric craft banked into a sharp turn, shrinking in the distance as they set off on a strafing run down one of the empty boulevards of the dead metropolis. Hathor could see only the flash of the twin blast-cannons as a twinkle in the distance. But from experience she knew the destruction that must be raining on the under-brush now clogging the empty streets.

As if in imitation of the passing fliers, Hathor activated her own craft's lifting drive. A decep-tively gentle radiance bathed the top of the dock-ing station as the shuttle rose. But the lichen blackened and died about a sixth of the way down from the top.

The shuttle moved with all the speed and flair of an elevator—definitely a case of "slow and steady wins the race." But it was the only means of admission to Ra's planetoid palace. The head god's paranoid search for security had placed the Tuat StarGate on the planet's surface. He'd even banned the short-range matter transmitters from the palace.

So, of one wished to visit Tuat-the-moon, one came by way of slow, tubby, easily scanned shut-tles. The damned things didn't even have the room to transport a decent strike team.

The shuttle's slow rise had taken it about fifty feet above the docking station when another pair of udajeets launched. Too bad they were atmosphere craft, without the range to reach the moonlet. Hathor smiled. Now, *there* would be the means for an impressive entrance. She'd have to talk to Ptah about supercharging one of the gliders.

The udajeets streaked straight for the shuttle, spreading out slightly to bracket it. Hathor's smile grew broader with reminiscence. Hot pilots were still the same, always ready to pull a stunt. Besides, she knew these two. The second-wave udajeets came from her own faction, her first followers.

The gliders had passed almost before Hathor realized they'd fired on her. Her shuttle yawed as blast-bolts tore at its golden fabric. The slow-moving, wobbling craft had only doubled its altitude as the udajeets banked around for a second pass.

Hathor thrust out a hand, running it over a newly installed panel. Control surfaces glowed to life. With a lifetime's facility she controlled the shuttle's lift with one hand while setting up parameters with the other.

A large red dot appeared on her navigation image. The udajeets were almost on top of her again. With their frail, airy construction they looked like a pair of butterflies attacking a brick. But they could wheel and fire, wheel and fire, while the brick was trapped on a single, slow-moving course. Sooner or later the attackers would hit something vital, and the brick would fall and crash.

Unless . . .

The udajeets were firing. Hathor moved her left hand over a large, glowing control surface. The red dot on her nav display followed her hand's movement. The dot touched one of the udajeets, moved ahead of it—

Hathor brought down her finger on the glassy plate. Bolts of blaster fire ripped from each apex of the pyramid. Three blasts struck the glider she'd targeted. The more aerodynamic but flimsier craft came apart like a butterfly with its wings torn off.

The other fighter flashed past, banked . . . and hesitated before coming around for another attack. They were much higher now, nearly at the limit of the atmosphere craft's performance range. If the warrior didn't score a crucial hit, Hathor would get away.

But the shuttle was quaking as it flew. One more hit could mean a long, fatal fall. Still, the attacking pilot hesitated as he came around.

Hathor's right hand flew across the flight controls, swinging the shuttle at right angles to its upward trajectory. Without the lift of the drive, the pyramidal vessel flew about as well as a cobblestone. Hathor lurched as the shuttle pushed slightly forward—and very quickly down.

But Hathor had aimed the craft so her attacker would have to pass the fields of fire of all five of her blasters. The udajeet came on, committed to its attack. Twin blasters flashed under the rakish wings.

Five blasters lashed out from each corner of Hathor's craft.

The shuttle staggered again as a hole was torn in its nose. The udajeet shattered as five bolts concentrated on its pilot's cabin.

Hathor fought her half-crippled craft, bringing it around so the drive surfaces pointed toward the planet again, engaging maximum lift, stopping her plummeting descent just in time. Throughout that struggle a grim smile curved her lips. She hadn't been able to get Ptah to increase the performance of the shuttles. But he had made sure her personal craft was armed.

Using the matter transporter inside the stone pyramid, Hathor transferred directly to the bridge on *Ra's Eye*. Ptah stood at the captain's place. Hathor noticed that all of his technician crew people carried blast-lances.

"Mutiny or assassination attempt?" she asked her erstwhile husband.

Ptah's mechanical shoulder rose in a shrug. "We're not completely sure yet, but the latter appears more likely. Most of our warrior complement seems shocked at the attack on you. They've been disarmed, and the udajeets have stood down. First flight was ordered to land."

"I wondered why no one was flying to my aid," Hathor said pointedly.

Ptah's waxy flesh looked as hard as his metal side. "No one was flying until I was sure they wouldn't be attacking you, too." His mechanical shoulder rose again. "Besides, I knew you could handle two udajeets with the equipment you had. And I was proven correct."

"I suppose we should be glad that the assassins weren't in Gunnery," Hathor finally said. "Those pilots—they were from my faction, weren't they?"

"Perhaps the better description is that they were from the late Sebek's faction," Ptah said. "Although they had seemed quite devoted to your cause."

"We'll have to hope the rest of the warriors will follow me." Hathor turned to the navigation officer. "Lift us. We're heading for Tuat-the-moon. I want a continuous scan on the palace's defensive batteries. If they give a hint of energizing, I want Gunnery to blow them away."

The marble walls of the central palace dome were scarred and spalled from repeated exchanges of blast-bolts. The pile of furniture at one end of the hall—including a golden throne—marked the position of the last rebels. Hathor watched a holographic image from one of Ptah's spy-eyes as one of her squad of Horus guards—recruited from three separate factions—brought his blast-lance to bear from around a corner and fired. The bolt of energy slashed through the makeshift barrier and caught one of the rebel guardsmen in the chest.

"One down, five effectives left," she counted. "And the two leaders in the chamber beyond—with Thoth."

"I can't show you what's transpiring in there,"

Ptah apologized. "They've destroyed my observation modules."

"I'm surprised they haven't tried the hostage gambit," Hathor said.

"Not with your reputation," her one-time husband pointed out. He frowned. "You're sure you want to go alone?"

She nodded grimly. "At this point I'm unwilling to have *anyone* at my back."

The attempted coup had recruited a surprising range of support because it had proceeded not in the name of Apis, the ringleader, but of Ra.

Who'd have imagined the Bull could be so clever? Hathor thought. *He tapped into the anger against me as an usurper—rebuilding what Ra had decommissioned. And, of course, all of us have a lively fear of how Ra would react if he did return.*

She had left Troth as master of the palace for the duration of the test voyage. And it was only her unexpectedly quick return that had foiled the plotters. They had only begun, seizing Thoth and the palace armory, when *Ra's Eye* had reappeared in the system.

The assassins aboard the battleship had been forced to rush. And there was still too much resistance to the coup on Tuat-the-moon. The conspirators hadn't even gotten close to the defense batteries.

With Hathor's return the *putsch* died—as did many of Apis's followers.

Now only this bare handful remained, trapped. Ironically, Ptah reported that the seemingly dead-end chamber where the leaders had taken sanctuary actually connected with a secret passage he'd built for Ra.

Hathor proposed to use the hidden entrance in an attempt to save Thoth.

"You could just as easily send a squad of guards," Ptah protested.

"Thoth is the one who revived me—I owe him my best effort," Hathor replied.

Grudgingly, Ptah showed her the nearest entrance. The secret way was dimly lit and surprisingly clean—in better shape, say, than the shuttle docking facilities.

Moving quietly, Hathor reached the panel which Ptah had assured her led to Apis's last redoubt. She stepped back, arming her blast-lance. Her first bolt blew in the secret entrance. The second took off Apis's head, blowing his bull mask—and its contents—halfway across the room.

The other occupant was a muscular man who still wore the side-lock of youth. The dye on the Eye of Ra tattooed around the young man's own right eye was still raw. He'd just recently entered the warrior caste, and had risen to the rank of god commandeer quite quickly.

Hathor knew his face. She had promoted him to take Sebek's place when she had taken over the crocodile god's faction.

The new Sebek was good—he had his own blast-lance armed and aimed at her chest. But Hathor had both aimed and triggered her weapon.

Sebek went down, his midsection charred, cooked meat. He sank to the marble floor, still alive as Hathor kicked his weapon from his nerveless hands. She knocked her appointee flat. His eyes were glazed but still conscious as Hathor aimed her blast-lance at his face. "Thoth!" she called. Sebek's eyes trailed off to his right.

Hathor turned. Thoth lay cold and stark on the floor. Several blaster burns had seared his body, wounds which hadn't been treated. There were also marks of torture, as if the plotters had tried to force him to come in on their coup.

Thoth had been unconscious when they'd finished him off. The top of his head was simply gone. It was the easiest way to deny the rescue of Ra's sarcophagus. Humans might be easily repaired. But even Ra's technology could not rebuild a brain from scratch.

Hathor's lips skinned over her teeth in a rictus as she returned to Sebek. His eyes met hers in terror as she positioned her blast-lance over his head. Hathor triggered her weapon, then triggered it again and yet again. By the time she was finished, not only was Sebek's head gone, there was a bowl-sized depression in the marble floor receiving the thin trickle of blood from the nearly cauterized stump of his neck.

Hathor then went to kneel by Thoth, closing his bulging, distorted eyes. If she had been one to heed omens, this would definitely be a bad one.

The revolt was definitely over. Hathor had appeared from the sanctum chamber of the coup leaders to take the last rebel guardsmen from behind. But the Cat's face was not happy as she rejoined Ptah.

"You have two days to do whatever additional repairs you can to *Ra's Eye*," she said. "Then I set off for Abydos. We can't stand any more incertitude about Ra's fate. It seems I daren't leave for fear of revolt. Yet I daren't stay for the same reason. When *I* know how the situation stands—whether we need a successor—then I will know how the deal with the others."

She stepped up to Ptah. "I name you master of the palace in my absence. May you succeed better than my last nominee."

"Speaking of nominees, shall I name a new Sebek?" Ptah asked lightly.

Hathor stared into his eyes. "You can do as you will," she said. "Always bearing in mind that I will come back."

In two days, losses among the crew had been fleshed out and the troublesome circuits on *Ra's Eye* replaced.

Surrounded by a full retinue of guards, Hathor marched through the docking station to board her ship. But someone stood waiting at the end of a hall attached to one of the ship's internal airlocks.

Hathor gestured for the guards to stop and stepped out of the open box they formed. Standing by the lock was the ghastly machine-human parody who had once been her husband.

"What are you doing here?" Hathor asked.

The waxy-pale flesh side of Ptah's mouth turned up in a grin. "The last time you set off from Tuat, I was notable for my absence," he said. "I thought this time I'd be notable for my presence." He raised his human arm. "Merely to wish you fare-well—and good luck."

Hathor nodded, then continued onward. Beyond the hall the ship's heavy airlock door closed and cycled.

And even as the docking station shook from the force of liftoff from *Ra's Eye*, Ptah held his place, still smiling his eerie half smile.

CHAPTER 15
INTO THE FLAME

Jack O'Neil stretched out as best he could, considering the narrow confines of his camp cot. If his sleeping arrangements were on the small side, the tent he was sharing was more cramped still. A far cry from his quarters as head officer on Abydos.

At least he had some friendly company. When Adam Kawalsky had realized his old commander was out of a tent as well as a post, he'd offered his own billet. "With all the people they're pouring in here, I'll have to double up anyway," Kawalsky said. "And, begging the colonel's pardon, I'd rather have you than some snot-nosed Army first-loot right out of the Point. Half of Keogh's officers look like teenagers."

"It's the security angle," O'Neil said sourly. "West is getting people right out of training because they've been vetted pretty thoroughly—and they don't have any connections in the service. Less chance of any of these guys getting drunk with his buddies and leaking info on this operation."

Kawalsky frowned. "Yeah, but if the cow flop hits the fan . . ."

O'Neil just shrugged. "We'll just have to hope

these boy soldiers will treat it as a training exercise with live fire."

The colonel's mood was not as flippant as his words. Most of Keogh's command were troops one step up from raw recruits. If trouble really erupted here on Abydos, the Army brats would be facing Skaara's boy commandos. They'd balance out pretty even in terms of training—and Skaara's boys had some combat experience, albeit brief. The Abydans would weigh up way short on the technology front, but Skaara and his followers had proven themselves very resourceful at getting weapons.

No, the deciding force in any armed confrontation would be the original nucleus of the Abydos expeditionary force—the combat Marines commanded by Jack O'Neil.

The colonel glanced at his lanky lieutenant. How would Kawalsky feel about fighting his recent comrades-in-arms? O'Neil shifted uneasily on his bunk. Hell, he didn't even know how *he* felt about it.

"So," he said aloud, "how are you and Feretti settling in over in Supplies?"

"It's like we've died and gone to hell," Kawalsky replied promptly. "Just from looking around and counting heads, I figure we've got maybe three battalions here. From the supply picture you'd think we were trying to equip D-Day."

O'Neil grinned. "Remember what Napoleon said about armies traveling on their stomachs."

Kawalsky gave a disgusted grunt. "That's the

only way our boys *could* move if they had to carry all the crap we're stockpiling."

"Speaking of stockpiles, Keogh wants to send back all the hand-held missiles I managed to assemble."

"The anti-udajeet armory?" Kawalsky frowned.

"He's convinced that if we end up fighting, it will be our friends in Nagada," O'Neil said. "And they, of course, won't have air support." He glanced at his lieutenant. "Now, I can't countermand a direct order from a superior. But I don't have to tell you to hurry. I'm sure you have lots of priorities. Just don't move stripping our air defense to the top of the list."

Kawalsky's frown deepened. "That's not as easy as it sounds. Those crates of missiles take up a lot of space. We're having a hard time keeping all our food supplies under canvas right now. There's just so much space on this plateau. We've got guys trying to set up a regular motor pool. That means maintenance bays, and they're going to start digging storage tanks for fuel. Keogh doesn't want to depend on tanker trucks out in the open."

O'Neil's lips twitched. "Great. All the inconveniences of home."

"The other problem is that there are a lot of truckloads of stuff coming *out* of the StarGate, but nothing much is going in—back to Earth." The lieutenant paused for a second. "I mean, not since the strike at the mine."

"So you think some conscientious supply sergeant will truck off our air defense to accommodate a few more boxes of Meals, Ready to Eat?"

" 'Fraid so, sir." Kawalsky, however, suddenly grinned as a thought struck him. "If they could find them. There's going to be a lot of earth moved. Who knows, maybe some of it will cover those rocket crates."

O'Neil laughed out loud. "Just as long as you remember where they're buried. If we end up needing them, we'll probably need them in a hurry."

Further conversation was interrupted when a young lieutenant wearing an orderly's armband burst into the tent. He executed a salute with the robotic precision of a recent cadet. "Colonel O'Neil, *sir*! General Keogh's compliments. Your presence is requested in the command tent. Immediately."

"Hope that means I'm allowed to pull on my boots first," O'Neil said, sitting up on the cot and returning the green soldier's salute. "The sun may have gone down, but I'll bet the sand is still pretty hot out there."

He tied his boots, then slipped a field jacket over the T-shirt and fatigue pants he was wearing. "Lead away, Lieutenant."

Gas lamps lit up the command tent like a Christmas tree. O'Neil hid a frown. He'd preferred to keep the amount of illumination down, a habit from his commando days out in the field. No sense turning the camp's brain center into a beacon for snipers.

Keogh had wrought other changes besides the lighting, his battle flag, and the presidential picture. An honest-to-god desk had been shipped over, teak by the look of it, with a matching tall-back leather chair complete with hydraulic suspension. O'Neil had gotten by with a camp table and folding chair.

Still, perhaps the trappings of authority helped the general as he half crouched behind his teak barricade, listening to the protestations of two UMC executives.

"I tell you, I *saw* it." Lockwood was almost gobbling as he spoke. "That Skaara character blasted a hole in the warehouse wall!"

Walter Draven presented a calmer front, but his face was grave. A good poker player facing a very dubious hand. "We both saw it, General. Frankly, I was shocked to find such a weapon in native hands."

Keogh swung in his chair and returned O'Neil's salute. "What do you know about this, Colonel?"

"I'm not sure what you're referring to, sir," O'Neil said carefully.

"We're talking about weapons—terror weapons—in the hands of the native militia!" Lockwood cried.

O'Neil frowned. "I don't know how that could be. Blasting a hole in a wall, you say? Maybe he stumbled across a couple of blocks of C-4 and det cord in our old base camp—"

"Negative, Colonel," Keogh snapped. "These two gentlemen are reporting that the natives have energy weapons like the ones you recovered after the fighting here on Abydos."

O'Neil shrugged. "I suppose it's possible. We recovered one of the cannons and some of the innards from one of the landed udajeets. They were in almost as bad shape as the one that had crashed after the crowd was done. Anything that represented Ra's authority got pretty well trashed that day. We also had two of those spear-like blasters—"

"That's what we saw!" Lockwood interjected.

Even Draven gave the man a look of disgust.

"Were there others that weren't accounted for?" Keogh demanded.

O'Neil tried a quick mental count. "There was the one lance that I took from Daniel, when Ra ordered him to execute us. We picked up another at the mine, when I zipped one of Ra's guards. There were four armed guards in the pyramid when we tried to sneak into the StarGate. And Anubis was carrying one when I faced him . . ."

"That's at least six," Draven said. "And you only brought back two."

"Plus there were at least two Horus guards who landed their udajeets and got caught on the ground when Kasuf led the people of the city to our rescue," O'Neil added.

"So there are a minimum of six of these energy weapons unaccounted for." Keogh swung to O'Neil. "Good lord, man! Why didn't you confiscate them?"

"At the time I had only two surviving subordinates and a civilian volunteer—Jackson," O'Neil pointed out. "Not enough to argue with the several thousand people who live here."

"All right, not then," the general conceded.

"But you could have initiated a search mission when you returned with the expeditionary force."

"You think I should have started turning the city upside-down for some weapons which theoretically existed?" O'Neil said. "Besides being high-handed, I think such an action would only stir up a hornet's nest of trouble."

"Nonetheless, for the safety of the mine and the UMC personnel here, that's exactly what these gentlemen have been asking me to do." Keogh gestured toward Draven and Lockwood.

"And what were these gentlemen doing in the city that they saw this demonstration of fire-power?" O'Neil asked.

Draven's poker face broke for a second—just the merest tic under his eye. "We were attempting to . . . negotiate an end to this insane strike."

It had started as a hunch but turned to solid certainty as O'Neil looked into the UMC man's eyes. Draven was indeed playing a bad hand!

"You tried to bribe Skaara into overthrowing Kasuf and the elders." O'Neil's voice was quiet, his tone almost wondering. "How could you do something so stupid? You had to know that Skaara is Kasuf's son—"

His voice cut off as he watched Draven aim an acid look at Lockwood.

"Well, obviously, you didn't." O'Neil turned from Draven to Keogh. "It would seem that Draven has gotten his foot—and UMC's—caught in the honey bucket. And now he wants us to pull him free."

Keogh sat very still, digesting this new information.

"Skaara is sure to tell Kasuf about Draven's approach, and when he does, UMC will be finished on this planet. The Elders will conclude—quiet rightly, I think—that Draven and company can't be trusted."

"General, you are here to insure that our operation at the mine isn't disturbed," Draven said.

"What's disturbed your operation is the fact that you shot yourself in the foot," an angry O'Neil pointed out.

"The question is whether or not you can allow a potentially hostile population to retain those energy weapons," Draven pushed.

O'Neil bit back his first angry words. "The only reason they'd use those weapons—however many working versions they may have—is because *you* pressed them into hostility in the first place!"

"Nonetheless," Keogh broke in, "they are hostile . . . now." The general looked around, his craggy face suddenly haggard. "Initiating a search-and-seizure mission may just present additional provocation, but—"

"But I don't see how you can avoid it," Draven said in cold triumph. "By the way, that's the message I've already sent to General West."

In keeping with his theories on protective camouflage, the West household occuped snug but not ostentatious housing in Officers' Quarters. Mrs. West had been asleep for several hours already.

But the general was still up, going over reports. A ringing telephone in his den cum office, even at this hour, was not out of the ordinary.

"General West," the voice on the other end of the connection said, "is this a secure line?"

"Yes," the general answered.

"My name is Vernon Ballard, sir. I'm security coordinator for UMC's operation in Ab—"

"I understand," West interrupted. No matter how secure the line, it was better not to mention too many details.

"I'm calling from Creek Mountain."

So, Ballard must have just stepped out of the StarGate—he was actually calling from inside the missile silo complex.

"Perhaps you could get to the point," West said.

"Mr. Draven—Walter Draven—sent me to tell you about the situation on—you know where. He's got a request, and a message. The message first. It's payback time for Chile."

"Ah," West said. In the shadowy intelligence world he worked in, favors were the coin of the realm. Favors given, favors gotten—markers called in. Chile was many years ago, one of his early successes—achieved with the aid of UMC resources. Whatever Draven wanted, it would not be small change.

"Suppose you explain the situation," West said. "Then I'll decide on the favor."

On Abydos, Jack O'Neil hurried through the armed camp for the motor pool. Even as he walked through the tented streets, soldiers were stirring, hours before reveille. General Keogh had not decided on a response to Draven and Lockwood's report. He was passing the buck up to West.

But just in case action was ordered, preparations had to be undertaken.

The general had also given O'Neil orders—certain unalterable demands that he'd have to pass on to the Elders of Nagada.

When O'Neil arrived at the motor pool, mechanics were already at work on the tanks that had come through the StarGate. The colonel stared at the 120-mm cannon, which seemed almost stubby compared to the massive turret.

Nonetheless, it would take only a couple of rounds from that gun to batter in the gates of Nagada. Hell, between the tank's gun and huge treads, it wouldn't take much more to get through the walls of the city. He wondered, however, how the Chobham armor would deal with energy bolts.

O'Neil shook himself out of his reverie. He was here to requisition a Humvee and get over to the city in the hopes of avoiding such combat experiments.

Keogh had been unwilling to lose his second-in-command, but O'Neil had argued passionately. Such government as the city had knew him and, hopefully, still trusted him. He also had the friendship of the leader of the suddenly much feared Abydos militia. If there was a peaceful solution to be negotiated, he had to try.

O'Neil declined the use of a driver. Setting off down UMC's mining road, he relentlessly pressed the vehicle to its highest speed. When he reached the dune that marked Skaara's watch station, he braked the vehicle and honked the horn.

No one answered.

O'Neil hopped out of the Humvee and stepped into the glare of his own headlights. "It's me— O'Neil!" he called up to continued silence. "Black Hat!" he added in Abydan.

After turning around in the light to show he was unarmed, O'Neil began climbing the face of the dune.

I'm going to feel really stupid if somebody shoots me for this, he thought.

The watch station was empty, although it showed signs of recent occupation. Prolonged use had brought some of the comforts of home. O'Neil saw the masked embers of a small fire— apparently with dried mastadge dung as the fuel. There were water skins and some neatly folded sand-colored blankets. They could offer shade from the suns by day and warmth by night.

The scanty gear had just been left where it was, but there was no sign of violence. Apparently, the militia members had simply been recalled.

O'Neil frowned. It seemed that Skaara took it for granted that some sort of force would be coming from the camp, and didn't want his people in a known position.

The colonel skidded down the hard-packed sand and returned to his vehicle. Next stop, Nagada.

Impatience flayed O'Neil's nerves as he jockeyed the vehicle beyond the mine pit. He felt torn between the need to get as much speed as possible and the danger of flipping the vehicle and killing himself.

At last the bulk of the sleeping city rose before him. No giant trumpet mooed a warning of his arrival. O'Neil had wondered if there was a curfew for the oversized noise maker. In the silence that followed when he turned off the engine, however, O'Neil caught a much less welcoming sound.

It was the metallic rattle of a round being jacked into firing position in an automatic pistol.

Hands out, O'Neil again stepped into the twin cones of illumination thrown by his headlights.

A voice cried out in recognition, "Black hat!"

But the doors didn't open.

O'Neil stood for what felt like forever, trying to keep still, to act unthreatening. What he really wanted to do was run in place and hug himself against the desert cold, which seemed to be leaching the very life out of him through his field jacket.

He had almost decided to sit on the still warm hood of his vehicle when a voice called, "O'Neil! Thank God it's you!"

It was Daniel Jackson.

The gates swung open.

O'Neil sipped at a bowl full of water. His throat was raw from hours of talking. He handed the bowl to Daniel Jackson, who had to be even more parched. Not only had he translated O'Neil's words to Kasuf and the Elders, but then he'd had to convey their words to the colonel.

And the upshot of this conversational marathon? Nothing.

Kasuf and his colleagues wanted UMC off Abydos. They hated Ballard, the company's security man, distrusted Draven, and actively despised Lockwood. General Francis Keogh didn't get high marks from the local government members, either. Everyone remembered that his green-clad soldier had been helping to guard the rest tent when Zaid fell to his death.

O'Neil had tried to be as diplomatic as possible, but Keogh's demand had been emphatic. All blast-lances in the city had to be turned over to U.S. forces.

Skaara, who was sitting to one side of the assembled Elders, broke into loud argument. At least he was able to offer his view directly in English. "Those spears—we captured them. They are our best weapons, next to your guns. See what Draven and his friends would have given us!"

He beckoned, and one of his militia lieutenants appeared from the darkness of the sidelines. He bore the burned and melted remains of a rifle. One glance told O'Neil that this was an antique Garand, the sort generally used by National Guard units in parades.

"What comes next? Will Keogh demand the return of your guns—the ones we dug out of the sands to use against Ra? If the Horus guards come again, are we to resist them with stones and walking staffs?"

"If Keogh comes looking for those blasters with troops and tanks, that's about all you'll have to resist *him*," O'Neil pointed out. "I can count on two hands the amount of government-issue weapons you have. I can estimate that you have maybe six blast-lances at most. That's if your people didn't break any of them because they were toys of Ra's—or if the energy charge on the weapons didn't all run out."

He turned to Jackson. "You've got to convince them that Draven and Keogh won't be kidding around. Draven seems to think he's got a lock on General West giving the okay. And if the orders come through, this isn't going to be like a nice student protest from your college days. Those tanks have real cannons, and Keogh's soldiers will have real guns—not to mention nervous trigger fingers. If shots are exchanged, well, I'll just remind you—we're a long way from government oversight."

A sheen of sweat appeared on Daniel's upper lip as he argued the ways of earthly *realpolitik* with the Elders. But in the end Kasuf and the others would not give in.

"They might have turned the weapons over to you, as a commander they know and trust," Daniel said, defeated. "They just have too many doubts about Keogh."

The light of one of the suns was just about to break over the horizon when the desultory argument was interrupted by a prolonged *mooooooooooooo*.

O'Neil, Daniel, Skaara, and a couple of the more spry Elders climbed onto the rope bridges that stretched over the gates. From this height O'Neil could see the vast cloud heading toward the city. This wasn't a windstorm, it was merely dust thrown up by treads and wheels—the signs of tanks, armored personnel carriers, and Humvees plowing through the roadless wastes of Abydos to present an ultimatum to Nagada.

"I guess the orders finally came from General West," O'Neil said quietly.

"I guess Draven—and maybe Keogh—feel all the better that you're trapped in here while this goes down," Daniel said bitterly.

"Nothing *has* to happen!" O'Neil turned directly to Skaara. "You don't have to fight! Can't you turn over those weapons?"

Skaara shook his head. In the pre-dawn murk, O'Neil could see young men—militia warriors—taking their places on the walls and on the taller buildings. "It is not for them to ask."

A pair of helicopter gunships came whining ahead of the advancing cloud.

Skaara tugged O'Neil's sleeve. "Could you truly attack friends you fought beside?" His voice was nearly a whisper.

O'Neil's throat felt like stone. "If"—he coughed, then tried again—"if those were my orders."

Overhead, the giant horn mooed again.

"Do they think we haven't noticed?" O'Neil said to Daniel.

But the Abydos natives around him were turning *away* from the oncoming force, looking in the opposite direction.

Another cloud was rolling toward Nagada, huge and roiling, its upper layers crackling with lightning high in the atmosphere. Mutters of consternation and fear ran through the observers.

"Wonderful. Keogh's sending his force right into the teeth of a sandstorm," O'Neil gritted.

Daniel Jackson's face was tight with apprehension. "They're saying this isn't natural."

"Then what can it be?" O'Neil wanted to know.

The answer came a moment later, as Cloud Number Two thundered closer. The flickering bolts of lightning high in the air resolved themselves into a coherent shape—the form of a titanic pyramid.

Skaara gasped. Several of the elders moaned. Daniel just stared, white-faced.

As O'Neil gazed upward, he whispered, "God-*damn!*"

It was half a curse and half a prayer.

CHAPTER 16
MEETING ENGAGEMENT

On the bridge of *Ra's Eye,* Hathor still shook in a cold rage. The scanner technicians had been quite clear. Their subspace readings had allowed them to follow the track of Ra's stardrive. He had arrived at Abydos. There were no drive-traces of him leaving.

But more physical scans had shown a dispersed, invisible-to-the-human-eye ring of matter surrounding Abydos. The ring was composed of irradiated quartzose crystal. It was not a natural phenomenon. Even months after the fact, Hathor's technicians were able to identify the particles as remnants of Ra's flying palace.

At last Hathor had to confront the fact that Ra was truly dead. Had he met some sort of navigational disaster? Her technical underlings were baffled by the irradiation of the crystal fragments. Could it have been some sort of repair that hadn't worked?

The cat goddess found it impossible to credit the *fellahin* of Abydos with Ra's passing. Where could they have obtained the wherewithal to harm a starcraft?

Nonetheless, whether they knew it or not, they had witnessed the death of Ra. If they had correctly interpreted the flash in the sky, there would be whispers of freedom. Hathor would have to put those whispers down—and she would do so in her own name, as the new empress. Plans quickly resolved through her mind. Abydos was a backwater world, uninviting. But it did possess the quartzite mine. As her other rivals had fief worlds, Abydos could become her base. She could bring Ptah here, set him to fashioning weapons.

Perhaps she could even recruit strength from among the *fellahin*. They couldn't become Horus guards, of course, but they could make useful blaster fodder. Ra had done the same when he first appeared on Earth.

The first order of business was to make an impressive arrival. Her scanner technicians had found perfect meteorological conditions. Hathor had brought *Ra's Eye* into the upper atmosphere, seeded the clouds of an insignificant storm front, used a few blasts from the secondary batteries to ionize the area, and rode down in a thunderstorm.

Impressive, yes. But the energy discharges around her had blinded the ships scanners until they were almost on top of the city.

Lieutenant Peter Collier bit off a curse as his helicopter jinked in a sudden gust of wind from the oncoming thunderstorm.

"Trust the brass to order us out onto a desert into the teeth of a sandstorm," he muttered. "I just hope they got this thing put together right."

The jet turbine overhead whined as he fed more power to the rotors. Collier was another newly minted lieutenant, fresh out of training. He toggled the radio in his helmet, trying to contact the other chopper. "Foxtrot Victor," Collier called. The pilot in the other craft was Captain Ralph Vance, a grizzled veteran who had a little experience in these oversized egg beaters.

"What?" the captain demanded as Collier called in.

"Sir, shouldn't we be trying to get some altitude with those clouds coming our way?"

"We're supposed to be flying reconnaissance— making sure there aren't any rag heads preparing surprises for our line of march." The older officer stopped chewing out the green lieutenant, apparently checking his controls. "What the hell is with this radar?"

Then in a voice of true shock the captain cried, "Ohmigod!"

A bolt of lightning shot from the dark, advancing cloud. The rotors flew off the lead chopper, and its engine spewed flame as raw aviation fuel squirted out and ignited. It made Foxtrot Victor look as if a rocket were pushing it downward as the copter plummeted to the ground. The radio link was dead silent.

Collier tore his eyes from his crashing companion, looking upward to see an impossible apparition seem to congeal out of the clouds.

It was a flying pyramid, and it seemed to be the size of a young mountain. But it was obviously a lot more dangerous than any mountain. The damned thing had zapped Captain Vance and his crew. "Yo! Gunner!" he cried into his intercom mike. "Light up everything we got in the way of rockets. We got a big mother of a target out there!"

He jockeyed his joystick, trying to swing around to an attack vector. All the time Collier felt like a house fly buzzing around a cow turd. How much damage could his rockets do to this thing?

Only one way to find out. "Fire!"

The copter was equipped with air-to-ground missiles, tank killers, although the locals weren't supposed to have any tanks. Collier's first two shots scored without making any appreciable dent in the golden-glowing facet where they landed.

But farther toward the apex, well above where the rockets had hit, a slit appeared in the pyramid craft. Collier didn't notice it until a bolt of ravening energy flashed from the opening toward his chopper.

And then, of course, it was too late.

Hathor stood silent on the bridge of *Ra's Eye,* her eyes devouring the holographic image of the sky before her starcraft.

"Scanners!" she ordered, "I want a close-up of that aircraft!"

A new image appeared, a little smaller than the reach of her outstretched arms, giving better detail on the remaining flying machine. To Hathor's eye, used to the trim lines of the udajeet, this craft had a gangling look. It reminded her of the big, buzzing insects that flew over the Nile's waters in the swampy Faiyoum.

A pair of bright trails erupted from under the

big craft. Hathor didn't know if the weapons hit or missed. *Ra's Eye* pressed on without missing a beat. Nor were there any damage reports.

"Gunnery," she ordered, "train one of the secondary batteries on that thing and eliminate it."

According to Ra's computer records, Abydos had been visited within the decade for collection of another shipment of energy quartz. There was no way in the universe that the local *fellahin* could progress from copper pickaxes to flying machines—even such primitive fliers as these—in that amount of time.

If these things were not built on Abydos . . . A chill tingled down Hathor's bare back. Ra himself was a hybrid creature, as he'd once admitted in a moment of intimacy. His human form was—well, "possessed" was too strong a term. Perhaps "shared" came closer. In any event, an intelligent creature from beyond Earth lived in the beautiful boy god's body.

Hathor knew such alien creatures existed. She had seen the almost human (but not quite) beings who had served Ra before he arrived on Earth. And, of course, she had slaughtered them probably by the millions on Ombos. Their only monument was the ruins on dead Tuat.

Could it be that another set of aliens had blundered on Ra's empire? Aliens powerful enough to destroy Ra himself?

But if the enemy had such powers, why did they fly on contraptions that seemed barely able to stay in the air?

A bolt from one of the secondary batteries

licked out to consume the crude contrivance. It fell to pieces in midair. "That seems to be the pilot!" Hathor cried as a form tumbled out of what appeared to be a shattered cockpit. "Focus on it and enlarge again!"

The pilot appeared to have two arms and legs, most of the body configuration being muffled in a loose-fitting, blotched suit. But the head! So large and bulbous, and the eyes appeared to bulge out like a bubble of crystal . . .

Hathor thought the aliens must be insectoid.

A piece of wreckage smashed into the limply falling body, shearing off part of the head—no, it was a helmet! What she had thought were eyes turned out to be a face plate—and the features behind it were definitely human.

But how could this be possible? None of Ra's minions would allow mere *fellahin* to build such machines. And Ra himself would never allow the development of such weapons on any of the fiefs. Where could non-divine humans progress so far without being put down?

The answer came to her almost in a blaze of revelation. Her lips drew back in an incredulous smile. "They come from the First World—they're descendants of the humans who revolted after the First Time."

All those years, alone, unsupervised, they'd built up their own technology. And then they must have rediscovered the StarGate. Somehow they had found their way to Abydos—right as Ra came to collect the tribute of quartz-crystal.

And even more incredibly, despite their primitive technology, these invaders had somehow destroyed Ra.

She should be grateful to these rogue humans.

But, of course, she'd have to destroy them.

The scanners expanded their range to the ground below, revealing a column of ground vehicles streaming toward Nagada.

"Ammit eat my soul," Hathor muttered. "There must be a thousand warriors down there—more!"

If she had the resources of the homeworld behind her while facing the rebellious minions . . .

Hathor pushed the inviting notion away. These wild humans were invaders here. They would have to feel the wrath of the empire. And even a thousand warriors couldn't stand against the weaponry of *Ra's Eye*.

"Gunnery! Prepare all secondary batteries." The cat goddess stared down at a line of lightly armored vehicles acting as the advance guard. Then came boxier vehicles churning sand with some sort of endless tracks.

The column was spreading out, apparently moving into some sort of line of battle. Not that it would do them much good.

Farther back, four heavier armored vehicles advanced in a diamond pattern around another of the boxy vehicles. Hathor's eyes narrowed. She could think of only one reason for such a strong escort.

Thrusting a hand into the image, she indicated her first chosen target. "Scanners, transmit this location to all secondary batteries that can bring their blasters to bear.

"Gunnery, at my command—fire!"

Francis Keogh did not believe in general officers attempting to lead attacks from the front. On the other hand, he was not going to sit in a fortified camp while two battalions engaged a rabble of natives armed with six science-fiction weapons, perhaps twice as many state-of-the-art assault weapons, and a few thousand copper pickaxes.

He had converted an armored personnel carrier to serve as his mobile command post, surrounded it with four Abrams tanks, and headed for the front. The security arrangements had seemed more than adequate—until a pyramid that looked more like a flying mountain had appeared out of a thundercloud.

Keogh had discovered this apparition when the driver of the APC had gone into a wild skid, staring out the vision slits in the front of the armored vehicle. Flinging himself out of his seat, Keogh leapt to the open hatch on the roof of the boxy troop carrier—they hadn't bothered to run in buttoned-down mode.

The general clung to the ladder leading to the hatch as the APC lurched again. He finally managed to climb up just in time to see the last of the reconnaissance gunships blown out of the sky.

Keogh screamed down to his radio man. "To all units! Disperse! We're too bunched up in column! That damned thing will blow us to kingdom come! Fall back on the camp!"

Damnation, he thought, *why hadn't O'Neil managed to get a couple of SAM units out here?*

Although he did have to admit, the missiles would probably require nuclear warheads to make any impression on that awesome bulk.

The vehicle under his feet yawed again, nearly flinging Keogh out of the hatch he clung to. The general swung around to see his command attempting to scatter. Vehicles peeled off, desperately attempting to climb the faces of the dunes.

Keogh's tank escorts elevated their guns, firing anti-armor missiles up at the pyramid, which seemed to hover over them like the shadow of doom.

For a wild moment Keogh considered dropping back into the troop carrier and closing the hatch. But what good was an inch and a half of aluminum armor against the might of a goddamned *starship*?

He stared upward, open-mouthed. The blasted thing *was* hovering—and it seemed to be shifting around, to bring one of its titanic faces to bear. Keogh could see dark lines against the glowing gold-quartz wall. Firing slits for whatever unimaginable weapons they possessed.

He felt much the same emotions as the ant who sees a human foot descending his way.

But like all good generals, Keogh's last thought was of history.

Now they will *lump me with that other Keogh—the one with Custer.*

A glare of incredible brilliance seemed to fill the sky above.

And we aren't even distantly related.

*   *   *

Hathor grinned in satisfaction. The commander's transport and its four armored escorts had disappeared under the radiation of dozens of heavy blasters. Heat shimmers rose from the five hulks surrounded by vitrified sand.

"Cut off the enemy's head, and the rest of the body is rendered harmless," she said.

The rest of the military caravan was not forming a line abreast, as she had first thought. Instead, its component vehicles slewed round, plunging helter-skelter across the sands.

Although they zigzagged and tried to spread out, offering targets as dispersed as possible, the invaders' destination was obvious from the altitude maintained by *Ra's Eye.*

They were heading for the great pyramid in the deep desert, the docking station—the Abydos terminal for the StarGate network.

"If they hope to retreat to their homeworld, they're doomed to disappointment," she murmured.

But then, the invaders were doomed in any event.

"Full thrust to the docking station," she ordered her navigation officer. Like some sort of mythical desert being, *Ra's Eye* raced over the sands, dragging its own wind with it.

The ship quickly outdistanced the ground vehicles. In seconds it was skimming across the plateau that accommodated the docking station.

Hathor quickly saw that the rocky shelf was also apparently serving as the invaders' home away from home. *Ra's Eye* passed over a good acre's worth of tents, blowing most of them down. She spotted human figures running for their lives.

And then the gleaming limestone of the pyramid lined up beneath her craft.

"Commence docking," she ordered.

In spite of its size, *Ra's Eye* shuddered slightly as it lowered itself on the station. The heavy drives caused great turbulence. The unfortunate humans outside would have been better off in a sandstorm.

The ship settled.

When Ra's yacht had landed, it seemed to cling to the sides of the pyramid, as if the stones had been gilded with a magically appeared flying palace.

For *Ra's Eye,* the monolithic docking station was more like a mere pimple beneath its bulk. The landed battlecraft's vast footprint effectively doubled the ground-level area of the original construction.

The roadway UMC had blasted and bulldozed out of the pyramid was crushed out of existence. The entrance hall had disappeared, lost behind a gleaming quartzose crystal wall.

Hathor nodded in satisfaction.

The invaders had nowhere to retreat to. They were trapped on Abydos to be dealt with at leisure.

All access to the StarGate was literally sealed beneath the bulk of *Ra's Eye.*

CHAPTER 17
EARLY INNINGS

Lieutenant Adam Kawalsky and Corporal Feretti stood in one of the base camp supply tents, inventorying ammunition. From the rumors they'd heard of Keogh's plans, the lieutenant figured there'd soon be a need for more bullets. He thought they might as well beat the rush—especially since they, like most of the Marine complement, had been left behind in camp.

Feretti was almost climbing over the stacked cases of bullets under the tent, offering a moving definition of the word *hyper*.

Kawalsky felt a certain sympathy for the noncommissioned officer. Men who desired a quiet, peaceful life didn't join the Marines, much less end up in this particular outfit. On the other hand . . .

"Feretti," Kawalsky finally said, "you can't be wishing you were out there on the sharp end. I mean, Keogh's soldier boys may well end up shooting at kids we helped train."

"You got it, sir." Feretti halted in his scramble to the top of the mountain of cases. "I *don't* want to fight with the locals. Hell, I like those kids. But it burns my butt that we get demoted to company clerk—and the rest of our outfit ends up guarding the supplies."

"Remember the halls of Montezuma," Kawalsky said with a smile.

Feretti gave him a blank look. He'd always thought the halls of Montezuma was a latrine—where you went when hit with Montezuma's revenge.

Kawalsky sighed. "Mexican war—back in 1847, Winfield Scott landed in Veracruz with twelve thousand men and marched for Mexico City. For a year's worth of campaigning, the Marine contingent with him guarded the supply wagons. They reached the capital, but to crack the city's defenses, Scott had to take the fortress of Chapultepec. Guess who got the job of storming the joint?"

Feretti threw him a snappy salute. "Marines, front and center."

Kawalsky nodded. "So, we may be guarding supplies now, but soon enough we may end up pulling Keogh's ass out of a crack."

His words were obscured by a rumble of thunder. And no sooner did he stop speaking than the tent was blown down on their heads. From outside they heard sudden cries and shouts of alarm.

"Oh, man," Feretti complained, wrestling against canvas gone suddenly balky with a strong wind. "If this is another one of those sandstorms, we've got trouble by the ton. These tents won't stand up to it, and there's too many of us to take shelter inside the pyramid."

"Not to mention Keogh's two platoons out thataway—right in the teeth of the storm." Kawalsky dropped to his knees under the canvas, crawling along the floor until he reached the edge of the collapsed tent. "I still don't understand how this thing came straight down instead of being blown away."

Out in the open at last, he stared up into the sky at the golden-glowing apparition, unmindful of the gale-force wind tugging at him.

"Oh." That was all Kawalsky had to say.

When Feretti snaked his way out from under the canvas, he offered additional comments. "Holy jumping Jesus Christ!" he breathed. "Ra's back!"

"O'Neil is pretty sure the nuke he beamed aboard Ra's flying palace did that freak in," Kawalsky said, taking in the mass of the settling pyramid. "This looks like Ra's big brother."

He turned to his old teammate. "Back into the tent."

"Begging the lieutenant's pardon," Feretti replied, "but I don't think a millimeter's worth of canvas will give us much in the way of cover."

"I'm not looking for cover, I'm looking for crowbars," Kawalsky replied.

The corporal yanked up the fallen canvas cover. From the look on his face, it was the halls of Montezuma all over again. Feretti had no idea what Kawalsky was up to. But he was ready to follow orders.

Before they plunged into the ruined tent, Kawalsky took a second to explain. "We need the crowbars to open those cases to Stinger missiles the colonel stockpiled."

Feretti still held the tent edge, his eyes involuntarily going to the vastness clamping down over the StarGate pyramid. "Hand-held missiles . . . against *that*, sir?"

Kawalsky shook his head. "The missiles aren't for that," he said. "They're for what comes next."

Aboard *Ra's Eye*, Hathor found herself caught on the horns of a tactical dilemma. Her battlecraft was the single most powerful war machine on Abydos—anywhere in Ra's empire, for that matter. But her strongest weapon had just lost much of its utility—because it no longer had mobility.

She had torn through the enemy's troops and flattened their camp in her first passage. But she'd had to land to cut the Earthlings's StarGate connection. And *Ra's Eye* would have to stay in this position to keep the enemy cut off.

Back on Ombos, she'd simply have left a contingent of Horus guards to seize the StarGate and hold the pyramid. But *Ra's Eye* didn't have a sufficient infantry complement to allow for a blocking force.

In the meantime the Earthling vehicles continued to scatter, along with the vast majority of the invading warriors.

They had to be harried—to be hammered.

"Scanners!" she barked. "Report on the wind situation outside. Has the disturbance from our passage moderated yet?"

The responsible technician frantically stroked control surfaces and examined readouts. "Lady Captain, the storm is abating."

"Excellent. Open the launching decks."

The thick deck plates under Hathor's feet shuddered as massive sections in the outer hull of *Ra's Eye* slipped away to reveal the ranks of massed gliders.

"Udajeet pilots, take your places," Hathor ordered. "Launch immediately."

From over the gates of Nagada, Colonel Jack O'Neil watched the fate of Keogh's battalions as the colossal pyramid passed over the column.

This thing is jumbo-sized trouble, he thought as the pyramid swatted Keogh's air elements out of the sky. *It's not only much bigger than Ra's flying palace, but it's also obviously designed for military purposes. The blast-cannon aboard that thing make the weapons mounted on the eagle-gliders look like cigarette lighters.*

O'Neil focused his binoculars on what had to be the force's mobile command post, just in time to see a searing whip of energy smash the armored vehicles like toys. He continued to observe, acid roiling in his stomach, as the force disintegrated.

It was incredible—and horrible to see. One second the Army strike group was moving like a machine with the highest of tolerances—say, a Swiss watch. The next moment it was as though that watch had dropped to the pavement from a second-story window.

All that was left were a few swiftly bouncing, broken components.

The two battalions, composed mainly of half-raw soldiers just out of training, ceased being military units and was turned into a cloud of fugitives.

It was as though by blasting Keogh in his APC, Ra's minions had vaporized the general's entire command.

In a way, O'Neil could sympathize with the soldiers' dilemma. It was manifestly no good to stand and fight with that flying mountain blasting away at them. However . . . "It won't do them any good to run," O'Neil muttered. "Where do they think that monster is heading?"

"I thought it was headed straight here," said a shaken voice at O'Neil's elbow. Daniel Jackson turned a pale face to his former comrade.

"Maybe it was, before the crew spotted Keogh's people. But with those tanks and helicopters, it's obvious we don't belong here. So that big mother is heading for the pyramid—with the added benefit of joy-riding right through what's left of Keogh's force."

O'Neil saw the incomprehension on Daniel's face. "Look, it's simple strategy. If possible, get astride your enemy's supply line. In this case, that's pretty simple."

He put his eyes back to the binoculars. The killer pyramid was far in the distance now—about the location of the base camp. O'Neil refocused the lenses. Yes, the damned thing was settling.

"Now it's official," he announced. "They're not just astride our communications line, they're sitting on it. We've got however many tons it takes to make up that behemoth between us and the StarGate. We can't get out—and I for one don't expect much help to be coming in."

O'Neil repacked his binoculars and started across the rope bridge toward the nearest tower.

"Where are you going?" Daniel asked.

"Where do you think?" O'Neil nodded toward the fleeing fragments of the Army strike force. "I'm the only commander those poor bastards have got."

Daniel stared. "You can't seriously consider going out there alone."

From beyond the Egyptologist, Skaara entered the conversation. "My people will come," he said.

O'Neil darted him a sharp look. "You were just ready to fight those guys. But now you'll come and help rescue them?"

Skaara pointed toward the dull glow on the horizon—the golden gleam of the pyramid ship. "That was before *they* came. We don't know what your people will do to us, Colonel. But we know what Ra's people will want. And we will not be slaves—not anymore. We will fight them—and if you will lead us, we will follow you."

"Considering that you're the closest thing I've got to an organized force—excepting whatever my Marines are doing out at the base—I accept." O'Neil turned to Daniel. "Translate for me to Kasuf. He'll have to evacuate the city—get all the noncombatants into the desert and under cover."

The colonel turned a speculative eye in the direction of the grounded pyramid. "Remember the damage those glider-jets caused when they strafed the city? I'm sure that behemoth out there comes equipped with a lot more."

O'Neil reached the tower and started down.

Skaara shouted orders to his militia lieutenants. The young soldiers were already swarming down from the walls, gathering around the Humvee behind the city gates.

The Marine climbed into the vehicle, followed by Skaara. Then Daniel scrambled aboard.

O'Neil gave him a surprised glance.

Jackson returned his look with a lopsided grin. "I think I'm crazy, too," he said. "But after you've fought for something you believe in, it's hard to go back to teaching—especially when other people may be out there dying."

But when Sha'uri went to board the Humvee, Daniel started raising objections. She favored her academic husband with a loving but impatient smile.

"You can talk about fighting," she said. "But I'm the one who came prepared."

From under her cloak Sha'uri produced a 9mm Beretta pistol—one of the government-issue sidearms left behind from the first Abydos expedition.

Daniel could only shrug in defeat.

Most of Skaara's troops were assembled now. Some of them opened the gates.

O'Neil started the Humvee's engine. Behind him, the city was just beginning to awaken—and to learn of the new danger. He drove out, covered by the long shadows thrown by the walls in the light of the first rising sun.

"We need a rally point," the professional warrior told his amateur aides. "I suggest the watch point Skaara set up outside our camps. The militia kids know it—and so do our people."

He turned to Skaara. "You can't ride with me. That will be putting all our command eggs in one basket."

Skaara nodded, apparently understanding the earthly idiom. "I'll ride with you a little way," he said, pointing at a pillar of smoke rising in the near distance. It marked the resting place of one of the oncoming Army vehicles. "From there I'll lead my people to the watch point."

O'Neil shrugged. It wasn't too far. He waited while Skaara conveyed his decision to his lieutenants in Abydan. They looked toward the smoke and nodded.

Then O'Neil sent the Humvee jouncing forward. They quickly outdistanced the young militia members, even though the Abydans were advancing at a ground-eating trot.

The Humvee's motor whined as it jounced and jostled the passengers, seeming at points merely to graze the sand below its wheels. O'Neil tried to avoid dune crest lines, where he'd be silhouetted against the rising suns. His twisting course did its best to stay in the shadows.

They swung around a swale of sand to confront the source of Skaara's pillar of smoke. It was a gutted armored personnel carrier. Part of its aluminum armor roof was completely gone, vaporized. The troop carrier had rolled on its side, and the engine had evidently blown up, igniting the fuel tank.

Two of the four-man crew had nearly made it away. They lay scorched and unmoving a little distance from the wreck.

O'Neil pulled his vehicle up. "You sure you want to wait here?" he asked Skaara.

The young man nodded his head. "It's as good a place to start as any other."

He lightly hopped out of the vehicle.

O'Neil started off again, but he glanced back to a wordless cry from Daniel.

Skaara was kneeling by the dead men, collecting their guns and ammunition.

The recon Marine gave a curt, approving nod. "Sorry, professor, but this is no time to be squeamish. Before this fight is over, we're going to need every gun we can get."

Walter Draven had never really admitted his slight tendency to claustrophobia. "Who's afraid of Santa?" he'd joke. That was much more easily done in a large, airy Washington apartment, however. On Abydos, in the room that housed the StarGate, it was harder to laugh off the feeling that one was in the bowels of a pyramid surrounded by a huge weight of dressed stone. Stone underneath, stone to either side, tons and tons of it overhead, pressing down . . .

Martin Preston had once explained how the ancient Egyptians had built their huge constructions, with angled stone blocks so that the massive weights involved pressed against each other rather than straight downward. An interesting theory, but Draven was sure the ceilings in the dark high overhead were just waiting to buckle and fall.

Only the most urgent of reasons would keep

him in here—especially since he was trapped with Eugene Lockwood for a companion.

The mine manager now stood beside him in sulky silence. Draven's overstretched nerves had been unable to stand listening to any more of Lockwood's justifications and idiot plans for dealing with the locals once UMC got the "whip hand." Lockwood had used the phrase at least five times in almost as many sentences. Finally, Draven told the silly idiot to shut his mouth and keep it that way. Lockwood first looked shocked, then angry. But at least the stream of nervous mouth noise had ended.

Draven looked around the room. In one corner stood a trio of UMC security people in gray camouflage suits. They huddled together, deep in conversation, their weapons either dangling negligently in hands or propped nearby within easy reach.

By the StarGate itself stood the local security chief, Vernon Ballard. He'd returned by military jet to Colorado. And the first thing he'd done after returning to Abydos had been to place an armed guard on the StarGate. Ostensibly, this was to prevent infiltration of any local terrorists to Earth.

In cold fact, however, the armed guard was against two troublemakers—Daniel Jackson and Jack O'Neil. Luckily, the orders from General West had come through while O'Neil was still in Nagada. Draven was just as glad that the start of hostilities would catch the Marine colonel behind enemy lines. With luck, he might even be taken hostage and expended.

For all his faults, however, O'Neil had been willing to take orders and keep quiet. Jackson was a more dangerous type, an idealist—and as Keogh's troops moved against his precious Abbadabba, he became even more dangerous—a frustrated idealist.

Draven would not put it past the Egyptologist to try to get to Earth, either to get a conflicting report to West—one they'd prefer not to get out— or even to try spilling the story to the press.

"Do you really think he'd desert his native wife to do that?" Lockwood asked. He sounded like something out of a bad Western movie, talking about a squaw man.

If left with no other option, any man might try something desperate.

And if Ballard's people didn't seem much worried over an errant professor, the security chief certainly took his duty seriously. Ballard stood on the ramp leading up to the StarGate, his camos pressed and an assault rifle at the ready in his hands.

The two UMC executives also had an ostensible security purpose. They were there to be on hand to identify Jackson. But there was an entirely different reason why they—and the heavy truck taking up most of the chamber—were standing by the StarGate.

Keogh had two battalions of troops, tanks, and even a couple of helicopters. His available force should be enough to cow the locals and their uppity Elders into toeing the line. If not, then there'd be fighting. Too many losses among the

Army personnel, and questions would be asked. And what if some unsuspected disaster struck?

Draven had arranged for a truck to be loaded with Lockwood's most damaging files, which were then buried under their remaining supply of quartz. If necessary, he proposed to abandon Abydos, then smuggle the whole load past the military people at Creek Mountain.

Not, he assured himself, that such extreme measures would be necessary. But it was best to be prepared for all eventualities.

He glanced at his watch. "They should almost be there."

A low rumbling came from the distance. Draven glanced toward the entrance to the pyramid, uncomfortably far away and out of sight. Thunder?

"Is that the guns on the tanks?" Lockwood asked nervously.

Ballard and the mercenaries cocked their heads. "Doesn't sound like artillery to me," the security chief said.

The room seemed to get colder. There was a positive draft coming from the entrance. Some kind of storm? Draven wondered.

"Hope this isn't a sandstorm," Ballard said. "That would foul Keogh's approach on the city."

Another of the mercenaries spoke up. "I hear a sandstorm is what set up the first party here to get their butts kicked."

Ballard silenced his man with a glare.

That wind is *getting stronger*, Draven thought.

Then the very rock around them began to shudder.

"Earthquake!" Lockwood yelped. He sounded as if he were announcing the end of the world.

Whatever was going on, it didn't seem natural. Draven turned to Ballard. "Activate the StarGate."

Ballard abandoned his position. He didn't want to be in the way of the sudden wash of energy that extended from the arcanely carved torus ring of the gateway. When Draven had first seen the effect, he'd been reminded of a scene from his childhood, gently blowing into a soap-filled ring. He hadn't quite created a bubble, but the film of soapy water had billowed outward in an amazing display of surface tension.

Except, in the case of the StarGate, it would require a god's lips to create the same effect.

Draven shrank against the wall. The hired gun-men seemed unaffected. One leaned into the cab of the truck, awakening the driver, who'd been dozing in the cab.

The StarGate cycled into operation. All eyes were drawn to the incredible show of light and energy. So they missed the four Horus guards materializing with a bluish glare in the matter transmitter.

Draven's first hint of danger came as the merce-nary security men were blown to gobbets of flesh by blast-bolts fired at close range. He stood frozen as the falcon-headed warriors wiped his soldiers out. Draven had seen pictures of the strange hel-met-masks. But that was far different from having a falcon's head turn, scan you with greenish eyes, dismiss you as unimportant because you had no weapon, and turn to the next target.

Ballard opened fire and downed one of the attackers. The combined fire of the other three, however, left him a smoking ruin.

And the matter transmitter flashed to deliver four more of the unearthly assailants. As they advanced, blast-lances at the ready, one of the first wave moved to cover the terrified truck driver.

Draven sidled toward the operational StarGate. Three—maybe two steps, and he could dive into the rippling energy interface, warn the people on Earth . . . get out of here.

He'd taken another step when Eugene Lockwood came out of his semi-coma. "D-don't shoot!" His voice sounded more like the squealings of a stuck pig. "We're civilians!"

The StarGate was still tantalizingly out of reach as the hawk heads—and blasters—turned their way.

Before the flare of energy that did him in, Draven had half a second to curse boneheaded subordinates.

CHAPTER 18
STRIKE AND COUNTERSTRIKE

Hathor observed the holographic display on the ceiling of the bridge. The technicians had expanded the scale to serve as a tactical display. The fighting forces were exhibited as various colored sparks—red for her people, green for the enemy. At the center was the StarGate pyramid, surrounded by a square of red representing *Ra's Eye*.

A cloud of red sparks radiated from the battlecraft, pursuing madly darting green sparks—udajeets on search-and-destroy missions against the invaders' ground vehicles. Within the red walls around the pyramid, red sparks flashed into existence—and green ones disappeared.

"Lady Captain," one of the technicians reported, "the Horus guards have just reported. The chamber of the StarGate is now in our hands."

Hathor nodded in satisfaction.

"One loss."

That wiped away Hathor's smile. "Split the force. Half will search the rest of the chambers for any other enemy troops." She paused. "The other half will secure the far side of the StarGate, with the search force acting as reserve."

Her eyes returned to the tactical display. "What's that concentration over by the city?"

A clump of green sparks had appeared, moving slowly across the desert toward *Ra's Eye*.

Another technician ran her fingers over glowing control surfaces, achieving a local focus. "Infantry, Lady Captain," she reported.

"We can afford to ignore them," Hathor decided. "All udajeets are to concentrate on destroying vehicles first."

She'd learned her lessons well on Ombos. Destroy the enemy's technology first. Mopping up foot soldiers becomes much easier when they can't transport themselves or any heavy weapons.

Mop-up, however, would have to wait until the enemy was first smashed.

On this world . . . and then on the world they came from.

An udajeet flashed over O'Neil's Humvee, and all aboard ducked. But the antigravity glider was after bigger game. Its blast-cannon flashed, and something exploded from beyond the next dune.

O'Neil kept the little all-terrain vehicle in the shallows of the sand—and the shadows.

"They've certainly got control of the air," Daniel said.

"For the time being," O'Neil responded. "But if Kawalsky and Feretti are on the job, we should be able to make the sky much hotter for them."

The vehicle's short-wave radio crackled to life. "All units, listen up!" a voice shouted. "This is First Base!"

O'Neil, Daniel, and Sha'uri all had to grin. Even

over the radio they recognized the staccato speech rhythms of Corporal Feretti.

"There are antiaircraft missiles available," Feretti went on. "We're going to use some to try to set up a safe area at the base of the plateau—by Firebase Three. We think that Big Mama up there won't be able to depress her guns enough to take pot-shots at us. The rest we're loading into trucks, and we'll try to get them out to you."

O'Neil picked up the microphone from the little set. "First Base," he said. "Feretti, this is O'Neil. Do you copy?"

"Thank God, Colonel! The lieutenant was afraid you'd gotten smeared."

"Not yet," O'Neil responded, watching another glider swoop up. "What's the situation there?"

"In a word, nuts," the radioman replied. "That big mother starship is overlapping about half of the UMC encampment. I'm afraid Mr. Lockwood's air-conditioned office has been knocked flat."

"We already knew it was hot around here," O'Neil sent back. "Now it's time to let these guys know." He frowned. "You remember the watch point Skaara's militia used? Send a truckload of missiles that way. We've got some infantry reinforcements arriving."

"Reading you five by five, sir," Feretti said.

"I'll try to rendezvous at the base of the plateau—Firebase Three," O'Neil said. "ASAP. O'Neil out."

He tromped on the accelerator, speeding up, but still taking the route with most cover.

"Daniel!" Sha'uri cried, pointing off to one side. "There!"

In the distance, rising like a mountain of gold, they could see the top of the pyramid ship.

O'Neil jockeyed the wheel. "Give us something to aim for," he said.

In the remains of the military camp, Adam Kawalsky helped to heave another case of Stinger missiles out from under the collapsed supply tent. Colonel O'Neil had been insistent on securing the weapons. So there had been a tent on top—the weapons were actually in an underground bunker. And thanks to the storm and the gales of the starship's passage, considerable digging was required to get the cases out.

Additional eager hands appeared to pull the case out of the hole. One guy wore a sweat-encrusted shirt with the UMC logo on it—one of the mine overseers. The other had the gray camo fatigues of the company's security guards.

They could have had tails and horns for all Kawalsky cared. He needed volunteers, and would take all he could get. "Hump that over to the edge of the plateau—there's a sort of trail down that way." He pointed, and the two new additions to the workforce staggered away.

More and more of the surviving gray-clad mercenaries were gravitating toward his operation. Kawalsky thought he understood. They were soldiers of a sort, after all. Strongly self-motivated, perhaps, to take a job like this. But they needed officers and orders. And this was one of the few corners of the camp where orders were still being given.

A picket line of Marines guarded the rocket dump, some armed with rifles, others with the green tubes that held the ground-to-air missiles.

Kawalsky had also established a firing party in one of the dug-in strong points that O'Neil had established at the edge of the camp. The firebase also covered one of the trails that led off the plateau.

People were bringing in the damnedest things. Keogh's thrust had virtually stripped the base of military transport. But some of the UMC people had managed to rescue wheeled and tracked vehicles from the surviving portions of their camp.

Kawalsky now had several trucks and a bulldozer at the edge of the rocky rises. The earthmover was pushing down part of Keogh's encircling wall in an attempt to create an exit ramp for the wheeled vehicles.

As the lieutenant directed two more men in manhandling a crate, Feretti came running up, carting a radio set with him. "I broadcast what you said, sir, to all units. And I got an answer from Colonel O'Neil!"

Kawalsky felt a smile stretch the skin on his gritty face. "Excellent news!"

Feretti nodded. "He said he's heading here to join us ASAP."

Kawalsky's shoulders rose a little higher, as if a burden had been lifted. He was a military man, too, after all. Maybe he'd feel better with someone around to give the orders, too.

*   *   *

Tense figures stood around the truck, all of them armed with Stinger missiles. The vehicle was half full of cased missiles, about as many eggs as Kawalsky wanted to risk in one basket.

It was time for this shipment of antiaircraft missiles to head out to the forces being pounded by the attack gliders. The problem was, who was going to take it? The truck was a soft, unarmored target, and if it went up, its precious cargo would probably explode as well. Which would, as Kawalsky's volunteer force now began to realize, cut down the driver's already slim chances of survival.

"Look, *somebody's* got to drive the damned thing," a Marine noncommissioned officer growled. "We can't send it out on automatic pilot."

The scattering of Marines and UMC mercs couldn't meet his eyes. The noncom wiped his sweaty face. In a second he'd have to order somebody, not the best answer to a suicide mission when you're dealing with desperate men with guns.

"I'll drive it," a voice came from overhead. A new team of two men were laboring down the steep slope, carrying another crate of missiles.

The noncom examined the volunteer carefully. He was a UMC supervisor rather than a fighting man, and frankly, he looked like a blond, shaved gorilla. Well, half shaved. The guy had pale stubble all over his face, and salt stains were crusted under the armpits of his shirt.

"You sure you know how to handle a truck this size?" the Marine asked dubiously.

"Call me Charlie," the volunteer said as he and his partner manhandled their crate down to the level. Flexing big but sloping shoulders, Charlie advanced to the Marine. "Drove a rig like this for a coupla years back home in Texas," he said. "I can handle it."

"And I'll go along—ride shotgun." The gray-clad merc with him stepped over to an open crate and removed one of the missile tubes. "If you don't mind."

Charlie turned abruptly to his companion. "You don't have to do this, Sullivan."

Sullivan merely shrugged. "I figure I can't screw things up much worse," he replied. "I'm coming along for the ride."

Charlie Morris swore as he tromped on the clutch, downshifting as sand sleeted from under the wheels of the truck. Yes, he *had* driven one of these pigs, but back in Texas they'd had paved roads, not dunes and wadis that curved crazily and had treacherous surfaces.

The only thing like a real road on this planet was the truck route that UMC had bulldozed and planed. And that, as both Morris and Sullivan knew, already looked like a war-surplus graveyard after the enemy's attack gliders had gotten through with the vehicles fleeing along it.

"I still think you're crazy to come along," he told Sullivan.

The mercenary only shrugged. "What the hell. You want to live forever?"

His flippancy faded. "That fella *needed* volunteers if they were going to get these rockets out where they'll do some good. You saw what happened to those poor Army bastards by dawn's early light."

The two of them had gone to the plateau's edge with binoculars to try to track the progress of the Army caravan. Instead, they'd been treated to a high-tech version of Custer's Last Stand.

At least their interest had probably saved their lives. They were well outside the confines of the UMC camp when the enormous pyramid ship had landed. Both Morris's tent and Sullivan's lay under the acreage crushed by the spacecraft's bulk.

Morris shrugged. "I just felt I had to do something. I mean, Lord knows I was busy enough helping to make this mess. Figured the time had come to try to pull things out of the crapper."

"Well, you broke the ice back there. After you came forward, other guys began to volunteer to take trucks out." Sullivan glanced over at the driver. "I'd say you were a *big* help."

Morris scowled in embarrassment. "I ain't no hero, you know. I just did what I thought had to be done."

"Understood," Sullivan said. "You just drive, and I'll shoot anything that looks hostile." They'd given him a gun—Marine issue—and he'd kept the missile he'd taken from the crate.

If that wasn't enough—

His thoughts were interrupted as something large and white flashed overhead. It looked like a giant moth, or—no. It was one of those hawk-shaped fighter-bombers that had flown out from the spaceship to target the Army vehicles.

There was a flash that left dazzling afterimages in Sullivan's eyes, and the sand ahead of the truck exploded in a pyrotechnic display.

Morris stared upward through the windshield, trying to catch sight of their attacker. "He's whipped around and he's coming back at us," he reported.

Sullivan gripped the tube containing the rocket and wondered how much good he'd do with it, trying to shoot out the side window of a jouncing heavy truck.

Morris brought his foot down heavily on the gas, the truck's wheels flinging sheets of dust as he sent the truck bearing straight for the oncoming glider. It was as though he was playing chicken with the attacking aircraft.

"Get ready to hop off," he told Sullivan.

"Why?" the merc asked. "You going to crash into him?"

Morris hit the gas again and twisted the wheel. The truck seemed to leap aside from the spot where it had been—the spot that the flier's blasters turned to smoking glass an instant later.

"You really are a hell of a driver," Sullivan began.

"Open your door—you're getting out in a second," Morris interrupted. He dropped speed, sending the truck into a slewing circle. "Now!" he yelled.

Sullivan had taken harder falls from faster vehicles. He skidded lightly over a surface that felt like sandpaper. There'd probably be some scrapes to tend tomorrow—if he survived that long.

He rose on one knee, still holding the firing tube for the missile.

Again, Morris had swung the truck around so it was charging straight for the approaching war glider. The two machines seemed to rush toward each other. Sullivan raised the weapon to his shoulder.

At the last moment Morris made the truck zigzag. The glider didn't even fire. It overflew the truck—then the blast-cannon that hung like engine nacelles under its wings suddenly shifted position, tracked the truck from behind, and hit it.

The twin-energy bolts must have both landed in the payload compartment, because the vehicle exploded with a force that even Sullivan felt, hundreds of feet away.

He had already triggered his missile. It lanced upward, hitting the udajeet right in the central body where the pilot sat. The shock wave from the new blast buffeted Sullivan, nearly knocking him flat.

The glider veered off in a graceless curve that intersected explosively with the top of a sand dune.

Sullivan pulled himself to his feet and started back in the direction of the plateau and the pyramid.

"One down," he said.

Not to put too fine a point on it, Gunnery Sergeant Rob Hilliard was bored out of his mind. It was bad enough being a road-block guard. But when the road block you were manning had no traffice passing . . .

Hilliard's brother was with the Border Patrol, working on the checkpoint on the main highway just north of San Diego. He checked the occasional truck or car for illegal cargo or passengers. But at least he was in the outdoors, with a chance to improve his tan.

Hilliard was stationed at the bottom of a hole in the ground where not too long ago, some big-ass rocket had been pointed at Moscow or some such city. The only illumination came from fluorescent strip lamps which gave everything and everybody an off-green tinge.

The hairs on the back of Hilliard's neck stood up as energy seemed to permeate the big chamber. "Incoming," he called, gesturing his six-man security team to the far wall by the blast doors. Countless repetition had reduced this to a drill like any other. They no longer hid behind the heavy steel door, but just stood there out of the way.

A gout of energy splurted from the ring of the StarGate, then sucked back in a sort of liquid vortex, as if the gate were a giant plug hole in somebody's bath. Then the energy field stabilized to a rippling glow bounded by the quartz ring.

"Kinda early for anyone to be coming through," one of the guards said, glancing at his watch.

Hilliard shrugged. "Maybe they ended the strike or whatever was going on over there, and are rolling early to make up for lost time."

The nose of a truck poked out of the gateway, seemingly covered in iridescence. Then it snapped into reality, nearly running into the far wall.

"Watch it there, buddy," Hilliard called. The driver's face was pop-eyed and gray-fleshed. He must have had one hell of a ride.

Hilliard's squad stood in line abreast, facing one side of the truck.

"You okay?" Hilliard asked.

His answer came as a totaly inhuman head rose in the cab beside the driver. It seemed to be a sort of blackish-gold bird's head that swiveled to look at him with greenish eyes. The olive-drab canvas that covered the cargo end of the truck was torn loose to reveal kilted men with similar helmet heads. They began leveling what appeared to be spears at the security team.

Damnation, Hilliard thought as he brought up his rifle. A quick head count told him he was already outnumbered, and his force was under the enemy's guns rather than defilading the StarGate.

As the shooting began, the sergeant was already falling back toward the blast doors. Bullets whined and ricocheted off the truck's body as what seemed to be miniature bolts of lightning struck the Marine guards.

Hilliard flung himself through the doorway and slapped the electronic control. The ponderous door began closing. Even as that happened, the monster-headed guards were leaping from the truck. The StarGate flashed, vomiting forth more figures. Hilliard aimed his gun at the opening and fired rounds one-handed while snatching up a phone. It immediately connected him to the officer of the day.

"Intruder alert!" Hilliard yelled into the receiver. "StarGate—"

Then a flash of intolerable brilliance lanced through the still open blast door and took him.

Hilliard's security team was not the sole defense of the StarGate complex. There were perimeter guards, and a whole platoon that slept in uniform with its boots on. This ready team was now roused, and, wiping sleep from their eyes, the defenders clutched their rifles and headed down the hall toward the missile silo that housed the interworld gateway.

Then figures out of legend appeared in the doorways lining the hall, and the firefight was on, bullets against energy gouts. The Marines had the advantage of numbers; the invaders had superior technology. In the end it was the Marines who gave ground, their officer screaming into his walkie-talkie for backup.

The intruders's weapons gave them a tremendous edge over the defense. A closed, locked steel door was little more than a delay to them, to be blasted out at the lock or the hinges.

But as the defenders pulled back, their numbers were augmented as off-duty guards came into the fight. They might not be perfect in uniform—some merely wore fatigue pants and T-shirts—but they all brought rifles to the party.

The incursion was held before the intruders could reach the elevators to other levels. More bullets were flying, and there really weren't that many blast-lances to meet them. The invaders from ancient Egypt began to pull back, concentrating their defenses on the access ways to the StarGate.

A lieutenant intercepted a detail of half-dressed Marines as they left their quarters. "You bunch, come with me," he curtly ordered.

The noncom who'd been in charge of the group glanced at the officer as the elevator stopped. "Sir? I thought the fighting was on the floor below."

The lieutenant gestured for silence as he led the men down a corridor, checking each room along the way. Then he kicked open the door to what looked like a conference room, ducking back as a lightning bolt snapped out at him.

"Figured they'd have somebody in here—there's a direct access to the StarGate from this room," he said.

The noncom detailed three men to clear the room. One got fried, the other two succeeded in shooting down the hawk-headed guard who had barricaded himself behind the long desk that made up most of the room's furniture.

More blast-bolts came from through a doorway marked EXIT, which gave onto a stairway.

"That's how our friend got up here," the lieutenant said, pulling a grenade from the front of his combat suit. He tossed it down the stairs. "Gunney, I want everybody back to the doorway."

The lieutenant stepped to the far wall of the room, a whiteboard setup surprisingly only dimpled by the firefight that had gone on a minute ago. Beside the board was a large button. When the lieutenant pressed it, the writing surface rolled up with a whine of heavy machinery. It was backed by a thick steel plate, and as it moved upward, it revealed a window.

The gunnery sergeant backed his people to the door, and the lieutenant took out another grenade. A second later, he was running out of the room, slamming the door. A dull boom marked the grenade's explosion, then they headed back in. The room was smoky and much the worse for wear. But the window was out.

And overlooking the StarGate room as it did, it allowed the sergeant and his men to catch the Egyptian defenders in the rear.

General West was in the air, flying to Creek Mountain, when he received word of the attack via the StarGate. "Lieutenant Jurgenson remembered that the conference room overlooked the StarGate complex, and led a squad up there to take the intruders in the rear. Those who survived have retreated through the gate."

"How about our own men?" the general inquired.

"Heavy casualties, sir."

The general's lips became a thin line under his

mustache. "As soon as you get things reorganized there, I want you to send a team through the Star-Gate," he ordered. "We've got to find out what's happening on Abydos."

By the time he arrived, the report dead line for the team had passed. There was no word from the people who'd passed through the gateway.

CHAPTER 19
TURKEY SHOOT

The suns of Abydos had risen higher, and shadows had grown scarce. It seemed as though the driver of the Sheridan tank that clanked to the crest of the dune had given up trying to hide. The tank's turret kept revolving as if on the lookout for hostile fliers, and the fighting vehicle's cannon tube was at maximum elevation.

The gun tracked to the right, and, as if on cue, one of the udajeet attackers came streaking in from the left.

Suddenly, human figures erupted from the sand, most aiming rifles at the low-flying glider. But two of the men had stubby green tubes which they raised and fired.

The Stinger missiles disintegrated the udajeet in midair.

Sergeant Oliver Eakins dusted himself off with a grin. He was a large, powerful-looking black man with closely cropped hair. "Got another one," he said. "That makes three so far. Guess it's time to move this show somewhere else."

The tank unbuttoned, and the sergeant in charge poked his head out of the hatch. "Easy enough for you to say," he grumbled. "You're not the one who has to sit out as bait for those buzz-boys."

Even as both of the men talked, their eyes kept scanning the sky.

They had met only a couple of hours ago. The sergeant's squad had managed to escape their APC alive after one of the gliders blasted the treads off one side of the vehicle. They'd been marching back to the base camp when the tank had encountered them, and they'd decided to pool their resources. The squad spread out to offer warning of approaching gliders, and the tank would try to shoot them down using the pintle-mounted .50-caliber machine gun mounted on the turret roof.

Their survival had been precarious at best. One udajeet had strafed them, though it had flown off after being damaged by machine-gun fire.

Still, neither sergeant would have bet on them making it through the day until the mining truck had appeared out of nowhere. It was driven by a Marine who frantically waved some of the infantrymen over.

"We're loaded with antiaircraft missiles," the driver had called. Two men in the back of the truck manhandled a crate off the tailboard. The canvas cover had been removed from the cargo area, and a third man stood braced, scanning the sky, a rocket tube in his hands. He wore the gray camouflage fatigues of UMC's mining police.

"Follow the instructions on the tube, and don't waste your shots," the driver admonished. "Head for the plateau, but don't go for the camp. Colonel O'Neil is trying to reorganize us at the foot of the rise."

"Colonel O'Neil?" Eakins knew the Marine Colonel was supposed to be the second-in-command of the Abydos Expeditionary Force. "Last we heard, he was inside Nagada." Eakins had refused to follow the Earthling practice of calling the city Abbadabbaville.

The Marine driver nodded. "Folks in there let him out, and are sending help, too."

Eakins looked surprised. "The guys we were supposed to fight?"

The Marine shrugged. "Hey, they hate the people inside that pyramid more than they hate UMC."

The case of missiles thumped to the sand. One of the loaders tossed down a crowbar. Eager soldiers broke the box open and began distributing the contents among the members of the squad.

"Good hunting," the Marine said as his men retrieved the crowbar. "Reports from First Base say there are a good fifty udajeets—that's what the locals call those glider things—flying search-and-destroy on all vehicles."

He glanced at the tank pulled up in the shadow of a dune. "It's not healthy to hang around armor right now."

Eakins patted the olive-drab tube in his hands. "Maybe. Or maybe we can make it unhealthy for any flying buzz-bomb to mess with them."

He smiled, a harsh, tight grin. "You tell your Colonel O'Neil we'll be coming in."

Eakins hefted the Stinger missile again. "And we'll be loaded for bear."

Moving at the pace of a marching man didn't

give them a whole lot of speed—especially since every good dune they found, they'd stop, dig in, and play "Little Lost Tank and the Troopers with Teeth."

After their third kill, however, Eakins said, "We've got to be close to First Base by now."

They crested the next rise to spot UMC's mining road—and farther out, Eakins saw the eroded rock of the plateau rising out of the sands. Topping that was the bulk of the hostile spaceship, gleaming in the sun where the StarGate pyramid had been.

"So that's where they went," the tank commander said grimly.

"And there's where we want to be," Eakins said, pointing to activity on the sands almost at the base of the ridge of rock, almost directly below where the ship had landed.

"Damn it, but I think this Colonel O'Neil wants to try a counterattack," Eakins said. The pyramid ship had made him run; its unearthly blasts and its udajeets had made him scared. For the chance to get back at them, Ollie Eakins would cheerfully march across hot sand and a dangerous road.

Besides, he wanted to see if any other of the scratch outfits developing on this battlefield had done better than blowing away three udajeets.

After a brief consultation, the leaders of the war band decided on a straight rush—down the dune, across the road, skirting the burned-out wreckage of yet another dead APC, then up to the crest of the next tall dune they could find. By then they should at least be in visual contact with O'Neil's force.

The foot soldiers broke into a trot, pounding down the face of the dune, then out onto the road. With a clank of gears, the tank followed. They were out in the open, completely naked, when one of the infantrymen stared up into the sky and cried, "Udajeet!"

Eakins whirled, trying to unship the missile tube he carried. Other men were doing the same, fumbling their weapons into firing position. The udajeet slashed down at them from out of the sky.

Then, from the top of the dune they were aiming for, came a blast of energy and a rush of a missile. Both struck the oncoming glider, which flipped in midair, skimmed the dune that Eakins and company had just vacated, then crashed and exploded in the sands beyond.

Incredulous soldiers stared as boys in Abydan homespun waved them on. More of the young men dashed across the sands, apparently going to investigate the crash site. "You're inside the defense perimeter," the kid who'd waved said in careful English.

"Why are you going to check the crash?" Eakins asked.

The young militiaman waved a spear-like weapon. Eakins realized that it must be a less powerful version of the blaster-nacelles on the gliders. "Many of the pilots carry these," he said.

With a smile the young man glanced at the tank churning its way up the hill. "But I think Colonel O'Neil will be very glad to see your weapons, too."

                    *   *   *

On the bridge of *Ra's Eye,* Hathor scowled at
the tactical display. Yet another of the far-ranging
red sparks representing her udajeets had
disappeared.

"The invaders were dying like ants under our
feet," she muttered, glaring at the shifting troop
distributions. "How could they so suddenly be
smashing our gliders from the skies?"

"Lady Captain, our pilots report that the
groundlings are firing some sort of rocket-weapons," one of the bridge crew said.

"Our pilots have supremely maneuverable, extremely fast aircraft," Hathor snapped. "Surely
they can stay out of the way of a few primitive
rockets!"

"The enemy targets them as they come in on
blaster runs," the crewman said.

"Then our people should attack at higher alti-
tudes instead of dropping on top of their targets—
and into the sights of these rocket-weapons."

The crewman paused. "Lady Captain," he said,
"our pilots are not used—"

"The fools aren't used to dealing with any opponents who might shoot back!" Hathor cut him off
in a rage. "What they are used to is flying low
over *fellahin,* scaring the *ka* out of them, and
herding them for their masters."

Hathor's fists were clenched so tightly, her
short nails were tearing holes in her palms. If she
just had a *few* of her veterans from the Ombos
campaign! They'd flown against more sophisticated weapons than these, and defeated the war-

riors who carried them. She grimaced. But that training, that skill—those numbers—had been dust for eight thousand years.

Now the Cat had to fight this battle with the resources she had available. She turned in concern to the hologram again. "How many of our udajeets are still in action?" she asked.

"Lady Captain—" This time the unwilling answer came from one of the scanner operators. "From our reports and scans, I'd estimate we've lost fifty percent of our air forces."

"*Half* of our udajeets?" Hathor said in shock. She'd allowed herself to be distracted by the fighting at the StarGates—both here and on Earth. The thrust to the homeworld of the invaders had been an overreaching move, she had to admit to herself. She'd hoped for more information about this planet of wild *fellahin,* but it seemed that those studying the StarGate had consigned it to a hole deep within the ground.

In the end she'd recalled her attack force, and was appalled at the losses they'd taken on their reconnaissance. If not for the fact that the Horus guards who'd searched the rest of the pyramid were available as a reserve, they might not have been able to destroy the counterthrust that arrived from Earth.

Even so, the losses to her scanty ground forces merely underscored her problems. Hathor lacked the strength in warriors even to sweep the plateau free of invaders. And the enemy was taking advantage of that weakness.

She looked long and hard at the steadily coa-

lescing collection of green sparks at the foot of
the docking plateau. The rocky cliff protected
them from direct observation, and as she'd already
discovered, the weapons of the secondary batteries could not be depressed far enough to bring
them into their field of fire.

But what could whoever was assembling these
forces hope to accomplish? *Ra's Eye* was invulner-
able to attacks mounted with such weapons as
they might have. They might as easily hope for
a sandstorm to help wear the battlecraft's quartz
armor away.

The situation was degenerating into a stale-
mate. The Earthlings' primitive arsenal precluded
the expectation of serious attack. But Hathor
could strike at the invaders only by exposing the
udajeets to primitive weapons which had proven
surprisingly effective.

Of course, she could recall her gliders, button
up, and leave the invaders to their own devices.
She had cut their communications with Earth by
seizing the StarGate.

But if those on Earth were willing to accept the
high casualties resulting from a really determined
push, they might recapture the Abydos side of the
gate and discover just how weak Hathor was when
it came to manpower.

Also, her hopes of inflicting a blockade on the
enemy had dimmed as she'd digested the reports
of a large force of infantry joining the invaders.
Udajeet pilots had also reported that Nagada
seemed to be in the midst of an evacuation.

The invaders wouldn't starve if the locals could

feed them. That meant camping over the StarGate until the Earthlings' machinery gave out—too long a wait, given the volatile situation on Tuat and the fief worlds. Hathor had to get back quickly with the definitive news that Ra was dead.

Unhappily, she contemplated the possibility of leaving Abydos but keeping the planet out of the Earthlings' hands. She could lift off, arm the main battery, and turn that weaponry loose on the plateau. The very heavy blasters could slag the pyramid and destroy the StarGate. With luck, the main battery salvos would even encompass the destruction of that worrisome force at the base of the plateau.

Hathor could then return to establish herself over the rival godlings on Tuat, and then, at some unspecified time, deploy sufficient force to bring Abydos to heel. With Abydos quelled, there would then be time to restore StarGate communications.

Then it would be Earth's turn. A possible scenario, but very . . . extreme. Too many variables arose. Could Ptah and the technicians available today restore an entire StarGate connection? From the work she'd seen on the refitting of *Ra's Eye,* the answer to that question was dubious at best. How long could she devote to establishing her position as empress? Three months hadn't been enough to ensure her leadership as Ra's regent. Let the *fellahin* of Abydos live wild for too long, and she'd be forced to exterminate the population of the whole planet.

Hathor forced her hands to relax, considering with dismay the bloody half moons created by her fingernails digging into the flesh. She had not come up with a solution to her problems. She'd needed time to think, to seek other options.

Before that, however . . .

Hathor turned to her bridge crew. "Recall the udajeets," she ordered.

Adam Kawalsky and a picked company of Marines lay low in the dug-in emplacements of Firebase Three, waiting for a target worth shooting at. He and Colonel O'Neil had both suspected that the firebase and the edge of the plateau were safe from the flying pyramid's energy weapons.

From their examination of both the spear-blasters and the blast-cannon, they saw that a barrel was necessary for these weapons. Such a requirement would doubtless apply to the heavier weapons aboard the ship from Ra's empire. But the very shape of the battlecraft, with its receding walls, would argue against the ability to direct fire to the very foot of the pyramid.

That was almost where Firebase Three was.

Then, too, both Kawalsky and O'Neil remembered how the udajeets had been handled during their first battle against a spaceship. The attack gliders had not operated independently, but had docked on the mother ship. Sooner or later, they believed, the same would happen with this heavier flight of gliders.

When they returned, *they* would be Kawalsky's target of opportunity.

Till then Kawalsky and his chosen few remained

hidden beneath sand, camouflage netting, and broiling heat, waiting.

"Lieutenant," Feretti asked, "you think they'll come back by evening? I mean, you wouldn't think it would do much good, trying to chase people in the dark."

"Feretti, I have no idea what will happen by evening," Kawalsky admitted. "Although I do hope it gets a little cooler around here." He wiped sweat off his face and took a sip of tepid water from his canteen. Even the plastic his lips touched seemed warmed by the sun.

"I'm not saying I want them to come by night," Feretti quickly said. "That would just make our job harder, right, sir? No, I wish they would come sooner instead of later. To tell you the truth, sir, I got a problem with waiting for things."

Kawalsky hid a grin. "Really, Corporal? You couldn't tell it by talking to you."

"Well, sir, you know, I try not to advertise," Feretti went on, completely unaware of the officer's sarcasm. "But if it's a case of sooner or later—"

His monologue was interrupted by a series of shots into the air from the dune crests that marked the outer perimeter of O'Neil's force.

"That's from Skaara's boys, warning us that the udajeets are incoming," Feretti said.

"Right," Kawalsky replied laconically. "Looks like you get your wish, Corporal—sooner rather than later."

In moments the flight of udajeets came close enough that the hidden men could see its approach. The gliders moved in a large, ragged formation, as if the pilots were unused to flying together—or too many wingmen had been shot down.

To Kawalsky they looked like a big, sloppy flock of homing pigeons returning to their coops instead of the hawk-like killing machines they'd been earlier this morning. There was something tentative, nervous about their flying. The lieutenant realized they were keeping a much higher altitude, trying to stay above Stinger range.

His usually good-natured face took on a wolfish cast as he grinned. They'd have to come down close if they wanted to dock.

On his first visit to Abydos, Kawalsky had been forced to endure repeated aerial attacks from udajeets while trapped outside the StarGate pyramid. Half of Skaara's friends, the original boy commandos, had died in that slaughter.

Kawalsky had promised himself that would never happen to troops under his command again. Now he was going to make that promise stick.

The udajeets smoothly lost altitude, aiming for the starship's open launch decks. Kawalsky's people were aiming, too. He'd carefully detailed sections of the ambush party. Some would go for the vanguard, others for the wings. Kawalsky himself was aiming dead center.

Stepping into the open, he tracked his first target with his missile tube, moved slightly ahead, and . . .

"Fire!" he shouted, triggering his own missile.

Stingers slashed up into the bellies of the docking craft, wreaking havoc among the unsuspecting pilots. Wings blew off, bodies went flying, gliders crashed into each other as they attempted to peel out of formation.

Kawalsky calmly picked up his second tube and aimed.

Above, some of the glider pilots attempted to maintain their vectors and land. Those were probably the wise ones—wise to get out of the way.

Other udajeet pilots, stung by the attack, went into wide, banking turns to overfly the ambush site and return fire. Instead, they ran into a virtual hedgehog of missile fire from the troops concentrated at the base of the plateau.

Several of the would-be counterattackers were knocked out of the sky. Others swung wide, hoping to come to the docking bays from a safer direction.

And one unfortunate pilot, the body of his glider burning in hellish colors, swept over the ambush site at speed, trying to bring his dying bird into the sanctuary of the pyramid ship.

"Hold your fire!" Kawalsky ordered crisply. "I think that sucker will make more trouble for them inside than if we bring it down."

The pilot must have been one of the better udajeet fliers. Despite the flames, the trailing smoke, and the wavering of his craft, he steered straight for one of the open bay doors. It was almost a perfect landing. *Almost.*

At the very last second, just as the pilot was braking the glider, one wing dipped. The wingtip caught about a foot below the opening, and the udajeet cartwheeled across the launching deck. It was as if the Earthlings had sent a killer rocket with a twenty-foot wingspan—and it had penetrated the ship's armor.

A godawful explosion shuddered the entirety of the huge pyramid. A gout of flame vomited from the deck's open hatchway, along with pieces of udajeets—*plural*. In its final throes their dying swan had taken along a couple of other gliders for company.

"Down and cover your asses, men!" Kawalsky yelled. He himself jumped into the earthworks in case some of the burning wreckage tumbling down the front of the golden starship should come ricocheting this way.

But as he burrowed in the dirt, there was a smile on Adam Kawalsky's face. Death might come at any time today, in many ways. But Kawalsky would die happy.

He'd made a promise to himself, and he'd kept it. He'd made the udajeets pay.

CHAPTER 20
ALTERCATIONS AND REPAIRS

Not all the udajeets caught in the fusilade of Stinger missiles crashed and burned. Several pilots came down in landings that were hard for their craft but successful in that most personal of criteria—they survived. They staggered to the base of *Ra's Eye,* screaming into the communicators built into their Horus masks.

Some were burned, some were bleeding. A few lucky, uninjured pilots had the presence of mind to take their blast-lances along. Not that their weapons would leave anything but scratches on the adamantine golden quartzose material that made up the hull. But at least they could protect themselves in the case of ground attack.

Kawalsky had dug himself out again and was on the radio to O'Neil with the main body of troops below. "There are maybe a half-dozen pilots who managed to walk away after bringing their gliders down," he said. "They seem to be congregated at the front of the ship, around about the centerline. Around about where the entrance hall would be on the stone pyramid inside."

"Are they trying to make some sort of stand?" O'Neil asked.

"From the way they're banging on the wall with

their spear butts," Kawalsky said, excitement quickening his voice, "I'd say they were expecting to be let in."

"Kawalsky, we're coming with everything we can push up this slope." O'Neil's voice sounded pretty excited, too. "If they open a door up there, you do everything you can to *keep* it open till we arrive."

In one of the lowest passages aboard *Ra's Eye*, a female crew-technician named Naila stared fearfully at the warrior confronting her. He had not activated his helmet mask, but his naked face, grim and coldly furious, frightened her more than any rendition of the Horus hawk. The man's eyes seemed almost as deadly as the tip of the blast-lance he aimed at her.

"The—the lady captain, she has given orders that none of the ground-side hatches are to be opened," Naila said, faltering.

The warrior's control slipped. "Ammit eat your soul! That's my *brother* out there! We were both taken into Ra's service—and we both pledged our fealty to Apis. That's who I swore my oath to, not some bitch who doesn't care about her own people!"

He glared at Naila. "What about you? Did you swear fealty to Ptah or to bloody-handed Hathor? Think hard—because if you didn't swear yourself to her, you wouldn't want to die for her, would you?"

The tip of the blast-lance poked painfully into

Naila's midriff. She stepped back, eyes wide, mouth dry.

"Now open that door! I may not know how to operate it, but I know how to operate *this.*" He gave her another painful prod.

"Last warning," the warrior growled, tightening his grip on the trigger mechanism.

Her face a grayish-pale color, Naila turned to the bank of photosensitive controls where the door would form. Her fingers stumbled for a second, and she had to start over.

The second time around, however, the correct code was entered. The biomorphic system of the quartz-crystal shifted to a new lattice structure.

And where a wall had once stood there was now a doorway.

"It's happened! It's happened!" Kawalsky called into his radio. "A door has opened in the enemy ship!"

He and his picked band burst from Firebase Three, assault rifles at the ready. Most of the stranded pilots were too busy gaining entrance to the ship to pay attention to anything else.

But a couple of the healthier escapees turned around, leveling their blast-lances. Bullets met energy-bolts, and fighters from both sides went down.

"Don't let them close the damned door!" Kawalsky yelled to his men. One of them still carried a Stinger. He primed the missile and sent it through the opening. Sparks and flame glittered in the interior.

Kawalsky turned at the racket of a heavy internal-combustion engine behind him. One of his men had climbed aboard an abandoned bulldozer.

"Let's seem 'em close it with *this* stuck in the way," the Marine howled over the roar of the engine. Swinging jerkily around, the earthmover lurched toward the portal in the quartz.

The surviving Horus guards concentrated their fire on the advancing machine, but the Marine driver kept the bulldozer's blade interposed between himself and the guards's blast-bolts. The heavy-duty steel glowed and fused as flares of energy hit it, but nothing came through. Ra's blast-lances were designed more for man-killing than demolition work.

The bulldozer hit the thin, tall doorway with a crash, slewing around as its blade caught on one side. The Marine who'd been controlling the machine jumped from the driver's seat as the defenders inside the pyramid ship finally got shots at him. Judging from the choked screams inside, the earthmover had managed to nail someone against a wall.

Kawalsky and his team swarmed over the bulldozer like monkeys—heavily armed monkeys—firing away. The defense melted. One or two blast-lances were still in action against them, then one . . . then none.

When Kawalsky finally led the way inside the spaceship, however, he did find a single Horus guard. At least, he figured the man was a guard. He was sturdily built but had no hawk mask. Instead his face showed terror as he supported a pale-faced girl beside a panel of glowing lights. The man held up her hand to the panel, shouting at her, pleading with her, in a language that Kawalsky didn't understand.

But it didn't matter what he said, unless this ship was equipped with one of those magic coffins Daniel Jackson had mentioned.

The girl was quite obviously dead.

Hathor was still reeling from the enormity of their losses in the air war when news of the latest disaster came in.

Barely twenty-five percent of her udajeets had survived after the Earthlings' ambush. The air forces she'd tried to conserve with her call-back order had been slashed in half again within sight of safety.

Not only that, but the better part of one of the pyramid's upper decks had been devastated thanks to the crashing glider. Control circuitry had been damaged, and her technicians weren't even sure they'd be able to get the cover panels to seal off the launching bays.

She shuddered. If that happened, it would mean cruising space with an entire deck open to vacuum. The bridge, higher up toward the apex of the pyramid, would be effectively cut off from the rest of the ship.

Then had come the news that they had another problem with openings in the ship.

"Lady Captain," one of the scanner crew reported in a tight, frightened voice, "we have a hull breach at ground level."

"What?!" Hathor's voice was deadly as she questioned the unfortunate technician. "How could that be? The invaders haven't the weapons to tear holes in our hull. And anything that could damage us so badly would have been felt."

Unless, she thought, *the udajeet crash was merely a cover for some sort of mine operation.*

She pushed that thought aside. Who could plan for an accidental crash like that?

The scanner technician's voice became more choked. "The breach wasn't caused by action from without, Lady Captain. It appears the main portal was opened—"

"I gave orders that all ground-side apertures were to remain closed." Hathor's voice was quiet but charged with fury. "Who was down there to open the portal?"

"Naila, one of the damage-control crew, was checking some circuits down on the lowest levels." The technician drew a deep breath. "There were surviving udajeet pilots outside—"

"I'm aware of that," Hathor said coldly. "But I'm also aware that an open portal is like an open invitation to the scum down on the sands to come and make a try for the StarGate. Have you been able to seal the portal?"

Sweat beads appeared on the technician's upper lip. "We've been attempting, Lady Captain, but there appears to be something caught in the opening—something substantial."

"You're saying the portal is *blocked?*" Hathor demanded. "Have you checked for boarders?"

As she watched the results of the technician's

scan, both of them went pale. Hathor activated
the communicator. "All warriors," she said. "This
includes all udajeet pilots. Collect small arms and
prepare to repel boarders. I repeat, repel boarders.
Boarders detected in lowest level of the ship. Star-
Gate guards, retain your positions. Beware of possible attacks."

At the same moment the external scan technician called out, "Lady Captain, the enemy forces
at the base of the plateau—they're climbing up."

Hathor swung around to the tactical display. If
that mass of manpower got aboard, her available
foot soldiers would not be able to handle them.

"Gunnery!" she called in desperation. "Secondary batteries, full depression. Continuous fire."

"Lady Captain," a thin, precise voice returned
over the communications link, "our calculations
showed that we could not target the enemy host."

"I want interdiction fire," Hathor said. "Your
salvos should come close enough to the lip of the
ridge to discourage that rabble from climbing up
here."

I hope, she said in her heart.

"Secondary batteries, firing," her gunnery officer replied.

Streaks of light appeared on the tactical display,
indicating where the batteries had fired. But the
coverage was weak, spotty, as if only half the
available blasters were firing.

"Gunn—" she began, but the precise voice of
Thoth's former servant was already reporting.
"Lady Captain," the gunnery officer said, "it ap-
pears our fire-control circuitry is defective. All

batteries above Launching Deck Four are not responding."

Launching Deck Four—where the udajeet had crashed.

"Damage Control, switch to backup circuits," Hathor barked.

"Lady Captain," a fearful voice came over the communicator, "there is no backup. In the press of refitting—"

In the press of refitting, Ptah thought he'd have me one last time—in a metaphorical sense.

The look on Hathor's face made several of her crew members flinch.

"Damage Control, see if you can repair the damaged fire-control circuits. Gunnery, you'll have to cover twice as much space with half as many guns."

Hathor was torn between a wish to retch and a desire to smash something—anything. But she could do neither. As captain of the ship, she was stuck on the bridge.

Ah, Ptah, she thought, *if—when—I get back, I will deal with you personally, painfully, and for a long, long time.*

Here and there discharges of energy tore at the ridgeline that marked the stony plateau's descent into the sands below. For the most part, however, the huge battlecraft's blaster batteries could not aim at a steep enough angle to interdict the ways up—or even reach them.

Still, the pyrotechnic effect was enough to quell even the most ardent spirits, much less men whose units had already been drubbed and shattered.

O'Neil came up with a force of volunteers—a large smattering of Skaara's boy militia, stiffened with Marines. Daniel Jackson accompanied him, as did Sha'uri. As they reached the top of the plateau, the very air seemed ionized. Ozone tore at O'Neil's nose. He walked across the dead zone in the ship's killing field to a portal blocked open by a still running bulldozer.

One of the Marines ran up to turn the machine off. Then they were inside the spaceship. The walls were of the same golden quartz, but it seemed rougher in texture, dull.

"I think we've found ourselves down in steerage class," Daniel said. "The decor was so much nicer in Ra's flying palace."

"Of course," O'Neil replied, "we never saw the engine room down there, either. I can tell you for sure the dungeons were on the unpleasant side."

A sand-colored figure stepped out from against one of the rough walls. "I'm on your side," Kawalsky said.

"What's the situation, Lieutenant?" O'Neil asked.

"We've made a quick reconnaissance against growing resistance," Kawalsky reported. "This main hall leads straight to the entrance hall for the StarGate, but there's a good-sized force of Horus guards dug in there. We've also discovered access to the next level up. As for the rest of this deck, it's cut up like a maze. And the other side knows the ground better than we do. The guards don't seem to be making direct assaults. Instead, some try to deny access to certain areas, while infiltrating behind us to ambush small groups."

"Let's see what we can see," O'Neil decided.

The assault party nosed its way down the main hall, checking every side corridor.

Daniel hung behind when he saw a plate inscribed with hieroglyphyics seemingly set into a wall. Sha'uri stayed with him, as did a pair of Skaara's militia boys.

"I barely understand a word of this," Sha'uri said.

"That's because these are some kind of techtalk hieroglyphics," Daniel finally concluded. "It appears to be instructions for electrical circuitry supposedly inside the wall—"

His scholarly disquisition abruptly ended with the sound of a death rattle from behind. Husband and wife turned to find one of their erstwhile guards already dead, the other expiring in the death grip of a Horus guard.

Sha'uri whipped out her pistol. The guard dropped the murdered boy and whipped up his blast-lance.

It had all happened to Daniel before. Sha'uri had tried to defend him with her gun; the Horus guard had blasted her. But here there was no sarcophagus of quick healing. Or it there was, Daniel had no idea where it was.

He launched himself into a wild tackle, smashing the lance aside. Energy gouted out in a wild shot, and the echoing blast of the pistol filled Daniel's ears.

He was going down, knocking the Horus guard to the floor. Daniel wrenched the blast-lance free. There was no resistance. As Daniel rose, he saw why. There was a bullet hole in the guardsman's chest.

Daniel turned to Sha'uri. She was frowning at him. "You could have gotten killed!"

"I knocked his spear away."

"Not from him," Sha'uri said, looking frightened. "From me! My bullet must have gone just past your head!"

"Did it?" Daniel frowned, trying to remember. "I guess I didn't notice. There were other things on my mind."

When the couple caught up with the main group, Daniel was carrying the blast-lance and a rifle slung over his shoulder. Sha'uri carried the other boy's rifle and her pistol.

The procession had stopped because yet another Horus guard had ambushed the point men. A black man in Army fatigues with sergeant's stripes lay dead on the floor. So did another of Skaara's militia. The main group had come up in time to riddle the guardsman with bullets.

"I think whoever's commanding this tub has personnel problems," O'Neil finally said.

"That guy seemed to be fighting just fine," Kawalsky objected.

"So did the guy who nearly killed Sha'uri and me," Daniel added.

"Individually, these guys are formidable," O'Neil agreed. "But there don't seem to be many of them. I began to suspect it when there wasn't an infantry sweep to clear out our base camp."

"That would have been standard operating procedure," Kawalsky admitted.

"Instead, we were allowed to save equipment and reconcentrate some of our forces, while the enemy tried to harry us with airpower." O'Neil frowned. "I'll bet most of the ground pounders on this ship went to take the StarGate—and they're still holding it."

"And the rest are playing guerrilla war with us, trying to pick us off one by one." Kawalsky looked disgusted.

"That's only if we play their game," O'Neil said. "Or, we could make them play ours."

"How?" Daniel wanted to know.

"We head someplace where they have to stand and fight us," O'Neil replied. "We've seen that things at the bottom of this ship seem on the grungy side. That leads me to believe that the bridge is probably up near the top." He checked his rifle. "Shall we go and find out?"

They'd risen more levels than Daniel wanted to count. Kawalsky and O'Neil climbed like machines. Skaara scampered up with a boy's boundless energy. Daniel grimly forced himself up a step at a time. And Sha'uri wasn't about to be left behind.

Some more members of the assault team had been lost, but several surviving members had picked up Ra-technology blaster weapons from dead crew warriors.

O'Neil had been right about two things. The accommodations had gotten nicer the higher they went. And the defense mounted by the Horus guards had grown fiercer.

The attackers had just passed through a deck with inhabited crew's quarters, after climbing through several floors where the apartments had been empty, neglected, and dusty.

Daniel could smell destruction wafting down the stairs from the deck above. He caught the stench of smoke, seared metal, and a pungent chemical odor. They mounted the stairs to find a flight deck in ruin. Burned-out hulks of udajeets stood stranded in slimy pools of chemical foam. The flames must have been fierce enough to affect the quartz-crystal that made up the walls, ceiling, and floors. In parts it was discolored, even cracked. One wall showed discoloration around the spread-eagled silhouette of a human figure.

"This must be where the glider crashed," Daniel said.

"At least it's pretty much open space except for the structural supports," Kawalsky joked. "Sort of like a municipal parking lot."

But even as he spoke, Horus guards materialized from behind several of the wrecks, aiming blast-lances at the intruders.

"Damn!" Kawalsky complained, "I *hate* when they do that!"

The hawk-headed guards had set up their ambush well. They'd caught the raiders away from the stairs, out in the open. And there were more of the Horus guards. As O'Neil had predicted, the enemy was assembling more and more warriors to stand and fight.

But there still weren't enough to stand before the numbers of the invaders. O'Neil and Kawalsky led Marines and militia kids in flanking movements, their bullets and blast-bolts driving the masked warriors back.

Even in victory, however, Daniel noticed that O'Neil looked puzzled. "Why were these guys fighting so hard over a wrecked deck?" he asked.

"Maybe we've been using this particular stairway too long," Kawalsky suggested. "So they've been getting prepared for us."

"Let's find a new way up," O'Neil said.

They set off more carefully across the open, scorched deck—point guard, flankers, the main body following with their guns ready.

The Horus guards fell back sullenly, sniping with their blast-lances.

O'Neil frowned. "They're trying to draw us in that direction." He nodded after the retreating warriors.

"Straight into another ambush," Kawalsky said. "Which way do we go instead?"

O'Neil chose a direction at random, and the raiders set off. But Daniel lagged behind, his attention caught by another of those plaques with hieroglyphic technical notes. But this one was on the floor, cracked and half-incinerated by one of the larger structural members.

Did this mean that the circuits which had been behind it were now revealed?

Daniel stepped around the thick pillar—to encounter an equally surprised Horus guard standing with his blast-lance grounded.

The masked warrior raised his weapon, but Daniel fumbled his into place and fired. The guard fell back, blasted.

Then Daniel noticed a diminutive female technician working on the open circuitry. She whirled around, screaming. The tool in her hand, a biomorphic piece of quartz-crystal, cycled through several changes as she faced him.

Daniel felt he had no choice. He fired his blast-lance again, and the technician was gone.

Then he turned the energy weapon on the exposed circuits.

I don't know what these do, Daniel thought as he triggered blast after blast into the incomprehensible circuitry. *But whatever hurts this ship helps us.*

On the bridge of *Ra's Eye*, Hathor came to a decision. Her guards couldn't stop the incursion of the boarders. But there was another way to handle the problem. The enemy was already on the deck that wouldn't seal against vacuum.

"Recall all warriors from Launch Deck Four," she ordered.

"Lady Captain, there is also a technician—"

"Notify all personnel!" Hathor said shortly. "Damage-control crews will seal the area."

Then *Ra's Eye* would lift off, rise high enough, and the boarders would cease to encumber the ship—because they would cease to be able to breathe.

At the same time the ship's main batteries would vaporize the plateau supporting the Star-Gate pyramid, the invaders sheltering there, and, of course, the StarGate itself.

The situation had become sufficiently extreme to merit the extreme solution.

"Engines, prepare lifting drive."

Ra's Eye began to shudder as the landing clamps unlocked from the stone pyramid below them.

"Gunnery, start energizing main batteries."

"Damage control, prepare to seal off the deck."

Hathor stood very straight. "On my order," she said.

Energy and information hummed through the ship. But at a critical junction about halfway between the bridge and the engine room, the control circuitry had been blasted and scrambled. Machine-language orders were lost or misrouted. Energy jumped circuits.

On the bridge, indicators began showing threatening fluctuations. Warning sirens began their howl. The ship was no longer shuddering but bucking wildly.

"Lady Captain," the navigation crewman said, her face going pale. "The engines—they're attempting to respond to extraordinary power drains. Energy is being routed to systems with no power needs."

Her hands fluttered over the photosensitive controls, which began dimming, then increasing to glaring with apparently no logic. "The systems won't—I can't—"

The young woman shouted into her communicator: "Engines, shunt all power from *SB*-29! Do it now, before we have—"

The lights in the bridge died, as did the holographic tactical display.

Hathor finished the sentence: "—A power cascade."

The hologram was gone, and there was only the dim phosphorescence of the emergency bridge controls.

Yet somehow Hathor saw an image, half a face that had an unhealthy glow, giving her an eerie half smile and a farewell.

It was the last face she'd seen on Tuat.

It was Ptah.

CHAPTER 21
TO THE VICTOR ...

The sound of Daniel's blaster-bolts brought the main body of the boarding party back at a run, weapons at the ready. They found him standing over two corpses, firing into an opening in the usually seamless crystalline quartz that formed the decks, walls, and ceilings of the enormous spacecraft they'd invaded.

Within the opening, the crystal lattice showed a complex pattern of veins. At least it had before Daniel's blast-lance had gotten to work. Now the tracery of veins was spalled and fused.

"We thought you'd gotten ambushed," Kawalsky said. "But it looks like the other way around."

Sha'uri stared from the sprawled guard to the fried technician. "You shot her?" she asked.

Colonel Jack O'Neil nudged the dead woman's hand with the toe of his boot, and the tool she'd been clutching dropped to the deck. It was a piece of the biomorphic crystal that supported so much of Ra's technology. But the recombinant lattice structure had taken the shape of a cutter, its blade vibrating at nearly hypersonic speed.

The colonel picked up the implement and scored a line in the usually impenetrable crystal of the floor. "Imagine what it would have done to

flesh and bone," he said. After a moment's search-
ing, he located the controls and stilled the blade,
slipping it into his pocket.

"Show's over," he said. "Let's find—"

The deck beneath their feet began to quiver.
And inside the circuit board, junction box—whatever it was—veins in the golden tracery began to
glow. It was like watching a microscopic light
show as energy impulses rippled and flashed
through the tiny filaments.

But as the energy pulses encountered the bub-
bled and fused mess that Daniel had created, they
cycled madly, diverted from their proper paths.
The fairy lights flashed and blinked as circuits
began to overload. Some of the veins went from
gold to red, looking like the heating filaments inside a toaster.

The whole construction they stood within began
to shake harder. Heat began wafting out of the
circuit box. Almost unconsciously the members of
the raiding party stepped back.

The glimmering of the wrecked circuits took on
a glaring hue. Sparks began to fly. An irregular
rhythm punctuated the trembling of the pyramid
ship, as if the floor beneath them were trying to
buck them off. The boarders stumbled away, and
just in time. An arc of energy spat out of the
opening with almost the force of a blast-bolt.

Kawalsky glared at Daniel. "What did you do?"
he demanded.

Daniel was trying to put as much space between
him and the flaring circuits as he could. "A little
sabotage—I thought."

The arhythmic tremor in the deck and walls had reached almost earthquake proportions. The whole construction seemed to heave up for a second. Then it slumped back down, hard enough to make everyone stumble. The sourceless illumination that usually lit the decks cut off and died.

At least on this particular level, light from the suns of Abydos filtered in through the vast openings of the launch decks.

"I think," O'Neil said, "that the ship was preparing for liftoff, which would have been very unhealthy for us on an open deck if we'd gone high enough. Let's get out of here."

They took the first upward-leading staircase they could find. At the top, they found the way half blocked by a thick panel of quartz-crystal. "Like a blast-door," Kawalsky murmured.

"More likely an airtight seal," O'Neil said as he ducked under. The slab was poised to come down, as if the power that had actuated its movement had abruptly been cut off.

Away from the open hatches of the launching deck, the corridors of the ship were pitch dark. The ever prepared Colonel O'Neil produced some flares. "I hope some of the rest of you brought a few," he said. "These aren't going to last us all the way to the bridge."

The bridge of *Ra's Eye* was a scene of controlled turmoil as Ptah's technicians strove mightily to overcome the effects of their leader's scrimping and the damage done to one of the main junction circuits.

"There are no backups," one of the crew cried, almost wailing. "We can't reroute those circuits. The transmission net won't stand it. If we try, we'll blow out other junctions!"

"Lady Captain," a voice came from the engine room, "I fear that has happened already."

"Damage Control," Hathor said, trying to come to grips with the situation, "how long will repairs take?"

A brief silence answered her. "Lady Captain, it will require at least as long as we took after the last mishap." The crew person's voice halted another moment. "Perhaps longer."

There was a brassy, burning sensation in the back of Hathor's mouth, as if someone had poured molten metal in there while she hadn't been looking. With a start she realized this must be the taste of defeat.

"Scanners," she said, trying to keep her voice level. "What's the situation outside?"

The interdiction fire from the secondary batteries had been halted as *Ra's Eye* attempted to lift off. And, of course, there was no power to resume firing now.

"Lady Captain." It was the voice of a frightened underling delivering more bad news. "Enemy forces are climbing the plateau. More are boarding us."

For a second Hathor felt as though the whole weight of the battlecraft were pressing against her shoulders. Not enough crew to resist, not enough power to escape. Balked by ancient machinery and her erstwhile husband's malice.

He never understood what there was between Ra and me, she thought.

Hathor jerked her chin up. Perhaps she might explain—when she came back to kill him.

"Engines," she said crisply. "Can we divert enough emergency power to run the matter transmitters?"

A moment's silence as technicians frantically calculated. "Yes, Lady Captain."

"Then do so. All inessential crew will be withdrawn to the StarGate. All warriors will continue to assemble on the upper decks, concentrating on slowing, if not destroying the first group of boarders."

She hesitated. "I will consider volunteers for a udajeet mission to discourage the enemy forces on the plateau from boarding."

A forlorn hope, she thought.

Hathor turned to her bridge crew, nervous technicians all. "I'll require all Engines, Power, Communications, and Damage Control personnel," she said. "Navigation, the rest of you—you can go as soon as we power up the matter transmitter."

The crew members other than the ones she had chosen immediately made their way to stand on what appeared to be a huge medallion of beaten copper set in the quartz of the deck. A similar disk stood vertically aligned overhead in the ceiling.

"Engines!" Hathor called. "Has power been diverted to the matter transmitter?"

"Yes, Lady Captain."

"Then prepare for the beaming of the first party." She stepped to the statue of Khnum that loomed over the transmitter circle. A golden necklace hung around the figure's neck, with a milky bluish gem set in the middle. Hathor pressed her fingers against the jewel.

From the medallion overhead, a brilliant blue radiance covered the crew members. Four metal rings seemed to float down to encircle them. And a pulse of blue light, intense as a laser, swept around the circumference of both copper medallions until the escaping crew members seemed encased in a tube of shimmering blueness.

An instant later, they were gone.

The battle to reach the bridge finally resolved itself into alternate slogging and slugging matches. The raiding party would haul itself up another flight of stairs to engage in increasingly more desperate battles with increasingly more frantic Horus guards.

Daniel was panting, his legs were numb, and he suspected he was developing a blister on his thumb from triggering his blast-lance. The numbers of the boarding party had dropped as more of their members had fallen. They were down to the core group of original adventurers: O'Neil, Kawalsky, Daniel, Sha'uri, and Skaara, plus a scattering of Skaara's boy militia members.

The ranks of the Horuses had thinned as well. Both attackers and defenders were now armed with blast-lances, though the practical-minded O'Neil wasn't averse to using home-grown technology—like hand grenades—when the enemy was too well barricaded.

They were encountering breastworks on every level now, as the numbers of upward-leading stairways decreased. There was also less room for the Horus guards to run, as floor space became measurably more and more constricted.

Daniel dazedly realized that they must be near the top. The deck they were on was essentially only a large room with a few structural members. Four stairways, one in each corner, gave access from the level below. But this floor's version of the Alamo was constructed in the center of the room, a square bastion comprising furniture, equipment cases, and what appeared to be control consoles torn from the floor.

Less than a half-dozen hawk-masked guards fired blast-lances at the intruders, who were shooting back from each of the four stairwells.

"What are they defending so hard in there?" Daniel muttered as he sent three consecutive pulses through a gap in the wreckage which one of the guards had been using as a firing slit.

"The last way out," Kawalsky replied. "I think it's a circular staircase there in the middle of the room."

Two of the guards fell, then three. Their remaining fellows were firing almost wildly, attempting to keep the intruders' heads down.

"There should be more of them." O'Neil almost seemed to be complaining. "Unless they're preparing a real greeting upstairs."

A muffled cry came from the deck above, and the guards still on their feet bolted up the circular stairs. All three were cut down as soon as they rose above the level of their concealing barricade.

O'Neil advanced with care—they'd had experience of guardsmen playing possum to leap up and drill the unwary. But the three masked figures in the square of furniture were definitely dead.

The Marine colonel cautiously reconnoitered the circular stairs. Nobody shot down at him.

"Everybody stay in your corners," he warned.

Then he took their last two grenades and tossed them up. Daniel watched as O'Neil leapt for cover on the far side of the barricade. Then the grenades went off with a flash, a bang, and a spray of shrapnel that would have diced anybody on the deck above.

"Now!" O'Neil yelled.

He was the first up the stairs. Kawalsky was second, but somehow Daniel moved his numb legs quickly enough to be third onto the starship's bridge.

The place was empty—except for a gorgeously formed female standing in the cyclinder of blue radiance that indicated a matter transmitter in action. The woman's lithe body was clad in a warrior's kilt and pectoral necklace, and her face was masked in a gold-crystal helmet in the shape of a cat.

It was over. The last udajeet of her forlorn hope attack had been blown from the sky. The last crew person evacuated—those in the engine room had their own matter transmitter. Even the last Horus guards had disappeared for the StarGate in a rush of blue radiance—except for the small blocking force below, who probably wouldn't be able to disengage in time anyway.

Hathor called to them, and saw the three cut to ribbons before they could reach the top of the stairs. Now she was the last aboard *Ra's Eye*. She pressed the gem control on Khnum's necklace, and was bathed in azure radiation.

Outside her blue cocoon, flashes erupted on the bridge as the invaders prepared their way with some sort of bombs. Still Hathor held off her transit until the raiders actually confronted her. They stared, which was only to be expected.

But Hathor was staring as well. The third invader to enter the bridge was a kind of man she'd never seen before.

When Ra's telepathic call for subjects had gone out, it had drawn most heavily on the populations nearest to the site of his proposed capital. Proto-Egyptians, Berbers, Nubians, and the inhabitants of Arabia and the Near East heeded his summoning.

It never reached northern Europe.

So, despite her travels to other worlds of Ra's empire, her brushes with alien races who had also served Ra . . . Hathor had never met a man with fair skin and blond hair.

"Who—?" This unlikely vision spoke in a language close enough for her to understand. He stared at her cat mask. "Hathor?" he finally said.

She tapped the tumbler switch on her necklace, and her helmet mask disappeared.

"Know, Golden Man, that I am Hathor," she

said. "We shall meet again. And you and yours shall suffer for this humiliation you have given me."

The matter transmitter finally cycled, and she was pulled downward to the StarGate room, down below the surface of Abydos, faster than the speed of light.

"Who the hell was that?" Kawalsky said, slack-jawed.

"Hathor," Daniel said. "Depending on which legends you follow, she's either the goddess of love or slaughter."

"Well," Kawalsky said judiciously, "I guess she's got the build for either job."

The matter transmitter was silent.

"I want as many people on that medallion as can fit safely," O'Neil said, stepping over to the Khnum statue. "I guess this is the Down button." He glanced at the group crowding the beaten copper plate. "And leave room for me."

They arrived in the room of the stone pyramid devoted to the matter transmitter just moments after Hathor had vanished.

But as they marched on the room of the Star-Gate, Daniel heard male voices raised in argument. "The bitch has left us here to die!" one man cried. "Destroy the StarGate, and we're trapped here. If the invaders don't kill us, the *fellahin* will tear us limb from limb!"

"And if we follow Hathor—well, that's suicide, too," another voice replied. "And it may be more unpleasant than a soldier's death."

The Horus guards didn't have time for any more argument. The raiders stormed the room and blew them away.

Then Kawalsky moved to cut the power leads for the light blast-cannon aimed at the Star-Gate's base.

"I guess they were supposed to trigger this when we arrived," O'Neil said.

Daniel nodded. "Except they got too involved in arguing about their own survival."

The colonel checked his blast-lance. "Jackson, you and Sha'uri stay here to direct the next wave. Kawalsky, myself, and the others will be going right through. If we come out right on the bad guys' asses, they won't be able to do too much damage at Creek Mountain."

Daniel grabbed O'Neil's arm. "If you step through there, you won't be going to Creek Mountain. You won't end up on Earth at all."

He pointed at the carved symbols clamped in the seven chevrons which dotted the outer ring of the gate. "Trust me, I know the coordinates for Earth. And that's not what the gate is now set for."

Daniel began patting himself down. "Anybody got a pen and paper?" he asked. "We've got to get a record of this combination. Then I'll set the gate for home." He glanced around at the Abydans in the room—the vast majority. "I mean, planet Earth."

Jack O'Neil stepped through the StarGate to deliver his report, and nearly got his head blown off by a platoon of Marines with nervous trigger fingers.

On the other side of the silo blast doors, General West had a regular crisis center going. "You beat the invaders?" he demanded.

"I'd say they didn't have enough numbers or machines to rate as an invasion," O'Neil said. "A scouting force maybe. Although if we hadn't been there, what they had would have been enough to reduce Nagada to rubble."

"But you beat them," West repeated.

"I regret to report that General Keogh died in action," O'Neil said formally. "We took heavy losses—especially in our armor and vehicles. But in the end the enemy was forced to abandon their position and retreat through the StarGate."

"Through the StarGate?" West frowned. "But they didn't come here."

"No, sir." O'Neil held out a scrap of paper, hastily scrawled upon. "This is important intelligence, sir. The coordinates for a new StarGate location." He hid a grin. "Jackson says we have to stop thinking of the StarGate as an intercom and remember that it's attached to a whole network. This is a new number we can dial."

"If we don't disconnect the phone," West growled.

O'Neil glanced around the room and finally saw the traces of fighting. Bullet holes pocked one wall, and the ceiling was fused from the discharge of a blast-lance.

"But if we disconnect now, sir, we'll lose the

chance to examine the starship the enemy left be-hind on Abydos."

West's eyes tracked his like a pair of antiair-craft cannon.

"A working starship?" he demanded.

"Temporarily incapacitated," O'Neil admitted. "Certainly beyond the capacity of an Egyptologist or combat Marine to figure out. You may have to reorganize the StarGate investigation team to make sense of it. And they'll probably need more physicists—and maybe some people from NASA."

He allowed a little excitement into his voice. "But think about what we could find, sir—tech-nology a quantum leap ahead of ours. There's a deck full of those antigravity gliders—undamaged. Incredible computers—and just imagine the data they've got stored. Technological processes, infor-mation on other star systems—"

"Heavy weapons," West interrupted.

O'Neil nodded. To each his own.

"How soon can we start moving this ship over here?" West wanted to know.

"Ah, sir," O'Neil replied, "maybe you'd better inspect the site before you make plans."

West frowned but nodded. "Maybe I should make an on-site evaluation."

Then you'll see that the spoils of war won't fit in a truck, O'Neil thought.

The problem, he saw, was that the general was still thinking in planetary terms.

Once you've been out through the StarGate, your scale of reference changes forever, O'Neil realized. *Like it or not, you see a bigger picture.*